WAKING UP IN VEGAS

JE ROWNEY

LITTLE FOX
PUBLISHING

Also by JE Rowney

I Can't Sleep
The Woman in the Woods
Other People's Lives
The Book Swap
Gaslight
The House Sitter
The Work Retreat
The Other Passenger

For further information, please visit the author's
website.
http://jerowney.com/about-je-rowney

Disclaimer:

This novel is a work of fiction. While real-world locations
are used in a fictionalised setting, all characters, places, and
businesses within this story are entirely fictitious. They are not
representative of any real persons, places, or organisations. Any
resemblance to actual persons, living or dead, or actual events, is
purely coincidental. If any names of persons, places, or
organisations within this novel coincide with real-world entities,
it is by chance, and no inference should be made regarding their
connection to the real world.

Please don't plan your Uber journey according to travel
times reflected in this fictional novel.

ISBN: 978-1-917398-02-2

ONE

THIS MORNING

Jess's eyes snapped open, her body instinctively recoiling from an intense, biting cold. Panic surged through her as she found herself submerged in ice, the chill penetrating to her very bones. Her teeth chattered uncontrollably, and her limbs felt leaden, barely responsive.

"W-w-what the h-hell?" she stammered, her voice a raspy whisper.

As her senses sharpened, she became acutely aware of two things: the unmistakable clinking of poker chips floating around her, and the fact that she wasn't as cold as she should be if she'd been in ice for long. How long *had* she been here?

The realisation sent a different kind of chill through her. Someone must have put her here recently. Were they still in the suite?

Jess attempted to sit up, fighting against nausea and dizziness. The ice shifted, chips cascading over her bare, goosebump-covered arms. As they clinked against each other, she noticed something odd - they were blank, no casino logos or values. Plain, multicoloured discs. Worthless.

She was still wearing last night's dress, a sequined number now soaked through and clinging to her like a second skin. It was meant to be her "wild night out" dress, the one she'd bought specifically for this trip, her first time in Vegas. Now it felt like a mockery of her expectations for this bachelorette weekend.

"Get out," she muttered to herself, willing her sluggish limbs to move. "Come on, Jess. Move!"

With trembling hands, she gripped the edges of the tub, her fingers slipping on the icy porcelain. It took three attempts before she could haul herself up to a sitting position. The sudden movement sent poker chips skittering across the bathroom floor.

As she struggled to stand, Jess's mind raced. Who had done this to her? And why? The suite had seemed secure when they'd checked in. It was the Bellagio, one of the most prestigious hotels in Vegas, not some shitty motel. Had someone broken in? And if so, why would they do this? Or was it one of her friends? A crazy bachelorette prank gone too far?

Jess grabbed a plush hotel towel, wrapping it around herself with clumsy, shaking hands. She rubbed her arms vigorously, desperate to generate some warmth. Gradually, feeling began to return to her extremities, bringing with it a painful tingling sensation.

She made her way to the sink, gripping its edges for support. The face that stared back at her from the mirror was a stranger — mascara smeared, lipstick smudged, and was that a bruise forming on her cheek? Her usually sleek blonde hair hung in wet, tangled strands around her face. This was not the composed, responsible middle school teacher she saw every morning. This was someone else entirely, someone wild and reckless.

"Rachel? Lisa?" she called out, her voice stronger now

but still quavering. "Megan? Olivia?"

Silence.

In the bathroom, Jess looked around for clues or something to warm herself up. She spotted a hairdryer on the counter and grabbed it, switching it on to its highest setting. The rush of hot air was heavenly against her icy skin. She ran it over her arms, legs, and hair, feeling life slowly return to her body.

As her physical discomfort subsided, confusion and fear took its place. What happened last night? This was supposed to be her bachelorette party, a final girls' trip before she tied the knot with Miles. She thought of her fiancé back home, probably just waking up for his morning run. Should she call him? No, she decided. He'd only worry, and she didn't even know what to tell him yet. Miles had always been protective, sometimes overly so. It was one reason she'd been so thrilled about this trip - an opportunity to unwind, to be the spontaneous, carefree Jess she'd been in college, before the responsibilities of adulthood and her career as a teacher had settled on her shoulders.

But how did she wind up in a tub filled with ice? And more importantly, who had put her there?

Jess leaned against the counter, her mind racing. Would any of her friends have done this? She tried to imagine a scenario where it made sense but came up blank.

Lisa, her friend from college, was always ready for a prank, but this one seemed too much, even for her. Jess remembered how excited Lisa had been about the trip, eager to shake off the stress of her recent divorce and rediscover her fun side. Would she really go this far?

Megan was too cautious: the level-headed one in their group. The data analyst in her would have calculated the risks and deemed this too dangerous. Initially, she had reservations about the trip, concerned about work and project deadlines. She wouldn't plan pranks like these.

Olivia? The freshest face among their social circle, Olivia had been eager to prove herself, to show she could keep up with their long-established dynamic. She might get carried away after a few drinks, but this seemed extreme.

And Rachel... Rachel had organised this entire trip. She'd been so excited about giving Jess the "ultimate Vegas experience." Surely, she wouldn't do anything to ruin it? Rachel had always been the adventurous one, but this was beyond anything she'd ever done before.

But if not her friends, then who? A stranger?

The thought gave her a shiver that had nothing to do with the ice. Had someone broken into their suite? Or had they invited someone back after a night of partying? Jess strained to remember, but the events of the previous night were a blur.

She took a deep breath, trying to calm her racing heart. There had to be a logical explanation. Maybe it was an unknown Vegas tradition or a misguided hangover cure. But even as she thought about it, she knew she was grasping at straws.

One thing was clear: she needed to find the others.

If someone had done this to her, her friends might be in danger too. Or maybe they had answers to the questions swirling in her mind.

With renewed determination, Jess straightened up. It was time to face whatever waited for her beyond the bathroom door. Taking a deep breath, she approached it, suddenly afraid of what she might find on the other side.

Jess turned the handle, stepping out into the suite beyond. The room was a disaster zone. Clothes were strewn everywhere, empty bottles littered every surface, and playing cards carpeted the floor like fallen leaves. The heavy curtains were drawn, but slivers of harsh Nevada sunlight sliced through, illuminating swirling dust motes.

"Girls?" Jess called again, her heart racing. "Is anyone here?"

As she surveyed the surrounding chaos, Jess thought about how far this was from her orderly classroom back home. The responsible teacher in her wanted to clean up, to restore order to this mess. But she pushed that instinct aside. Right now, finding her friends was the priority.

A muffled sound came from somewhere in the suite. Jess froze, straining to hear where it was coming from. Her pulse quickened as she realised she wasn't alone. Whatever had happened last night, whatever wild turn their Vegas adventure had taken, she was about to find out. She just hoped that when the fog of confusion cleared, she wouldn't regret what she discovered.

TWO
LAST NIGHT

The sleek black limousine glided down the Las Vegas Strip, its mirrored surface reflecting the neon lights of the city. To either side of them, the frontages of impressive hotels bordered the boulevard. The medieval castle towers of Excalibur gave way to the city skyline and the miniature Statue of Liberty at New York New York. To the other side, an enormous Coca Cola bottle stood beside the MGM. The five women strained to see out of one side of the limo and then the other as they travelled through the Nevada evening.

"It's the happiest place on Earth," Olivia said, in a dreamlike state.

"Disneyland for adults," Rachel laughed.

Jess wrapped her arm around her best friend's shoulder and drew her in for a hug. "This is so perfect," she said.

"You'd better believe it," Rachel said. "Because tonight we are going to take over this town."

"Damn right!" Lisa shouted, before slapping a hand over her mouth. "Sorry," she said. "I might be a little overexcited."

"In Vegas, there's no such thing," Rachel said with a grin.

As they approached the Bellagio, the spectacular water show was in full force. The women pressed their

8

faces to the windows, oohing and aahing at the synchronised performance.

"Wow, look at those fountains!" Jess exclaimed, her eyes wide with wonder. This was her bachelorette party, and Vegas was about to become their playground. It was beyond anything she could have imagined, and the night hadn't even begun.

Rachel, Jess's maid of honour, squeezed her hand. "Just wait, honey. This weekend is going to be unforgettable!"

The limo turned away from the boulevard, circling around to the side of the massive, luxurious hotel. The path climbed a winding hill past a columned walkway on one side and the fountain display on the other. The imposing façade of the hotel came into view as they rounded a final corner, making Jess suck in her breath.

"This is.... amazing..." she sighed. "Rachel, I..."

Rachel pressed her index finger against Jess's lips.

"We deserve this," she said. "All of us. Our lives have been crazy the past few months, and you are an excellent excuse to get together and forget about all that. We are here to celebrate you, and to celebrate the happiness in our lives."

Jess nodded, a lump forming in her throat.

"Thank you," she mouthed.

"Come on," Megan cut in. "Let's not ruin our make-up. I want to get out of this very gorgeous and impressive limo and get into that very gorgeous and impressive hotel."

As they pulled up to the drop off point, a uniformed valet opened the door for them, and the five women tumbled out.

"I can't believe we're actually here!" Lisa said, helping the driver unload their luggage.

"You don't need to do that," Rachel said, kind-heartedly. "We're going to leave a good tip, so you don't have to break a nail."

Lisa laughed and linked arms with Rachel, and Jess joined the chain.

The warm Las Vegas air enveloped them as they made their way to the grand entrance, the scent of desert flowers mingling with the faint aroma of chlorine from the nearby pools. The Bellagio's facade loomed before them, its Italian-inspired architecture a testament to luxury and opulence.

As they stepped through the revolving doors, the cool air-conditioned interior was a welcome respite from the Nevada heat. The lobby stretched out before them, a vision of stately columns and vibrant floral displays. The ceiling, adorned with Dale Chihuly's iconic glass flowers, drew their gazes upward.

"This is amazing," Jess breathed, her eyes wide as she took in the intricate sculpture above.

Rachel nodded towards the artwork. "That alone cost ten million dollars."

"It's beautiful," Megan sighed. "Everything is so beautiful."

Olivia, the newest addition to their friend group, spun in a slow circle, trying to take it all in. "I feel like I'm in a movie," she gushed. "Like we're about to embark on some glamorous adventure."

"Tonight, we are," Rachel smiled.

The five women made their way to the check-in

desk, their heels clicking on the polished floor. Other guests milled about, but in that moment, it felt like they were the only ones there, the stars of their own Las Vegas story.

"Reservation for Jessica Parker," Rachel said, flashing a confident smile at the concierge.

As they waited, Jess looked around at her friends. Olivia was holding Megan's hand, pointing through to the vibrant flowers in the conservatory just beyond the lobby. Lisa, however, seemed distracted, her eyes darting around nervously. As Jess made eye contact, Lisa pulled Jess aside, her voice low and urgent.

"Hey," Lisa whispered, her eyes ensuring the others couldn't hear. "I don't want to, you know, be a downer or anything, but... Did Miles say anything... unusual to you before we left?"

Jess blinked, taken aback by the odd question. "Unusual? Like what?"

Lisa opened her mouth to respond, then seemed to think better of it. "Never mind," she said quickly. She gave a small smile that Jess couldn't quite believe was genuine. "I'm sure it's nothing. Looks like Rachel is nearly done schmoozing. Let's go see our rooms!"

The concierge handed over their key cards to Rachel, and she passed them out.

"It feels like I got a Golden Ticket," Olivia giggled.

"Your luggage will be brought up shortly. Is there anything else you need?" the concierge asked.

"No, thank you," Rachel replied with a polite smile. Her eyes sparkled with a hint of mischief as she added, "I think we've got everything we need for an unforgettable weekend."

The concierge nodded knowingly, a slight smirk playing at the corners of his mouth. "Very well, ladies. Enjoy your stay at the Bellagio. And... may luck be on your side."

As they turned away from the desk, Jess felt a bubble of excitement rise in her chest. This was really happening. She was in Las Vegas, surrounded by her best friends, about to embark on the weekend of a lifetime. The elegant marble beneath her feet, the soft murmur of excited voices around them, and the faint tinkling of slot machines in the distance all seemed to pulse with possibility.

"Ready for this?" Rachel asked, linking her arm through Jess's again. Her voice was low and excited, full of promise for the adventures to come.

Jess looked at her friends - Megan's usual reserved demeanour melting into eager anticipation, Olivia practically bouncing on her toes with excitement, and Lisa... Lisa's smile seemed forced, her eyes still darting around as if searching for something. It was her first weekend away, hell it was her first big night out since the divorce. Of course she was bound to feel out of sorts.

"Ready as I'll ever be," Jess replied, her voice trembling slightly with a mix of nerves and exhilaration. She squeezed Rachel's arm, silently thanking her best friend for organising this extravagant getaway.

Making their way towards the elevators, the enormity of what lay ahead began to sink in. Vegas, with all its glitz, glamour, and promise of excitement, was theirs for the taking. Little did they know just how wild their weekend was about to become.

The elevator ride was a blur of giddy laughter and excited chatter. Megan was already enthusiastically describing her outfit choice for their night out, while Olivia regaled them with stories of her one previous trip to Vegas. It had involved a lot of blackjack and slots, but not much winning, from what the girls could tell. While Olivia talked, Lisa stood quietly in the corner.

As the elevator ascended, Rachel leaned in close to Jess, her voice hushed and excited. "I have so many surprises planned for you this weekend. You're going to love it!"

Jess nodded, her excitement tinged with a hint of concern as she glanced at Lisa. She made a mental note to check in with her friend later, knowing how hard this weekend must be for her so soon after her divorce.

The doors opened with a soft ding, revealing a hallway that screamed luxury. Plush carpets muffled their footsteps as they made their way down the corridor, the anticipation building with each step.

"All right, ladies," Rachel announced as they reached their destination. "Jess and I have the two-bedroom Bellagio Suite. The rest of you have Tower Deluxe Rooms just down the hall."

"Don't go yet," Jess beckoned. "Come in with us first. Let's have a drink?"

"The first of many, I hope," Megan smiled.

"I'll drink to that," Oliva agreed.

Rachel pressed the keycard against the lock and

pushed the door open.

As they entered the suite, Jess's eyes widened. It was nothing short of spectacular – an expansive living room greeted them, with floor-to-ceiling windows offering a panoramic view of the glittering Las Vegas Strip beyond.

"Wow, Rachel," Lisa's voice cut through the chorus of impressed gasps. "You've really outdone yourself. If I were maid of honour, we'd probably be splitting pitchers at O'Shea's right now. Or back home at Crazy Tom's."

Jess turned to see Lisa's face, a complex mix of emotions playing across it. There was admiration there, but also something that looked a lot like regret.

"I mean," Lisa quickly added, her laugh sounding a bit forced to Jess's ears, "this is amazing. You're giving Jess the bachelorette she deserves."

Jess stepped over and squeezed Lisa's hand, trying to convey her understanding without words. "Hey, O'Shea's would have been perfect too. As long as I'm with you guys, that's all that matters. Crazy Tom's though... I don't know." She grinned, and Lisa returned the smile.

"Thanks, Jess," Lisa said.

"I'm here for you, okay?" Jess said. "Regardless of what we're celebrating. I'm here for you."

Lisa nodded. "It means a lot. Thank you."

The group began to explore the suite, exclaiming over its luxuries; it was truly overwhelming.

The living area boasted plush sofas and armchairs, a dining area, and a fully stocked bar in one corner.

Two separate bedrooms branched off from the main space, each with its own lavish bathroom.

"This is insane," Olivia breathed, running her hand over the sleek furniture.

Megan peeked into one of the bedrooms. "Wow, Rachel. You really went all out."

Lisa grinned. "I can't believe we each get our own room, too. I appreciate this, Rachel. This weekend is going to be epic!"

Rachel, already at the bar, began pouring champagne into slim, elegant flutes. "I figured for Jess's last hurrah as a single woman, we should do it in style. Now, let's toast before you all check out your rooms!"

The women gathered around, raising their glasses high. Despite having separate rooms, they knew they'd be spending most of their time together, either in this luxurious suite or out on the town. For now, though, it was the perfect launching pad for their Vegas adventure.

"To Jess," Rachel proclaimed, "and the most unforgettable bachelorette party ever!"

Their glasses clinked together, the sound mixing with their excited laughter. As they sipped their champagne, Rachel's eyes sparkled with mischief.

"Speaking of unforgettable," she said, setting down her glass and reaching for her purse. "I have one more surprise for you all."

The other women watched curiously as Rachel rummaged through her bag. With a flourish, she pulled out five laminated passes, each adorned with a holographic VIP symbol.

"Guess who scored us access to the most exclusive hotspots in Vegas?" Rachel grinned, holding up the passes. "With the full, all-inclusive package."

The girls squealed in delight, gathering around to examine the passes with awe. Lisa's face lit up with pure joy, her eyes sparkling as she ran her finger over the holographic design.

"No way!" Lisa exclaimed, her voice filled with genuine excitement. "Rachel, this is incredible! How did you manage this?"

Jess watched as Lisa beamed at Rachel, not a trace of envy in her expression. Despite everything she'd been through recently, Lisa's happiness for her friends seemed completely sincere.

Rachel winked, clearly pleased with the reaction. "I have my ways. Let's just say a friend of a friend owed me a favour."

Lisa turned to Jess, grinning from ear to ear. "Can you believe this? We're going to have the most amazing night!"

Jess couldn't help but smile back, touched by Lisa's enthusiasm. She pulled her friend into a quick hug, grateful that Lisa could set aside her own troubles to fully embrace the celebration.

Jess hugged her friend tightly. "Rachel, this is amazing! You've thought of everything."

As the others chatted excitedly about the night ahead and what they were going to wear, Jess felt her phone buzz in her pocket. She frowned at the screen – it was Miles, her fiancé.

"Hey, I need to take this," she said, her eyes darting for somewhere she could have privacy.

16

Rachel appeared to read her friend's mind as she gestured towards the balcony.

"Miles," Jess mouthed, stepping out and sliding the glass door shut behind her. The contrast was immediate and jarring. The crisp, air-conditioned coolness of the suite gave way to the stifling heat of the Vegas night. Even in darkness, the air was thick and heavy, enveloping her like a warm, damp blanket. She felt a bead of sweat form at her temple almost instantly.

As if the heat wasn't enough, the view took her breath away. From the vantage point high in the Bellagio, the iconic Las Vegas Strip unfurled before her like a shimmering river of light. Directly across, the Eiffel Tower of Paris Las Vegas stood proudly illuminated, its warm golden glow a beacon in the night. Next to it, the hotel's signature hot air balloon hovered, a whimsical touch against the dark sky. There was the glitzy front of Planet Hollywood to its right, advertising a new Vegas residency from one of Jess's favourite singers. Maybe she would have to return to check it out.

Jess's eyes were drawn downward to the front of the Bellagio, where the grand fountains had been dancing earlier as they passed by. Now, the expansive pool lay still, its surface reflecting the myriad lights of the surrounding hotels and casinos, creating a mirror image of the vibrant cityscape.

Far below, throngs of people moved along the sidewalks like colourful ants, their excited chatter rising up as a distant hum. Cars crawled along the Strip, their headlights adding to the perpetual glow of the city that never sleeps.

The cacophony of sounds washed over her – the hum of the throng on the sidewalk, the honking of impatient taxis, and the constant underlying buzz of a city alive with possibility.

Jess inhaled deeply, the warm air filling her lungs. The scent was a unique mixture of desert heat, and the faint aroma of expensive perfumes and cuisines from the high-end restaurants below.

Breaking from the spell of the Vegas night, she glanced at her phone, Miles's name glowing on the screen. With the pulsing energy of Sin City thrumming around her, she answered the call.

"Hey, babe," she said, a smile in her voice.

"Hey, Jess," Miles replied, his tone a mix of concern and affection. "Just wanted to check in. How's Vegas treating you so far?"

"It's amazing, Miles. We just got to the hotel, and you wouldn't believe this suite Rachel booked for us."

There was a moment of silence before Miles spoke again. "That's great, honey. I'm glad you arrived safely. Just... be careful, okay? Don't let Rachel get you into any trouble."

Jess frowned, confused by his tone. "What do you mean? Rachel's my best friend. What kind of trouble could she possibly get me into?"

Miles sighed. "I know, I know. It's just... sometimes she can be a bit... wild. I don't want you getting caught up in anything you might regret. It's Las Vegas, after all. I've heard all kinds of..."

"Miles," Jess broke in, her voice firm, "Rachel's been my friend since college. I've known her longer than you have. I've known her longer than I've known you. If you're taking me on, you're taking me with my friends. Trust goes both ways, you know."

"You're right," Miles conceded. "I do trust you, Jess. Just... I don't know... keep your eyes open, okay? And if anything feels off, call me immediately."

"Of course," Jess replied, still puzzled. "I'll be fine, Miles. We're just here to have some fun."

Part of her was flattered by her fiancé's concern, but part of her was surprised by his comments about Rachel. Rach was the one who had introduced them. Miles and Rachel worked together, and whatever complicated association they had, neither of them had ever let it impact upon their relationship with Jess. Why was Miles concerned now, of all times?

"Okay, hon," Miles said. "I love you."

"You too," Jess said. "So much."

Despite being happy to speak to her fiancé, Jess couldn't shake the feeling that there was more to Miles's warning than he was letting on. She stared at her phone for a moment after they had hung up, a tiny lump beginning to grow in her stomach.

THREE
THIS MORNING

"Holy shit!" The words escaped Jess's lips before she could stop them, a far cry from her usual measured teacher's tone. The scene before her was so surreal, so utterly bizarre, that for a moment she wondered if she was still trapped in some fever dream induced by her icy bath.

The Las Vegas sun beat down mercilessly on the balcony, its harsh light exposing a tableau that looked like something out of a Hunter S. Thompson novel. Lisa, one of her closest friends since their wild college days, was sprawled on the sun-baked tiles. Always the put-together one of their group, Lisa looked like she'd been through a war.

Her slinky red bodycon dress, a departure from her usual conservative attire, was now a crumpled mess. It had ridden up scandalously high, revealing more of her long legs than Jess had seen since their spring break in Cancun. One stiletto heel was missing, the lone survivor lying a few feet away like an abandoned glass slipper. A large wine stain marred the fabric near her hip, a Rorschach test of their forgotten night.

What caused Jess's jaw to drop open, though, was that Lisa was handcuffed to a man Jess had never seen before.

"Lisa?" Jess's voice was barely above a whisper, as

if speaking too loudly might shatter this surreal scene. "What the hell is going on here? Who is this? Lisa?"

Lisa's eyes, usually a clear, intelligent blue, were bloodshot and unfocused as they struggled to meet Jess's gaze. Her skin, normally glowing from her rigorous skincare routine, looked pale and clammy in the morning light. Her carefully styled blonde hair was a rat's nest in the morning sunlight.

"Jess?" Lisa's voice was rough, confused. "Why are you soaking wet?"

Jess looked down at herself. "I woke up in a bathtub full of ice," she replied, her voice shaking slightly. There was no real way to explain it, at least not yet. "I'm still trying to figure out what happened."

As the words sank in and she started to regain full consciousness, Lisa looked down at the handcuffs, then at the man beside her. Horror dawned on her face. "Seriously?" she whispered, her voice trembling. "Jess, I... I don't know who he is. I... I can't remember anything from last night."

Lisa's expression was one of sheer confusion, and Jess didn't have any answers or explanations to help her out.

Jess stepped onto the balcony and crouched beside Lisa in what she hoped was a reassuring gesture. The heat rising from the tiled floor was a striking juxtaposition to the chill still clinging to her damp skin.

"Don't panic, Lis, but I can't either. I promise everything is going to be all right." As she spoke, Jess realised she needed to hear the words just as much as Lisa did. Finding new strength, she continued. "Okay, let's take this one step at a time. First things first - we need to find out who your new friend is."

Lisa groaned, her eyes struggling to focus on Jess. Still groggy, she instinctively tried to cover her left hand, where a pale band of skin marked her recently removed wedding ring. It was a gesture Jess had seen many times since Lisa's divorce, a reflexive action born of habit and lingering pain.

Jess felt a rush of protective anger. Lisa had been through enough with her divorce; she didn't need this added complication. She turned to the unconscious man, shaking his shoulder roughly. "Hey! Wake up!"

The man stirred, moaning. He looked to be in his late twenties, with a mop of curly dark hair and the kind of tan you only get from living in the desert. His eyes fluttered open, revealing a mix of brown and green that might have been attractive under different circumstances.

"What's happening?" he mumbled, then noticed the handcuffs. His eyes widened in shock. "What the hell?" The sight had clearly been enough to jar him wide awake.

Lisa jerked away from the man as much as the handcuffs would allow, her free hand instinctively moving to smooth down her dress. "Who are you? Why are you handcuffed to me?" she asked.

The man shook his head, wincing at the movement. "I... I don't know. I can't remember anything. Where are we?"

Jess intervened, her voice stern despite her own confusion and fear. She drew on her experience of dealing with unruly students, hoping it would lend her an air of authority she didn't feel. "You first. Name.

22

Now."

"Alex," he said, still looking dazed, but responding to Jess's tone. "My name's Alex. I work... I think I work at the casino. In the Bellagio." He rattled the handcuffs, the metal chain clinking ominously against the cuff in the morning air. "Pretty sure I've lost that job now."

"What do you mean?" Jess asked, her heart racing. Her brain was trying to piece together the implication of his words.

Alex sighed, looking defeated. "Casino workers aren't supposed to end up in situations like this. Handcuffed to a guest? That's... definitely grounds for termination."

"You think?" Jess said. "That still doesn't explain how you got here."

Lisa's eyes widened as she seemed to fully grasp their predicament. "How did this happen?" A flicker of fear, or perhaps excitement, crossed her face as she glanced at Alex. Jess recognised that look; it was the same one Lisa used to get when she was about to do something reckless back in college.

Alex shook his head, running a hand through his tousled hair. "Everything's so fuzzy. It's like trying to remember a dream."

Jess nodded instinctively. "That's exactly what it feels like. You too Lisa?"

Lisa turned to Jess, her eyes wide with fear. "Exactly, yes. Jess, what's going on? Why can't I remember anything? Why can't any of us...?"

Jess leaned against the balcony rail and flinched as the

heat sizzled against her damp skin. "I'm still trying to figure out what's going on. This is batshit crazy. Do either of you remember *anything* from last night?"

Both Lisa and Alex shook their heads, looking increasingly distressed and confused. The three of them sat in the morning heat with countless questions and no answers.

"Okay," Jess said eventually, trying to keep her voice calm despite the panic building inside her. She needed to be the voice of reason, the responsible one, just like she was for her students. "We need to figure this out. We need to find the others and piece together exactly what happened last night. And you," she pointed at Alex, "are going to help us. Because right now, you're our only lead."

Alex nodded slowly. "I... yeah, of course. I want to know what happened just as much as you do. I'll help however I can. Right now, though, I'm as lost as you are."

Lisa looked at Alex, her eyes narrowing slightly as she studied his face, as if trying to dredge up any memory of him from the night before. Finding none, she turned back to Jess, her voice filled with worry. "Seriously, Jess, you need to dry off. You're shivering! Who did that? Who put you in the ice?"

Jess wrapped her arms around herself. "I don't know; I don't know anything. I didn't see anyone when I woke up. I thought... I don't know, maybe I hoped it was one of you girls. Maybe Rachel...?" She looked at Lisa for a reaction, but her expression remained confused. "I should look for the others," Jess said. "You're handcuffed, and I was on ice. I can hardly wait to see what's happened to the rest of the group."

"Don't say that," Lisa said. She shook her head, wincing at the movement. "Jess, what happened to us last night? I don't remember anything after we left for the club."

"I don't know," Jess replied, her voice almost breaking. She reached out and squeezed Lisa's free hand. "But we need to find the girls and piece this together. Either this is a misjudged prank, or something very wrong happened. We need to figure out how we ended up like this."

Lisa opened her mouth and closed it again, as if she was going to speak and thought better of it. She shifted uncomfortably, the movement causing Alex to wince as the handcuffs pulled at his wrist.

Jess raised an eyebrow. Lisa opened her eyes as wide as she could. It was as though the two of them were communicating in terrible sign language, with Lisa's hesitant glances and Jess's subtle head tilts forming a silent conversation.

Finally, Lisa asked: "Should you... call Miles?"

Jess felt a pang of guilt at the mention of her fiancé. She should have contacted him first, shouldn't she? As soon as she got out of the tub, wouldn't it have been best to phone Miles? He could help, surely. Even as Jess thought this, it seemed absurd. How could Miles do anything? And the idea of explaining this mess to him when she didn't understand it herself... "I... let's try to find out what's going on first. Before we worry him," Jess replied, avoiding Lisa's knowing gaze. "This could all be nothing."

"An enormous pile of nothing," Lisa sighed. Still,

she gave one quick nod that Jess interpreted as understanding - whether or not it was agreement. Alex glanced between them, clearly sensing unspoken tension.

As the three of them looked at each other, the gravity of their situation settled over them like a heavy blanket. Down on the street below, the sounds of the Las Vegas Strip beginning to stir for another day of excess and excitement seemed to mock their predicament. Even at half-past nine in the morning, the city was coming to life.

The glittering promise of Las Vegas, and the excitement of Jess's bachelorette party, seemed like a distant memory now. Instead, they were left with a mystery that seemed to grow more complex by the minute, and a gnawing fear of what they might discover as they unravelled the events of the previous night.

FOUR
LAST NIGHT

After her phone call with Miles, Jess stood on the balcony a moment longer, looking down upon the glittering city. The bustling sounds of the Strip below seemed to fade away as she tried to process Miles's words. What could he possibly think that Rachel would do to warrant such a cryptic warning? She drew in a long breath, trying to calm her racing thoughts.

At the front of the hotel, the fountain show erupted again in a stunning display, but Jess barely noticed. Her mind was a whirlwind of confusion and conflicting emotions.

On one side was Rachel, her best friend since college, the one who had meticulously planned this extravagant weekend. On the other was Miles, her fiancé, the man she was going to spend the rest of her life with, warning her to be careful.

He was overprotective, overreacting. She had come to Vegas to have fun with her girls, and that was exactly what she planned to do. Taking one last look at the city lights, Jess turned back to the suite where her friends were waiting.

As Jess stepped back indoors, the cool air-conditioning was a welcome contrast to the warm Las Vegas night she'd left behind on the balcony. The excited chatter of her friends filled the room, a counterpoint to the unease that had settled in her stomach after Miles's call.

"Everything okay?" Rachel asked, noticing Jess's furrowed brow.

Jess forced a smile. "Yeah, just some last-minute wedding stuff. Nothing to worry about."

Rachel didn't look entirely convinced, but didn't push the issue. As Jess glanced around the room, she noticed Lisa watching her intently, an unreadable expression on her face.

"All right, ladies," Rachel announced, clapping her hands together. "It's time to get our glam on. I want to see you all looking like the VIPs you are!"

The energy in the room immediately shifted back to excitement. Lisa grinned, clutching her VIP pass. "I can't wait to see what everyone wears. This is going to be epic!"

"Where are we heading first, Rach?" Olivia asked, jittering with anticipation.

"It's a little place I know just down The Strip called the Cherry Pop. You are going to have so much fun, Liv. All of us are."

"Cherry Pop," Olivia pondered with a grin. "It sounds perfect."

Megan checked the time on her phone screen. "Let's meet back here in an hour. 8pm? That should give us plenty of time to get ready before hitting the first club."

"You're going to have to give me a hand with my hair if we only have an hour," Lisa grinned.

"Going for the full blowout?" Meg laughed. "You're going to look amazing."

"She deserves a blowout after the past few months," Jess said.

Lisa nodded, wordless.

"Come on," Megan said, looping her arm through Olivia's. "Let's unpack and get party ready."

As the girls headed to the door, Lisa lingered for a moment, catching Jess's eye. "Everything really okay with Miles?" she asked quietly, her tone casual but her gaze searching.

Jess nodded, a bit taken aback by Lisa's interest. "Yeah, of course. Why wouldn't it be?"

Lisa shrugged, her expression neutral. "No reason. Just checking." She turned away quickly, following Olivia and Megan out of the door before Jess could say anything else.

The three girls headed off, chattering excitedly as they made their way to their own rooms. Jess watched them go, unable to shake the feeling that there was more to Lisa's question than simple concern for a friend.

As the door closed behind them, Rachel turned to Jess. "All right, spill. What did Miles really say?"

Jess hesitated, torn between her unease and not wanting to dampen the mood of the weekend. "It's probably nothing," she said finally. "He just told me to be careful and to keep an eye out. You know how he worries."

Rachel rolled her eyes. "Typical Miles. Always stressing over nothing. C'mon, let's get moving. By the time we're out the door, you'll have totally forgotten about his paranoid BS."

Jess couldn't help but smile at Rachel's trademark

no-nonsense approach, but she still felt conflicted. On one hand, she trusted Rachel implicitly - this was her best friend who had gone all out to make this trip perfect. On the other hand, Miles's warning had seemed so earnest. But why would he caution her about Rachel, of all people?

Jess shook off these thoughts as gave Rachel a last hug before wheeling her suitcase into her luscious bedroom. This was Las Vegas, a city she'd dreamed of visiting since she was a teenager. The view from their suite had been tantalising, but now she was eager to experience it all up close. It was natural for Miles to worry about her, surely. In just a week, they would be married. Tonight, though, was for her and her girls.

Standing alone in the spacious bedroom, Jess took in her reflection in the expansive mirror. Her hair, usually pulled back in a practical ponytail, now cascaded in soft waves around her shoulders. She ran her fingers through it, marvelling at how different she looked already. The anticipation of the night ahead sent a thrill through her body.

She reached for her makeup bag, laying out an array of products she rarely used in her day-to-day life onto the dressing table. Tonight was special, and she was determined to look the part. As she applied a shimmering eyeshadow, she thought about how far she'd come from the small-town girl who used to dream about Las Vegas lights.

The vanity was quickly becoming cluttered with the contents of her toiletry bag: mascara, lipstick, various tubes and compacts. The air was thick with the scent of her favourite perfume, a special occasion fragrance she'd packed just for this trip.

Barely discernible, she could hear the muffled sounds of her friends getting ready in their own rooms, punctuated by occasional bursts of laughter and excited chatter. She pictured them running from room to room, helping each other prepare for the night ahead, and smiled to herself. This was what she had always imagined a bachelorette party would be like – surrounded by her best friends, dressed to the nines, ready to take on the glittering world of Las Vegas.

With a final sweep of mascara, Jess decided her makeup was complete. Now for the pièce de résistance — the dress she had carefully packed for this very night. She unzipped her suitcase, gently pulling out the silver sequined dress that had been nestled between layers of tissue paper.

As she held it up, the sequins caught the light, sending sparkles dancing across the walls. Jess took a deep breath, pushing aside the lingering thoughts of Miles's warning and focusing on the excitement of the moment. It was time to transform into her Vegas self.

"Rach?" Jess called out, stepping towards her door. "Can you help me with this zipper?"

Rachel appeared almost instantly, already looking stunning in a gold dress that seemed to catch every bit of light in the room. Their dresses complemented each other perfectly, just as they had planned.

"Of course, hon," she said. "Turn around."

As Rachel zipped her up, Jess caught her friend's eye in the mirror. "I can't believe you put all this together, Rach. It must have been so much trouble."

Rachel waved her hand dismissively. "Please, it was my pleasure. You deserve the best bachelorette party ever."

Jess turned to face her friend. "Seriously, though. This suite, the VIP passes... it's all so extravagant. You're sure it wasn't too much?"

A flash of something - discomfort? worry? - crossed Rachel's face, but it was gone so quickly Jess thought she might have imagined it. "Don't worry about it, Jess. Tonight is about celebrating you and having the time of our lives."

Jess nodded, but her mind wandered again to her conversation with Miles.

"Not still thinking about...?" Rachel began, but Jess knew exactly what she was going to say, and answered before her friend could finish.

"Maybe a little," she said, honestly.

Rachel swept a stray hair from Jess's face and pursed her lips. "I told you. He's such a worrier. Don't let him stop you having fun."

Jess reached her hand up onto her friend's and squeezed it gently.

"Hey, Rach," Jess said, attempting to keep her tone casual. "You know, I've always wondered... what is it like working with Miles at your family's company? He never really talks about work. And... well, neither do you."

Rachel paused. Briefly, Jess thought she saw a flicker of unease in her friend's eyes. But then Rachel smiled, the expression smooth and practiced.

"That's a bit out of the blue," she laughed. "I don't talk about it because it's not as exciting as it probably seems. You know how it is in a big company," Rachel said, sitting on the edge of Jess's soft king-sized bed. "And Miles and I have always worked in different departments, so our paths don't cross that often."

Jess nodded, watching Rachel's reflection in the mirror. "But you must have interacted enough to think he'd be perfect for me, right?"

Rachel's smile softened, becoming more genuine. "Just a hunch, I guess. I know you so well that it seemed like a no-brainer. I'd seen him around, and I don't know... he seemed like a good-looking, decent guy. There aren't many of them about."

"And he is," Jess said.

"He is," Rachel agreed. "I was right, wasn't I? As soon as I introduced you..."

"We clicked straight away," Jess said, drifting off into the memory, almost forgetting the concern that had brought her to question Rachel.

"I don't think I saw you the whole night. You were glued to Miles the entire time," Rachel said, with no hint of resentment or disappointment in her voice. Instead, her tone was light, almost teasing, as if she were recalling a fond memory rather than a potential slight.

The warmth in Rachel's voice made Jess smile, remembering that first meeting. But there was still something nagging at her. "It's funny, though," she drawled. "You two never really became close friends, even with me in common and both working at your parents' place."

Rachel shrugged, her movements a little too casual. "Like I said, we don't really work together, even

33

though it's the same company. I feel as though we probably have different approaches anyway."

Rachel stood up and brushed down her dress, looking as though she wanted to change the subject.

"Different approaches?" Jess pressed gently.

Rachel met her eyes in the mirror. "Just different work philosophies, that's all," she said, breaking eye contact again. "You know Miles much better than I do. I get the impression he is very structured and methodical, while I... well, I prefer a more flexible, creative approach. Listen, let's focus on you tonight, not this. I want to celebrate my best friend's bachelorette, not rattle on about work all night."

Jess couldn't let it go. She turned to face her friend directly. "Rachel, is there something you're not telling me? About you and Miles?"

For a moment, Rachel looked caught off guard. But then her usual confident smile slid back into place. "Jess, honey, what are you talking about? Miles and I are fine. We just... we're different people, that's all. But we both love you, and that's what matters."

Jess nodded slowly, not entirely convinced. She opened her mouth to ask another question, but Rachel cut her off with a laugh.

"Enough about work, and enough about Miles," she said decisively, linking her arm through Jess's. "This is your bachelorette party, remember? No boys allowed, not even in conversation!"

The familiarity of their friendship pushed away Jess's unease, but didn't completely erase it.

"Okay," Jess said. "It's just... on the phone... he sounded so..."

Rachel shook her head.

"No more," she said. "You can worry about him when you have that platinum band next to that lovely sparkling thing of beauty on your finger right there."

Jess laughed, lifting her hand and watching as the light caught the diamond.

"It matches this dress so perfectly," she said.

"You are radiant, Jess. With or without the bling." Rachel said.

Looking at her engagement ring made a flood of emotions rise within her, and Jess was momentarily overwhelmed. "Rach, I just want to say thank you again. For all of this. For being such an amazing friend."

Rachel's eyes softened. "Oh, Jess. You don't have to thank me. You're my best friend. I'd do anything for you."

For a moment, they just looked at each other, years of shared history and friendship passing between them. Then Rachel broke the moment with a laugh. "Okay, enough mushy stuff. Are you ready to hit the town?"

Jess grinned, pushing aside the last remnants of her earlier worry. "Absolutely. Let's show Vegas what we're made of!"

As they left Jess's bedroom, laughing arm-in-arm, Jess felt a surge of excitement. Whatever lay ahead, she was about to smash it with her best friend by her side. The night was young, Vegas was waiting, and they were ready to make some unforgettable memories.

FIVE
THIS MORNING

On the balcony in the morning sunlight, Jess reached out a hand to pull Lisa to her feet. Alex, connected at the wrist, moved with her. He matched her movement as she rose, as though they were performing an intricate dance.

"Sorry," he mumbled as he stumbled into Lisa.

Lisa gave him a small smile and tried to move away to give him space. It was futile.

"Come in out of the sun," Jess said. "I'm going to look for the others. See if you can find a way to get those off."

She nodded towards the handcuffs and then patted Lisa's shoulder in what she hoped was a reassuring way. Lisa scooped up her missing stiletto and the three of them stepped off the balcony and back into the suite.

The main room, which had seemed like a palace of luxury when they had checked in yesterday, was now a scene of chaos.

Sunlight streamed from the balcony, illuminating the debris left behind by the bachelorette party. Empty champagne bottles lay scattered across the marble coffee table, some tipped over, leaving sticky residue on the polished surface. How much had they drunk here last night? And that was without whatever they had got through in the VIP clubs.

Discarded shoes were strewn haphazardly across the plush carpet. A feather boa, bright pink and now somewhat bedraggled, draped itself over a crystal lamp like an exotic pet. Jess couldn't remember ever having seen it before, but somehow that no longer surprised her. No doubt they had picked it up somewhere along the way, and there was a hilarious anecdote to explain it that she couldn't quite remember.

The contrast of the room's inherent opulence and its current state of disarray was jarring. The crystal chandelier overhead, which had sparkled so enchantingly when they checked in, now seemed to mock them with its pristine brilliance amidst the mess.

Jess ran a hand through her tangled hair, wincing as her fingers caught in the knots. Her mind was a fog, memories of the previous night frustratingly out of reach. The only thing she knew for certain was that she had woken up in a bathtub filled with ice and poker chips, and had found Lisa handcuffed to a stranger on the balcony. These facts were so bizarre they seemed more like a dream than reality.

She glanced towards Lisa and Alex – a stranger whose presence was yet another puzzle piece that didn't fit. Now they hovered, standing just inside the balcony door, as if neither of them knew what to do next.

Jess didn't either.

Lisa looked shell-shocked and Alex was awkwardly trying to make himself small and unnoticeable, despite being chained to someone he'd apparently just met.

What Jess did know was that she had to find her

girls. Olivia, Megan, and Rachel were as yet unaccounted for, and Jess had a feeling that they would not be tucked up asleep in their beds.

Jess's stomach churned with apprehension as she thought of her friends. What had *happened* last night? The fragments of memory that flitted through her mind were disjointed and confusing – flashes of neon lights, the sound of laughter, the clink of glasses. But nothing substantial enough to explain their current situation.

"Girls?" she shouted. "Rachel? Meg? Olivia?"

There was no answer.

Giving one last glance in Lisa's direction, Jess set off to search the suite for her friends.

Jess moved through the main room, her bare feet sinking into the lush carpet. Each step revealed new evidence of their wild night – an upturned cocktail glass here, a playing card there, a single high heel balanced dangerously on the edge of the ornate table. None of it seemed familiar to her, and still there was no trace of her girls.

Despite her own rude awakening and the way she had found Lisa on the balcony with the casino worker, Jess still had a glimmer of hope that Rachel would be in her bed, sleeping off the night's excesses. This could all still turn out to be one big joke, something that they could laugh about for years to come. That's what it was: the making of an anecdote. Imagine how Miles would laugh when she told him about the ice bath, Lisa and Alex... Jess came to a halt when she thought about her fiancé. The fact that she hadn't called him yet was still lingering in her mind. But of course, there was nothing to tell. Rachel would be in her room, and everything would be fine. They'd go out for breakfast in the village pub that Rachel had raved about and then hit the spa. It was going to be a perfect day.

Jess approached Rachel's bedroom door, feeling more positive. She rehearsed in her mind how to wake her friend and break the news about their bizarre morning. As she reached for the doorknob, a sound from the main living area behind her made her freeze.

It was faint at first, almost imperceptible over the pounding in her head. But as Jess strained her ears, the sound became clearer – a muffled voice, calling out from somewhere in the suite.

"Help! Someone let me out!"

Jess's heart leaped into her throat. She recognised that voice – it was Megan.

How had she not noticed Meg in the suite?

Jess turned heel, her eyes scanning the room.

"Meg?"

Jess flicked her eyes across to Lisa, to see whether she too had heard, but Lisa's eyes were fixed on Alex.

As if on cue, the muffled cry came again, cutting through the morning haze.

"Help! Someone?"

Jess rushed towards the sound, only to find her path blocked by a room service cart that stood outside a walk-in closet. As she pushed it aside, she examined its contents: a half-eaten plate of what looked like beef stroganoff, congealed and unappetising, and an empty champagne bottle, its label bearing the name of an expensive vintage brand that Jess recognised but couldn't remember ordering. Was this what they had done when they arrived back at the suite? Dinner and more drinks? Rachel did always say that you shouldn't go to sleep on a stomach full of alcohol and empty of food, but... stroganoff?

Jess pulled her face as the thought of Rachel brought another pang of worry. Where *was* she? What had happened last night to leave them in this state?

"Megan? Are you okay?" Jess called, yanking the closet door open. The smell of expensive perfume mixed with sweet, stale alcohol wafted towards her.

Megan stumbled out, her usually composed demeanour shattered. Her sleek black jumpsuit, last night magnificent in its elegant simplicity, was now a wrinkled mess, with mysterious stains spattering the fabric. In her hands, she clutched a sleek leather briefcase, her knuckles white from the tight grip. She stared at it with a mixture of confusion and surprise, as if she couldn't quite remember how it had come into her possession.

Her trademark bob, normally a perfect curtain of shiny chestnut hair, was a tangled disaster. One side stuck up at an odd angle, as if she'd slept on it wet, while the other was flattened against her head.

Megan's face, usually adorned with subtle, professional makeup, was a canvas of smeared eyeshadow and smudged lipstick. Her eyes, wide with panic, were bloodshot and puffy, with mascara streaks trailing down her cheeks.

"Jess?" Megan croaked, her voice hoarse. "What's going on? And why am I holding this?" She lifted the briefcase slightly, her eyes bewildered.

Before Jess could respond, a low moan emanated

from behind the Italian leather couch. She exchanged glances with Megan, before turning to investigate. She peered over to find Olivia sprawled on the floor, wearing what appeared to be an authentic Las Vegas showgirl costume, complete with feathers and sequins. The outfit sparkled in the strips of sunlight sneaking through the partially closed curtains.

"What the...? Olivia?" Jess knelt beside her friend, gently shaking her. The feathers of the costume tickled her arm. "Can you hear me?"

Olivia's eyes fluttered open, unfocused and confused. "Why am I wearing Big Bird?" she slurred before promptly passing out again, her head lolling to one side.

Jess felt a stab of concern for Olivia. Though the newest addition to their group, she had quickly become an integral part of their circle, her bond with them as strong as any longtime friendship. They had met just six months ago at the local yoga studio when Olivia had taken over the class that Jess attended. Olivia had breezed into the class she was teaching, all smiles and positive energy, instantly lifting the mood of the room.

It hadn't taken long for Jess to introduce Olivia to the rest of the group. Their new friend had brought a fresh perspective and zest for life that they all admired. Now, seeing her passed out in a showgirl costume, the sequins catching the light with every shallow breath, Jess felt a mix of worry and bewilderment. This wild Vegas trip was supposed to be her last blowout as a single woman; an unforgettable celebration with her closest friends before she tied the knot. Instead, it seemed to have turned into a night that none of them could remember.

While Jess was occupied with Olivia, Megan had locked eyes with Lisa.

"What the hell happened last night?" Megan asked, her voice thick with confusion. She glanced around the room, taking in the chaos.

Lisa shook her head. "None of us remember. I'm guessing you're in the same boat?"

Megan nodded, opening her mouth as if to ask more questions, then closing it again. What was the point? No one had any answers.

"Must have been one hell of a night," Lisa muttered, running a hand through her tangled hair.

Alex groaned. "You can say that again. I feel like I've been hit by a truck."

"You look just fine," Lisa blurted out, immediately blushing at her own words.

Megan raised an eyebrow, a small smile tugging at her lips despite the situation.

"Sorry," Lisa mumbled. "Guess this isn't really the time for flirting, huh?"

Jess sighed, her eyes scanning the messy room. "Look, everything's gone sideways, but we need to keep it together. That includes being able to laugh a little, even now."

She stood next to Olivia, taking in the surrounding disarray. The once-luxurious suite now resembled the aftermath of a tornado. What a difference a day could make.

Five women had arrived in Las Vegas for a bachelorette party just yesterday, giggling and full of anticipation. Now, in the harsh light of morning, she faced a room full of confused and possibly drugged companions.

Ice baths, handcuffs, briefcases, and showgirl costumes were hardly what she expected from her bachelorette.

Jess needed help to make sense of it all. She needed her best friend. She needed to find Rachel.

SIX
LAST NIGHT

Jess and Rachel stepped out of the bedroom and into the suite's opulent lounge area, the energy in the room palpably shifting. The Las Vegas skyline shimmered beyond the floor-to-ceiling windows, a glittering tapestry of neon promising a night of endless possibilities. Jess felt a flutter of excitement in her stomach, mixed with a lingering unease she couldn't quite shake, like a premonition she couldn't decipher.

The plush carpet muffled their footsteps as they moved through the room, the air heavy with the scent of expensive perfume and anticipation.

"You look amazing, Rach," Jess said sincerely, taking in her friend's radiant appearance. "Thanks again for organising all this."

Rachel beamed, pulling Jess into a tight hug. The familiar scent of her perfume enveloped Jess, a comforting reminder of years of friendship. "Anything for you, Jess. This is going to be a night you'll never forget, I promise."

As they embraced, Jess felt a surge of love for her friend, mixed with a twinge of guilt for doubting her, even for a moment. Whatever Miles's concerns were, surely they were misplaced. The warmth of Rachel's hug and the sincerity in her voice pushed away the last of Jess's doubts.

"So, spill," Jess said, sinking into one of the elegant sofas, the cool fabric a stark contrast to her flushed skin. "What's this big surprise you've been hinting at all day?"

Rachel's eyes sparkled with mischief as she poured them each another glass of champagne, the golden liquid cascading into crystal flutes with a soft hiss.

"Now, now. If I told you, it wouldn't be a surprise, would it?" She handed Jess a flute, the condensation cool against her fingertips. "Let's just say I've pulled a few strings. Tonight, we're going to see a side of Vegas that most tourists never get to experience."

Jess raised an eyebrow, intrigued despite herself. The champagne bubbles danced on her tongue, a fizzy counterpoint to the knot of anticipation in her stomach.

"Sounds mysterious," she said. "And a little scary."

Rachel laughed, the sound light and carefree, echoing off the high ceiling. "Oh, come on. Where's your sense of adventure? Trust me, it's going to be amazing."

As they sipped their champagne, Jess studied her best friend. Rachel looked stunning in her gold dress, the fabric clinging to her curves and catching the light with every movement, every inch the confident, successful woman. But there was something else too - a tension in her shoulders, a look in her eyes when she thought Jess wasn't watching. It was as if Rachel was carrying a secret, one that weighed heavily on her despite her outward exuberance.

"Rachel," Jess began, her voice soft, barely audible over the faint music playing in the background. "You know you can tell me anything, right? If something's

45

bothering you..."

Rachel's smile faltered for just a moment, a crack in her perfect façade, before returning, brighter than ever. "Of course I know that, silly. But nothing's bothering me. I'm just excited about tonight. For you."

Before Jess could press further, there was a knock at the door, the sound sharp and sudden in the quiet room.

"That'll be the others," Rachel said, jumping up with perhaps a touch too much enthusiasm, her gold dress shimmering as she moved.

Lisa, Megan, and Olivia burst into the room in a whirl of perfume, sequins, and excitement. The suite was suddenly filled with animated chatter as the women complimented each other's outfits and poured more champagne, the clinking of glasses creating a festive atmosphere.

"Here come the girls!" Megan heralded their arrival.

"We may have had a glass of the fizzy stuff while we were getting ready," Lisa admitted with a wink. "Blame Liv."

Olivia raised her hands. "I knew Rach would be plying Jess with the good stuff. We've got to keep up, right?"

"Touché," Rachel smiled, tipping her glass towards her friends. "So, are you ready for tonight's adventures?" she asked, a mischievous glint in her eye.

Jess grinned, turning to face Rachel. The excitement in the room was infectious, pushing away her earlier apprehensions. "As ready as I'll ever be," she said.

"Though I have to say, I'm a bit nervous about what you've got planned."

Rachel's eyes sparkled with promise. "Don't worry, it'll be great. I've got us VIP access to some of the hottest spots in Vegas. Places most people only dream of seeing."

"As long as you don't drag me to see the Chippendales, I'm game for anything," Jess said, wrinkling her nose. "No offence, but that's just too tacky for me. I'm not really into the whole six-pack thing."

Rachel smirked, her eyes twinkling with amusement. "Oh, I can tell that. I've seen Miles, remember?"

Jess gasped in mock outrage, swatting at Rachel playfully. The cool glitter of Rachel's dress brushed against her hand. "Hey! Miles is perfectly... adequate."

"Adequate? Oh, honey," Rachel said, shaking her head. "Don't worry, no Chippendales tonight. I promise you'll love what I've got planned. It's going to be a night you'll never forget."

As their banter subsided, Jess caught Lisa giving her an odd look. Lisa's red dress hugged her curves, a statement of newfound confidence after her recent divorce, but there was a hint of concern in her eyes.

"Everything okay, Lis?" Jess asked, noticing the subtle shift in her friend's demeanour.

Lisa hesitated, glancing at Rachel before answering. The pause was brief, but noticeable. "Yeah, of course. Just... are you sure you're up for whatever Rachel's got planned? It sounds pretty wild."

Jess felt a flicker of unease at Lisa's tone, a shadow

passing over her earlier excitement. "Absolutely," she said, trying to sound more confident than she felt. "You're okay, aren't you?"

Before Lisa could respond, Olivia bounded over, practically vibrating with excitement. Her blue sequin dress caught the light with every movement, embodying the energy of Vegas itself.

"Girls, we need to take some photos before we leave," she said. "For posterity!"

The next few minutes were a blur of poses and flashing cameras. Jess found herself smiling, caught up in the excitement of the moment. The constant clicks from their camera apps created a soundtrack of anticipation. But beneath the surface of the revelry, Jess couldn't help noticing how Rachel kept checking her phone. The subtle action was at odds with the celebratory atmosphere, a discordant note in the otherwise harmonious scene.

As Megan fiddled with her camera settings for *just one more group shot*, Jess's own phone buzzed in her clutch. The vibration seemed to cut through the noise of the room. She fished it out, her stomach dropping slightly when she saw Miles's name on the screen, a reminder of the world outside their Vegas bubble.

Rachel appeared at her elbow, her voice tinged with concern. "Everything okay?"

Jess nodded, perhaps a bit too quickly. The lie felt heavy on her tongue. "Yeah, just Miles again. I'll call him back later."

Rachel's eyes narrowed slightly. A flicker of something - suspicion? concern? – passed across her face. But before she could say anything, Megan called them over for the photo, her voice cutting through the tension.

"Damn, girl!" Olivia whistled, her eyes roaming appreciatively over Jess's silver sequin dress. "Miles won't know what hit him when he sees the photos."

Jess blushed, pleased despite herself. She still couldn't quite believe this was all for her - her last big night out as a single woman, surrounded by her best friends in the glittering heart of Las Vegas. The reality of it all suddenly hit her, a wave of emotion threatening to overwhelm her.

Rachel reached for the champagne, the bottle sweating, even in the air-conditioned room. She poured the bubbly into flutes, the golden liquid catching the light.

"A toast," she declared, raising her glass high. "To Jess's last fling before the ring!"

They clinked glasses, the crystal catching the light and sending rainbows dancing across the walls. They sipped their drinks in unison, a moment of perfect synchronicity. Jess felt the champagne bubbles tickle her nose, a physical manifestation of the excitement buzzing through her veins. The alcohol warmed her from the inside, adding to the flush of anticipation already colouring her cheeks.

"All right, ladies," Jess said, her voice filled with excitement and just a hint of nervous anticipation. She raised her glass, the remaining champagne glittering like liquid gold. "Are we ready to show Vegas what we're made of?"

The answering cheer from her friends was all the reassurance she needed. It echoed off the walls of the suite, a battle cry of friendship and adventure.

Whatever the night held - surprises, adventures, or even potential dangers - Jess knew she could face it with her friends by her side. These were the women who had seen her through breakups and promotions, who had celebrated her highs and comforted her in her lows. Tonight, they would be her anchors in the swirling chaos of Las Vegas.

With one last glance in the mirror, taking in her reflection - flushed cheeks, bright eyes, silver dress catching the light - Jess squared her shoulders and prepared to step out into the Las Vegas night. She was ready for whatever awaited them, be it glamour, excitement, or the unexpected.

As the girls gathered their things, chattering excitedly about the night ahead, Jess found herself hanging back slightly. She watched her friends move around the room, each of them embodying a different facet of their shared excitement.

Lisa, still a bit subdued but smiling, her red dress a statement of resilience after her recent divorce. Her eyes held a mix of anticipation and caution, as if she were steeling herself for whatever the night might bring.

Megan, practical as ever, double-checking she had everything in her purse. Her outfit, a chic pantsuit that somehow managed to look both professional and party-ready, was a perfect reflection of her organised nature. Yet there was a glimmer in her eye that suggested she was ready to let loose, to step out of her comfort zone.

Olivia, practically bouncing with anticipation, her

blue dress sparkling in the light with every movement. She was the newest addition to their group, but her enthusiasm was infectious, adding an extra spark to the night's energy.

And Rachel, the mastermind behind it all, her radiant dress illuminating the surroundings as she moved. She exuded confidence and excitement, but Jess was sure that there was something more lurking beneath the surface, a secret hidden behind her dazzling smile.

Jess felt a wave of love for these women, mixed with a strange sense of foreboding. The juxtaposition of emotions was dizzying, like standing on the edge of a precipice, exhilarated by the view but acutely aware of the drop. She shook her head, trying to dispel the feeling.

"Ready to go, bride-to-be?" Rachel asked, appearing at her side and linking their arms. The warmth of her friend's body against hers was comforting, a physical reminder of their years of friendship.

Jess took a deep breath, inhaling the mingled scents of perfume, hairspray, and excitement. She pushed aside her lingering concerns, choosing instead to focus on the thrill of anticipation coursing through her veins. She smiled at her best friend, feeling the excitement of the night ahead beginning to take over. "Ready as I'll ever be. Let's do this!"

As they headed for the door, Jess glimpsed their reflection in the mirror - five women, dressed to the nines, on the brink of a night they'd never forget. The image was striking - a tableau of friendship, excitement, and latent possibility.

Las Vegas spread out before them, a playground of adults, a city where fortunes could change with the roll of a die or the turn of a card. And tonight, they were ready to gamble it all - on friendship, on adventure, and on the promise of a night they'd never forget.

SEVEN
THIS MORNING

The harsh Nevada sunlight sliced through the gap in the curtains, painting a bright stripe across Jess's face. She squinted, her head pounding with the unmistakable throb of a hangover. As consciousness fully returned, so did the memories of the chaos she'd woken up to – the ice-filled bathtub, Lisa and Alex handcuffed on the balcony, Megan in the closet with the briefcase she was still clutching, and Olivia in that showgirl costume. But one crucial piece was still missing: Rachel.

"Rachel?" Jess called out. "Rachel, are you up?"

Silence answered her, broken only by the faint hum of the air conditioning. Jess slowly walked to Rachel's bedroom, her stomach churning with a mix of nausea and growing concern.

She pushed open the door, wincing at the slight creak of the hinges. The sight that greeted her only deepened her unease. The bed was untouched, still perfectly made from the day before, the Egyptian cotton sheets smooth and inviting. Rachel's suitcase lay open on the floor, designer clothes spilling out, but there was no sign of her friend.

Jess frowned, her earlier discomfort blooming into full-fledged worry. Whatever had happened, it wasn't like Rachel to disappear without a word, especially on a trip this significant. As maid of honour and Jess's best friend since college, Rachel had been the driving force behind this bachelorette weekend, sparing no expense to ensure it would be unforgettable. Considering the state that she and the other girls had awoken in, Rachel's absence was all the more jarring.

She had half-expected to find Rachel passed out in the same daze as the rest of the group, and half-hoped she would be fresh out of the shower and full of answers. Not finding her at all was unsettling in a way Jess couldn't quite articulate. Rachel had always been the organised one, the planner. Even in their wildest college days, she was the friend who made sure everyone got home safely, who remembered the important details. For her to be missing now, when they all needed her most, felt wrong on every level.

Jess ran a hand through her still damp hair, trying to quell the growing anxiety in her chest. There had to be a logical explanation. Maybe Rachel had gone out for coffee or breakfast, or to sort out some mix-up with their reservations. But even as she tried to force these rational thoughts into her mind, Jess couldn't quite escape the terrible feeling that something was off. Without the ice bath and handcuffs, and all the rest of the chaos, there might have been a simple explanation, but the morning was already so screwed up that Jess could only fear the worst.

She glanced back at the pristine bed, the scattered clothes, searching for any clue that might hint at Rachel's whereabouts. The faint scent of Rachel's signature perfume lingered in the air, a haunting reminder of her absence.

Jess returned to the living room, her gaze falling on Olivia, still passed out in her showgirl costume. The sequins sparkled in the morning light, creating a surreal contrast to the surrounding chaos.

The yoga instructor's infectious energy and adventurous spirit had been a welcome addition to their longtime friendship group. But now, as Jess looked at her friend sprawled on the floor, she wondered if Olivia's penchant for excitement had somehow contributed to their current situation. After all, Olivia had always been the one pushing them to step out of their comfort zones.

"Any luck with Rachel?" Megan asked, still clutching the mysterious briefcase. Her knuckles were white against the sleek black surface, and Jess could see her hands trembling slightly.

Jess shook her head, feeling a headache building behind her eyes. "No sign of her. Let's focus on getting Olivia up. Maybe she remembers something about last night. You don't think...?"

Jess stopped before finishing the question, Lisa, Megan and even Alex looking at her quizzically.

"Nothing. I just... It's stupid. Come and give me a hand."

Lisa rattled the cuff on her hand, forcing Alex to do the same.

"Of course, sorry," Jess said. "Meg?"

Megan nodded and came to Jess's side, finally letting go of the briefcase and leaving it on the glass coffee table.

As they turned their attention back to their

costumed friend, although she moaned softly, it was clear she wasn't quite ready to rejoin the land of the living.

"I'll keep an eye on her," Megan offered. "Keep looking around, Jess. There must be some clues."

Jess nodded, flicking her gaze to Lisa and Alex, who had settled uncomfortably on the sofa. Lisa was twisting the silver shackle on her arm as though it was a bracelet that had become too tight. Alex looked exhausted.

Jess's eyes scanned the chaotic living room once more, searching for any evidence. The morning sun had crept further into the room, illuminating the debris of their forgotten night; an overturned bottle of champagne was slowly dripping its contents onto the expensive carpet. Jess leant over and scooped it up. Damage limitation seemed futile, but her instinct was to do everything she could.

A glint near the entertainment centre caught her eye. She moved towards it, her bare feet crunching on something cold and smooth. Looking down, she saw the shattered remains of a phone. She knew at a glance that it belonged to Rachel.

Jess felt her stomach drop, an icy wave of dread washing over her. Rachel's phone. Rachel never went anywhere without it; It was practically an extension of her hand, always within reach for that important call or the perfect photo op. For it to be here, shattered on the floor...

With trembling hands, Jess picked up the damaged device. The screen was a spiderweb of cracks, but she could still make out Rachel's lock screen photo: the five of them, arms around each other, laughing at the airport just yesterday. Rachel must have updated it after they arrived. Their smiling faces served as a harsh reminder of how quickly their joyful trip had turned into a nightmare.

Was it only yesterday? It felt like a lifetime ago.

"Guys," Jess said solemnly.

"What is it?" Lisa said, craning from the sofa.

"Rachel's phone," Jess said, trying to hold in her emotions. "It's smashed up pretty badly."

"Oh shit," Megan said. "That's.... shit.... she..."

Jess nodded. "I know. Wherever she is, I don't think she left us voluntarily."

Lisa dropped her head into her hands, and Alex put his free palm on her shoulder.

"Hey," he said. "You're going to find her. People get lost in Vegas all the time. It was a wild night. I'm sure she'll turn up."

"She never leaves her phone," Lisa said, her voice cracking.

The pit in Jess's stomach grew deeper, fear clawing at her throat. What kind of trouble had Rachel got into? And more importantly, where was she now?

Jess's mind raced with possibilities, each more terrifying than the last. Had Rachel been kidnapped? Was she hurt? The weight of the situation pressed down on Jess, making it hard to breathe. She had to find Rachel, had to make sure she was okay. But where to even start?

With a muttered affirmation to herself, Jess forced herself to focus. There had to be something that could point them in the right direction. She turned the phone over in her hands, hoping for any sign of what might have happened to her friend.

Despite the damage, the fact that she could just about make out their faces through the cracks meant that the device still had some life in it. A notification blinked on the shattered screen: one new voicemail.

With trembling fingers, Jess tapped in Rachel's passcode. She frowned in confusion as she saw her own name on the screen. The timestamp showed it was from the early hours of the morning, but Jess had no recollection of leaving a message. Had she called Rachel? Why couldn't she remember doing so? Then again, why couldn't she remember anything?

Her confusion deepened as she noticed something odd about the contact entry. Instead of the usual "Jess" it said "Jess - EMERGENCY." When had Rachel changed her contact name, and why?

"Megan, look at this." Jess showed her the name.

"What the shit?" Megan said slowly.

"What? What is it?" Lisa got up, pulling Alex with her, and came over to the other girls. "Emergency?" she said. "How would she know...?"

"Something must have been going on that none of us knew about," Megan said.

"But that Rachel *did* know about." Jess gulped back a sob. "She's in trouble. We have to listen to this. Maybe this message... Maybe I said something that might help?"

Heart pounding, she pressed play and held the phone to the room so the others could hear. The sounds of the Vegas night filtered through the cell – distant music, the constant background hum of chatter. Her own voice, tense and frightened, crackled through the speaker:

"Rachel, it's Jess. I don't know what's going on, but something's not right. If you get this, be careful. I think we're in trouble. Don't trust—"

The message cut off abruptly, leaving Jess staring at the phone in horror.

"Don't trust who?" Jess asked no one in particular. "What did I find out?"

Lisa looked up at her with a pale face. "And why did you phone Rachel instead of talking to her directly?"

"If we were with her all night, you wouldn't have needed to phone her," Megan said. Jess could see that her analytic mind was already whirring in overdrive. "What time was that message? I guess we can assume that by whenever that was, Rachel was already missing."

Jess looked at the timestamp of the call – 3:17am.

"Nearly six hours ago," Jess said, reading out the time.

"So we need to work out what had happened in those six hours," Lisa said.

"Or what happened in the time leading up to then," Megan countered.

"You're both right," Jess said.

As she looked up from the phone, she caught sight of her reflection in the large mirror across the room. Her usually sleek hair was a tangled mess, her makeup smeared, and her expensive dress was wrinkled and damp. But it was the look in her eyes that startled her most – a mix of fear, confusion, and determination.

Jess tried to focus. Whatever had happened last night, whatever trouble Rachel was in, she was going to figure it out. She owed it to her best friend, to all of her friends, to unravel this mystery.

"We need to know how she disappeared, and what happened to us all after that. Maybe then we'll know where to look for Rachel," Jess said. Her voice was tense, but she was trying to stay in control of her emotions.

Jess set Rachel's shattered phone down on the glass table. Its cracked screen was a stark reminder of the potential danger. The urge to call Rachel was overwhelming, but futile.

"Above all, we need to find her," Jess said, her voice tight with worry.

Megan reached out her hand and took hold of Jess's.

"Hey," she said. "Maybe she's lost, or..."

"I heard my voice, Meg," Jess said. "If I tried to warn Rachel that we were in trouble, there must have been something bad going down. And why would she change my name to emergency?"

"Shit," Megan said again.

Alex shifted uncomfortably, the handcuffs clinking as he tried to create some distance between himself and Lisa without yanking her arm. His curly hair was dishevelled, and dark circles under his eyes betrayed his exhaustion.

He cleared his throat, his voice hoarse. "Look, I know how this looks, but I swear I have no idea how I got here. The last thing I remember is working my shift at the Bellagio. I was dealing blackjack, and then...

nothing. I feel bad for all of y'all but... I'd really like to leave."

Jess noticed Lisa's rapid breathing and trembling hand as she pushed a strand of blonde hair behind her ear. Lisa's eyes, wide with a mix of fear and something Jess couldn't quite place, darted between Alex and her friends.

"There's the slight problem of the handcuffs," Jess said.

"We need to get out of these." Lisa whispered, her voice trembling.

"It's okay, Lisa," Jess soothed, squeezing her shoulder. "We'll figure this out together."

"I can't believe I'm handcuffed to a total stranger." She looked pleadingly at Jess. "He could be dangerous for all I know. He could be involved in..."

"I'm not dangerous!" Alex protested, his face flushing. He turned towards Lisa, and Jess watched as they both froze for a moment, their faces unexpectedly close. Alex quickly looked away, tugging slightly at the handcuffs. "I'm just as confused as you are. I'm a regular guy, I swear."

"This isn't happening," Lisa said, her voice taut. "We need to get these off. Now."

Alex glanced at her, confusion and curiosity mingling in his eyes. "Yeah, I agree. I don't like this any more than you do."

Jess observed this exchange with growing interest, noticing the undercurrent of tension between Lisa and Alex. Despite the chaos, there was something in their interaction that hinted at a story neither seemed ready to confront.

As panic set in about Rachel's disappearance, Jess noticed Lisa nervously biting her nails - a habit Jess thought she'd kicked years ago.

"Lisa?" Jess said. "I know this is awkward for you. I'm sorry. Are you okay?"

Lisa nodded. "Me? Yeah, I'm... I'm fine. It's just..." She hesitated, her eyes darting around the room. "Actually, I'm really worried about Rachel. I feel like this is all my fault somehow."

Jess frowned, confused. "Your fault? How could it be your fault?"

Lisa looked on the verge of tears. "I just... I feel responsible. I should have kept a closer eye on her. I knew something felt off about last night, but I didn't say anything."

The intensity of Lisa's reaction surprised Jess. Sure, they were all worried about Rachel, but Lisa's guilt seemed... personal.

The tense atmosphere was interrupted by a low groan from behind the couch. Jess rushed over to find Olivia stirring, her showgirl costume askew.

"Liv? Can you hear me?" Jess asked, helping her friend sit up.

Olivia blinked slowly, disorientation clear in her eyes. "Jess? What... where are we? Why does my head hurt so much?"

Before Jess could respond, a sharp knock at the door made them all jump. The room fell silent, tension thick in the air.

Jess exchanged nervous glances with her friends. Inhaling and holding her breath, Jess cautiously approached the door. Her hand hovered over the handle as another knock, more insistent this time, echoed through the suite.

With her heart in her throat, Jess reached for the door handle, unsure of what - or who - she would find on the other side.

EIGHT
LAST NIGHT

The limousine pulled away from the Bellagio, a cocoon of luxury amid the pulsing energy of the Las Vegas Strip. Inside, the air was thick with excitement and the subtle scent of expensive perfume. Jess settled into the butter-soft leather seat, her heart racing with anticipation.

"Wow, more champagne!" Lisa exclaimed, already reaching for the ice bucket. Her manicured nails clinked against the crystal flutes as she distributed them.

Rachel, effortlessly elegant in the designer dress that probably cost more than Jess's entire wardrobe, smiled mysteriously as she popped the cork. "Only the best for my girl's last night of freedom," she said, filling the glasses with practiced ease.

As the bubbles fizzed and settled, Jess couldn't help but marvel at her best friend. Rachel had always been the glamorous one, with her family's wealth opening doors that Jess could only dream of. Even after years of friendship, there was still an air of mystery about Rachel's background that Jess had never quite penetrated.

"To Jess," Rachel toasted, raising her glass high, "and the most unforgettable bachelorette party ever!" There was a glint in her eye that Jess couldn't quite read. Excitement? Mischief? Or something else entirely?

As they clinked glasses, the limo merged into the slow-moving traffic of the Strip. The girls pressed their faces to the tinted windows, drinking in the sights. The neon lights of Las Vegas painted their faces in a kaleidoscope of colours.

"Thank frick it's Friday," Megan laughed as she drank deeply.

"You can say that again," Lisa agreed. "Whoever decided that we should work five days and have two days off had it completely the wrong way round."

"When I rule the world, which for your information I intend to do, we will only work two days a week, and have a five day weekend," Rachel laughed, raising her glass.

"You know, I almost believe you'll do that," Jess giggled. "I, for one, would vote for you."

"Darling, you would be my number two." Rachel patted Jess gently and the two of them shared a smile.

"Fine," Lisa said. "I'll be too busy to help you anyway, with my harem of new lovers and..." She burst into uncontrollable laughter before she could finish, and the others let her enjoy the moment.

"My boss will still have me working seven days a week, no doubt," Megan said, rolling her eyes dramatically.

"How's your job going, Olivia?" Lisa asked. "Still enjoying teaching yoga? I don't think I've been in for... how long has it been?"

Olivia's laugh sounded forced, a stark contrast to her usual bubbly demeanour. "Oh, you know..." she began, her eyes darting around the limo as if seeking an escape. "I've actually decided to take some time off. Find myself, explore new opportunities."

Jess frowned, catching the slight tremor in Olivia's voice. Something wasn't quite right, but before she could probe further, Rachel smoothly interjected.

"Speaking of opportunities," Rachel said, seamlessly steering the conversation away from Olivia, "you wouldn't believe the connections I've made here in Vegas. Maybe I have one for you, Liv."

The moment passed, but Jess filed away Olivia's strange reaction for later consideration. For now, she turned her attention back to Rachel, curiosity piqued.

"I still can't believe you pulled all this together, Rach," Megan said, her focus shifting back to the night ahead. "These connections of yours must be pretty impressive."

Rachel shrugged, a practiced gesture of nonchalance. "Oh, you know. When you spend enough time in Sin City, you get to know people."

"People like that insanely hot guy at the Bellagio who practically fell over himself to help us?" Olivia chimed in, wiggling her eyebrows suggestively.

Rachel laughed, but somehow it didn't seem entirely genuine. "I didn't even notice. He was probably just doing his job. Or trying to earn his tip."

Lisa snorted into her champagne. "Doing his job? Rachel, darling, that man looked at you like you owned the place."

"Maybe she does," Megan joked, but there was a hint of curiosity in her voice. "Your family's business interests are pretty diverse, aren't they, Rach?"

For a moment, tension crackled in the air. Rachel's smile tightened almost imperceptibly. "Oh, you know how it is. A little of this, a little of that. Boring stuff, really. Who wants to talk business on a night like tonight?"

Jess frowned slightly. In all the years she'd known Rachel, she'd never got a straight answer about what her family actually did. Influential, yes. Wealthy, absolutely. But the details always seemed to slip away like smoke whenever the subject came up. They owned a portfolio of companies, some of which Miles was involved in and some even he probably didn't know about. It always seemed, though, as if there was a lot more going on behind the scenes.

Before she could dwell on it further, Olivia let out a squeal of delight. "Guys, look at the Bellagio fountains now. They're even more beautiful at night!" The others crowded to the windows, watching in awe as the water danced and swayed in time to music they couldn't hear.

As they pulled away from the grand hotel, Lisa turned to Rachel with a mischievous grin. "So, spill. What's on the agenda for tonight? Any scandalous surprises planned?"

Rachel's laugh was just a touch too bright. "Perhaps," she said, with a hint of playfulness. "Just trust me. Tonight is definitely one you'll never forget."

The way she said it sent a shiver down Jess's spine. There was something in Rachel's tone, something that didn't quite match the carefree atmosphere in the limo. A weight to her words that seemed at odds with a simple bachelorette party. Or maybe it was just Miles's words casting a shadow on the night. Jess beamed a smile at her friend and resolved not to let anything put a dampener on their fun.

As they cruised past the front of the Mirage, its volcano dark and dormant, Jess caught Rachel checking her phone for what seemed like the hundredth time since they'd left the hotel. Her expression was tense as she read something on the screen, then she quickly locked the phone as she noticed Jess watching.

"Everything okay?" Jess asked, trying to keep her tone light.

Rachel's smile was dazzling, but there was a tightness around her eyes that hadn't been there before. "Of course! Just making sure everything's perfect for tonight. You know me, always the planner."

Jess nodded, but she sensed that something was off. The secretive phone checks, the vague answers about her family, the tension that seemed to radiate off her in waves... it all added up to something, but Jess couldn't quite put her finger on what.

"Look!" Olivia exclaimed, pointing excitedly as they approached Treasure Island. "There's the pirate ship!"

The massive replica vessel loomed large against the night sky, its rigging and masts illuminated against the backdrop of the hotel. Even from inside the limo, they could hear the faint sounds of cannon fire and swashbuckling music from the famous outdoor show.

"And look! Senor Frog's! Wow, remember when we went to the one in Orlando last year?" Lisa giggled, her eyes sparkling with the memory. "I still can't believe Megan ended up on that mechanical bull!"

Megan groaned, burying her face in her hands. "I thought we agreed never to speak of that again! I swear if we end up in there this weekend..."

"You'll do it all over again," Lisa hollered.

The limo erupted in laughter, the sound mixing with the clinking of their champagne glasses. As they left Treasure Island behind them, Olivia raised her glass for another toast. "To friendship," she declared. "May it weather any storm and survive any adventure!"

The others echoed her sentiment, their glasses meeting with a crystalline chime that seemed to resonate with promise. As they sipped their champagne, Jess couldn't help but feel a swell of emotion. Here they were, cruising down the Las Vegas Strip in a limo, surrounded by the glitz and glamour of Sin City, embarking on what promised to be an unforgettable night. Yet even amidst the excitement, that nagging feeling of unease lingered in the back of her mind, a silent counterpoint to the laughter and joy filling the limo.

Eventually, the vehicle slowed, and Rachel straightened up, smoothing down her dress. "All right, ladies," she announced, her voice filled with excitement. "We're almost there. This is the exclusive and not at all famous Cherry Pop Las Vegas. Are you ready for a night you'll never forget?"

As they chorused their agreement, Jess caught Rachel's reflection in the window. For just a moment, her best friend's face was a mask of worry and... was that guilt? But then Rachel turned, flashing her trademark dazzling smile, and the moment was gone.

The limo came to a stop, and as the driver opened the door, the pulsing beat of music flooded in. Jess tentatively looked out into the night. Blissfully unaware of the storm brewing on the horizon, the girls exited into the night, ready to paint the town red.

NINE
THIS MORNING

The pounding on the door jolted Jess from her thoughts. She glanced at her friends, their expressions reflecting her own confusion and worry. With a deep breath, she approached to answer, her bare feet silent on the deep, soft carpet.

She opened the door to find a stern-faced man in a crisp suit. He looked to be in his sixties, but he was as perfectly turned out and elegant as the hotel itself. The man's name tag read "Robert Chen, Hotel Manager." Before he spoke, Jess already knew that she was in trouble. Seeing Jess, Mr Chen's eyes widened, taking in her damp, wrinkled dress and smeared makeup.

Jess suddenly became acutely aware of her appearance. She could feel her still partially wet hair sticking to her neck and the uncomfortable dampness of her dress. She tried to stand up straighter, attempting to project an air of maturity and professionalism despite feeling like a bedraggled mess.

"Good morning, *Ms* Parker," Mr Chen said, his tone clipped but with a hint of uncertainty. "I'm afraid I must ask you and your party to vacate the suite immediately."

Jess cleared her throat, fighting the urge to wipe at her face, knowing it would only smear her makeup further. "I'm sorry, what?" she asked, attempting to maintain her steady voice. "We have the suite booked for the entire weekend."

Mr Chen's gaze flickered over her shoulder, taking in the chaotic state of the room behind her. His expression didn't soften. "I'm aware of your reservation. However, given the... disturbance last night and the state of the suite, we must insist you leave."

Jess felt an overwhelming wave of panic, along with a deep embarrassment at being seen in such a mess. She struggled to maintain her composure, acutely aware of how ridiculous she must look, trying to argue while looking like she'd just stumbled out of a pool.

"Mr Chen, could you tell me what kind of *disturbance* was reported? We're trying to piece together what happened last night."

The manager's expression hardened, his polite veneer cracking slightly. "Ms Parker, I think we both know you're well aware of the **disturbance**. Multiple noise complaints, reports of shouting, and what sounded like furniture being overturned. Not to mention the state of this suite, which you haven't even attempted to conceal."

Jess flinched at his tone, feeling heat rise to her cheeks. She glanced back at the chaos behind her - upended furniture, scattered clothes, empty bottles. It looked like a tornado had torn through the room. Whatever reports had been made, there was no denying they were true.

"I... we..." she stammered, struggling to find an explanation that wouldn't sound completely absurd. "We genuinely don't remember what happened, Mr

Chen. That's why we need more time. Our friend is missing, and we're worried something might have happened to her."

The manager's eyes narrowed, clearly sceptical. "Ms Parker, I've worked in Las Vegas hotels for over four decades. I've heard every excuse imaginable. People come here to escape their lives, to be someone else for a weekend. Sometimes they take it too far. But actions have consequences, even in Sin City."

Mr Chen's gaze swept past Jess, taking in Lisa and Alex still handcuffed, and Megan crouching next to their drowsy showgirl. His eyes tightened further.

"Ms Parker, let me be clear," he said, his voice low and stern. "You and all your friends must vacate not just this suite, but your individual rooms as well. The disturbances were reported throughout your party's accommodations."

Jess felt her heart sink. She hadn't even thought about the others' rooms. "But sir, we —"

"No buts," Mr Chen interrupted, gesturing towards Lisa and Alex. "And remove those handcuffs at once. This is a respectable establishment, not a... den of iniquity."

Behind her, Jess heard the rattle of the cuffs as Lisa shuffled uncomfortably.

"Three hours," Jess pleaded. "Just give us three hours to clean up and figure things out. Please."

The manager hesitated, his eyes once again taking in the chaotic scene behind Jess. Finally, he looked at his watch – something that cost more than the group made between them in a year – and sighed. "Two hours and forty minutes, Ms Parker. Not a minute more. You will be out of this hotel by one o'clock. And this applies to all of your party's rooms. When I return, I expect to find everything in order and all of you ready to depart. Is that clear?"

Jess nodded vigorously, relief washing over her. "Crystal clear, Mr Chen. Thank you."

As the door sighed shut behind the manager, Jess leaned against it, closing her eyes briefly. When she opened them, she saw her friends looking at her expectantly.

"Okay," she said, straightening up. "First things first. We need to get those handcuffs off you."

Lisa and Alex looked relieved, but all out of ideas.

"There has to be an easy way out of these," Lisa muttered, twisting her wrist uncomfortably.

Alex's eyes suddenly lit up, focusing on something in Lisa's hair. Without warning, he reached out with his free hand, his fingers gently brushing against her temple. Lisa froze, her breath catching in her throat at the unexpected closeness.

"Sorry," Alex murmured, his face inches from hers. "I don't know why I didn't think of this before. You have a bobby pin. May I?"

Lisa nodded mutely, hyperaware of his proximity. Alex carefully extracted the pin from her tangled hair, his touch lingering for a moment longer than necessary. Their eyes met, and Jess saw a redness to Lisa's cheeks that she was sure had nothing to do with their predicament.

With focused precision, Alex bent the pin and started working on the lock of his handcuff. His tongue poked out slightly in concentration, and Lisa stared, seemingly captivated by this small detail.

After a tense minute, there was a soft click, and Alex's wrist was free. He let out a quiet cheer of triumph.

"My turn?" Lisa asked softly, holding out her still-cuffed arm.

Alex nodded, gently taking her hand. His fingers brushed against her skin as he worked on the lock.

Another click, and Lisa was released. But Alex didn't immediately let go of her hand, and she didn't pull away. Their eyes met again, and Jess observed a spark of something passing between them.

"Thanks," Lisa said, barely whispering.

Alex smiled, looking a bit flustered himself. "Anytime. Though hopefully, we won't need to do this again."

They both chuckled nervously, the moment stretching between them until Jess's voice broke the spell.

"All right... it seems you have some, er, skills we aren't aware of, Alex," Jess said. Then she addressed the group. "We don't have much time. Lisa, Megan, Olivia. Do a quick sweep of your rooms. Get changed and grab anything important and check for clues. Alex, help me search this suite. We meet back here in ten minutes, no matter what. Go!"

Megan offered out a hand and pulled Olivia to her feet.

"You okay to walk?" she asked. "Still wobbly?"

Olivia took a couple of tentative steps.

"I'll be okay," she said. "But this isn't my outfit and

these definitely aren't my shoes."

She teetered a little, swaying against the back of the sofa before regaining her balance. The shoes were covered in the same sequin design as her dress, with lavish feathers at the back of the heels.

"It kind of suits you strangely," Megan smiled. "All that yoga came in clutch."

Olivia gave a half-smile.

"I'd be happier if I knew where this had come from, why I was wearing it and where the hell Rachel is," she said.

Megan nodded, "Me too, Liv. Me too."

Lisa came around the other side of Olivia and offered her an arm.

"Let's get back into our sneakers and out of these clothes. We can't do anything looking like Taylor Swift's Eras wannabees."

It was almost enough to make the group laugh, but the most they could manage was a round of quiet chuckles.

"Ten minutes. Switch up your clothes and have a quick look around, okay?"

They nodded. Before she left, Megan reached down for the briefcase.

"I'll see what I can do with this too," she said.

With that, the three girls left the suite and made their way back down the corridor to their own rooms.

Once they were alone, Alex looked at Jess, his face a mix of guilt and anxiety. "Jess, before we start... there's something I need to tell you. I didn't want to say anything in front of the group. It's kinda sensitive."

Jess felt her stomach tighten. "What is it?"

He paused before speaking. "I... I have a record. It's nothing major, just some stupid mistakes when I was younger, but it's why I can't afford to get into any trouble now. If I do, I'll probably never work in Vegas again."

Jess stared at him, processing this information. "Is that why you were so good at picking those handcuffs?"

Alex nodded, looking ashamed. "Yeah, it's a skill I picked up... before. I've been trying to turn my life around, working at the casino, keeping my nose clean. But now, waking up here like this... I'm scared, Jess. I can't lose everything I've worked for."

Jess sank into a chair, considering his words. "Okay," she said slowly. "I appreciate you being honest with me."

"I'd really like to just leave, if that's okay." Alex held eye contact with Jess.

"Alex, we are in some serious shit here. I understand what you're saying, and why you feel that way, but Rachel is my best friend." Jess paused, as if reconsidering. "Rachel and Lisa are my best friends. We were in college together and we've been there for each other ever since. They mean the world to me, and I know that if anything ever happened to me, they would stop at nothing to find me. I feel the same way about Rachel. If there's any chance at all that you have answers that we don't..." Jess flopped onto the sofa. "Please. I'm asking you, for Rachel. For Lisa. For me. Please. Will you stay?"

Alex let out a deep breath that he had apparently

been holding all the while Jess was speaking.

"Okay," he said. "Okay. But please, I need to keep a low profile. You have to understand that this could cost me everything."

Jess reached over and took his hand. "I do. And thank you. I know you don't know us, and I have no idea how you're mixed up in this, but... I hope you can help us. I really do. Thank you."

"I don't know if I'll be able to. It's all so hazy."

Jess stood up and began pacing the room. "All right. If anything comes to you, tell me straight away. For now, let's keep looking for clues. There has to be something here that can tell us what happened last night. And Alex, don't worry. We're all in this together now. We'll figure it out without getting you into trouble."

Looking around the room, Jess's eyes fell again on Rachel's phone. She picked it up. She couldn't call her friend, but perhaps there were other clues behind the shattered glass. Carefully, she entered the passcode once more and began to search.

As she scrolled through, a text message caught her eye. It was sent at 11:58 PM the previous night: "Midnight. The back room. Come alone."

Whatever had happened to Rachel, one thing was evident: she hadn't left them of her own free will. Someone else was involved, and that meant Rachel could be in more trouble than they had even imagined.

TEN
LAST NIGHT

The limo pulled up to the curb, and the five girls spilled out onto the Las Vegas sidewalk. The night air was electric, hitting them like a slap after the cool, champagne infused interior they'd just left. The music from the club pulsed through the air, its heavy bass vibrating in their chests even before they reached the entrance. A bold neon cherry hung above the entrance, with the name of the club, Cherry Pop, glaring out below.

"Seriously, look at that line!" Lisa exclaimed, taking in the scene with a look of astonishment.

The queue stretched around the block, a sea of glittering dresses and crisp shirts. Excited chatter filled the air, punctuated by laughter and the occasional squeal of recognition as friends spotted each other. The atmosphere buzzed with anticipation and possibility.

Jess inhaled the unique scent of Las Vegas - a mixture of desert air, cigarette smoke, and the faint sweetness of countless cocktails. The glaring lights of the Strip painted the night in a spectrum of vivid shades, reflecting off the sequins of her dress and casting a magical glow over her friends' faces.

Rachel grinned, nodding towards their VIP passes. "Ladies, this is why connections matter. Follow me."

As they bypassed the long line, making their way to

the VIP entrance, Jess felt a thrill of excitement course through her. Her silver dress sparkled like a mirror ball. She could feel the eyes of the waiting crowd on them, a mixture of envy and admiration.

"I can't believe we're actually doing this," she whispered to Lisa, squeezing her hand. The reality of the moment was finally sinking in - they were in Las Vegas, about to enter one of the most exclusive clubs in the city. And they were VIPs.

Lisa nodded, her eyes sparkling with joy. "I know! We've been hearing about Rachel's Vegas adventures for years. It's about time we got to experience it ourselves."

Rachel overheard and turned to them, her smile warm and genuine. "Tonight's the night, girls. And what better occasion than Jess's bachelorette? It's time you all saw my world."

As they reached the VIP entrance, Rachel confidently flashed their passes. The bouncer, a mountain of a man in a tailored suit, nodded respectfully and unclipped the velvet rope.

"Enjoy your evening, ladies," he said, his deep voice almost inaudible amid the music.

They stepped inside, and the club's atmosphere enveloped them immediately. The interior was a fever dream of luxury – crystal chandeliers hung from ceilings that seemed to stretch to infinity, their light refracting off mirrored walls and creating a dazzling, otherworldly glow. Beautiful people in designer clothes danced on elevated platforms, their movements hypnotic in the pulsing lights.

The air was thick with the scent of expensive perfumes, mingling with the faint aroma of top-shelf liquor. The bass thrummed through their bodies, making their hearts beat in time with the music. The energy was palpable, a living thing that seemed to pulse with each beat.

"Holy shit," Megan breathed, her eyes wide as she took in the scene. Even the usually reserved brunette couldn't hide her awe at the spectacle before them.

Olivia was already swaying to the music, her yoga-toned body responding instinctively to the rhythm.

"Wow, this is amazing!" she shouted above the noise.

Rachel laughed, linking arms with Jess and Lisa. "Remember, ladies. Leave your troubles at the door. Tonight, you belong to Las Vegas."

As Jess gazed around the club, a statuesque woman in a slinky red dress approached them, her walk smooth and confident despite her sky-high heels. Her presence drew admiring glances from men and women alike.

"You must be Jess," she purred, her smile dazzling. "I'm Cynthia. Rachel told me to expect you."

Jess shot a questioning look at Rachel, who shrugged nonchalantly. "Cynthia's a friend of a friend. She promised to show us the real Vegas."

"Pleased to meet you," Jess said, shaking hands with the stranger. "This all looks very real to me."

Cynthia's laugh was like velvet, smooth and rich. "Oh honey, you haven't seen anything yet. Stick with me, and I'll show you a side of this city that tourists never see. Come along."

Cynthia led them through the crowd, the sea of

people parting effortlessly before her. Jess almost felt like a celebrity, trailing in Cynthia's wake. They passed the main bar, where bartenders were putting on a show, flipping bottles and creating cocktails that looked more like works of art than drinks.

They arrived at a private booth, elevated above the main dance floor. The plush velvet seats were a welcome respite from their heels, and a bucket of chilled champagne awaited them. The seating area offered a perfect view of the entire club, allowing them to take in the spectacle while enjoying their own intimate space.

As Cynthia expertly poured their drinks, the bubbles rising in a perfect cascade, Jess looked around at her friends. Olivia was bobbing to the music, her body itching to hit the dance floor. Her blue eyes were wide, taking in every detail of the club.

Megan, ever the pragmatist, seemed to be studying their surroundings with a mixture of awe and calculation. Jess could almost see the gears turning in her head, no doubt estimating the cost of such extravagance. But even Megan couldn't hide the excitement that tinged her expression.

Lisa was beaming, all traces of her recent divorce troubles gone from her face. The red of her dress complemented the flush on her cheeks, and for the first time in months, she looked truly carefree.

And Rachel... Rachel was watching them all with a mixture of pride and something else Jess couldn't quite place. Affection? Anxiety? Her gold dress caught the light, making her look like a statue come to life.

Before Jess could dwell on it, Lisa raised her glass.

"To Jess!" she shouted over the music. "And to the best bachelorette party Vegas has ever seen!"

"I've never drunk so much champagne in my life," Jess laughed.

They clinked glasses, the crystal ringing out even over the pounding bass. As the bubbles tickled her nose, Jess felt a wave of pure happiness wash over her. This was exactly what she'd hoped for – all her girls were by her side for her perfect night.

"Speech!" Olivia called out, grinning at Jess.

Jess laughed, standing up in the booth. She wobbled slightly on her heels, steadying herself against the railing. The movement sent sparkles from her dress, dancing across the booth in a personal light show.

"Ladies," she began, her voice thick with emotion. "I can't tell you how much it means to have you all here with me tonight. Each of you has been such an important part of my life, and I couldn't imagine celebrating this moment without you."

She turned to Rachel. "Rach, you've outdone yourself with this. Thank you for always being there, for being the sister I never had."

Rachel smiled warmly before Olivia pulled her into a hug.

"We love you, Jess!" Olivia exclaimed, her enthusiasm infectious.

They settled back into their seats, sipping champagne and taking in the pulsing energy of the club. Cynthia leaned in towards the group.

"So, ladies," she purred. "Are you ready to see what Vegas is really about?"

The girls exchanged glances. This was why they

83

had come to Vegas - for adventure, for experiences they couldn't get anywhere else, and above all else, to celebrate Jess.

"Absolutely," Jess replied, her voice tinged with both excitement and a hint of nervousness. "Show us everything."

Cynthia's smile was warm, with just a hint of mystery that made Jess wonder what exactly lay ahead.

"Oh, sweetie. You're in for a treat. Vegas has so many hidden gems."

"We'd better slow down on the drinks," Lisa laughed, eyeing her nearly empty glass. "Or we aren't going to remember any of this."

Jess knocked back a deep mouthful of her champagne and raised her glass again. "I'll drink to that," she said, joining Lisa's laughter.

"I've got your backs, girls," Rachel said, her voice reassuring as she squeezed Jess's hand. "Just relax, have fun, and enjoy the night."

As Cynthia settled back in her seat, her gaze drifting over the pulsing crowd of the club, Jess couldn't help but study her. There was something about this woman - her confidence, her air of knowing secrets about Vegas that they could only guess at. It both thrilled and unnerved Jess. The energy of the night seemed to flow around them, a current of possibility and excitement. As her friends chatted and laughed, Jess felt herself being swept along in it all. Vegas, she was quickly learning, had a way of exceeding expectations, of turning ordinary nights into extraordinary memories. And tonight, she had a feeling, was going to be one for the books - for better or for worse.

ELEVEN
THIS MORNING

After their quick freshen up and search of their rooms, the girls reconvened in Jess and Rachel's suite. Each was now dressed in fresh clothes, but none of them looked any less worried. The air was thick with tension.

Jess stood near the window, her fingers nervously twisting the engagement ring on her left hand. Her normally bubbly personality was subdued, replaced by a steely determination.

As soon as everyone was present, they all started talking at once, their voices overlapping in a cacophony of worry and confusion.

"You won't believe what I found—" Megan began.

"Guys, my credit card—" Lisa's voice was tinged with panic.

"There was something in my outfit—" Olivia chimed in.

"Whoa, whoa!" Jess raised her voice, cutting through the chaos. Her teacher's instincts kicked in as she sought to bring order to the group. "One at a time, please. We need to approach this systematically if we're going to figure anything out." She took a deep breath, centring herself. "Okay, let's go around the room. Megan, you start. What did you find?"

Megan, her sharp eyes darting between her friends,

held up the briefcase she'd been clutching when Jess found her. Her fingers, usually flying over spreadsheets and data analysis reports, now trembled slightly as she spoke. "I managed to get this open. There's a flash drive inside."

A collective gasp went through the room.

"How did you...?" Jess looked impressed.

"Uh... it turns out it wasn't locked," Megan blushed. "I didn't do anything clever."

Jess nodded, trying to keep her composure. "Okay, well, we have a flash drive. That's... interesting. We'll come back to that. Lisa, you're next."

Lisa's face was pale as she stared at her phone, her perfectly manicured nails tapping nervously against the screen. Jess knew that the recent divorcee had been looking forward to this trip as a chance to rediscover herself, but now she looked more lost than ever.

"My credit card..." Lisa said, her voice close to tears. "It's maxed out. There are charges from last night that I don't remember making."

"Oh man," Olivia muttered, her vibrant personality momentarily dimmed by the darkness of their situation. Jess shot her a look, and she fell silent, biting her lower lip.

"Whatever it was, I'm sure we can help you work it out. It's going to be okay, Lis," Jess said. She tried to sound reassuring, but the information seemed to create more questions than answers.

Lisa nodded, tight-lipped and tense.

"Olivia, what about you?" Jess prompted, her voice gentle but firm.

Olivia pulled a crumpled piece of paper from her

pocket. Her hands, usually so steady, shook slightly as she smoothed out the note. "This was tucked down the top of that dumb costume when I took it off. 'The man in the hat knows'," she read aloud. "And... it's in my handwriting. But I don't remember writing it."

A stunned silence fell over the room. The weight of their predicament seemed to press down on them, making the spacious suite feel suddenly claustrophobic.

"What does that mean?" Lisa asked, her voice small and scared.

"Okay," Jess continued, trying to keep her tone steady. She could feel the others looking to her for guidance, a role she was accustomed to in her classroom but felt ill-equipped for in this surreal situation. "So, we have a cryptic message that Olivia wrote but doesn't remember, a flash drive, mysterious credit card charges, and still no sign of Rachel. This is... complicated."

Jess straightened her back and raised her chin. They had two and a half hours before they had to leave the suite. Somehow, in that time, they needed to figure out what happened last night, find Rachel, and untangle themselves from whatever mess they'd stumbled into.

As Jess looked at the worried faces of her friends, she realised that this was no longer just about saving her bachelorette party. It was about keeping the people she cared about safe - and maybe uncovering a truth that someone was willing to go to great lengths to keep hidden.

Megan, ever the problem-solver, turned to Jess. Her

analytical mind appeared to be formulating theories and connections already. "What about you and Alex? Did you find anything else in the suite?"

Jess hesitated.

"Yes," she said, picking up the fractured cell phone and opening Rachel's messages. "Look at this," she said, holding out Rachel's phone for the others to see.

Lisa leaned in, her eyes widening, reading the text behind the spiderweb of cracks. "'Midnight. The back room.' Do you think she went?"

"I don't know," Jess replied, her voice tight with worry. "But this could be why she disappeared."

Megan frowned, studying the message. "The back room of where? And who sent it?"

"It's from an unknown number," Jess said, scrolling up to check. "But it must be the back room somewhere we were last night. A club maybe?"

Olivia nodded slowly. "Yeah, I think most of the big clubs have VIP back rooms. But why would Rachel go alone? What could she be doing that didn't involve us?"

The group exchanged worried glances.

"I have no idea," Jess said. "We need to figure out where we were at midnight last night. It might lead us to Rachel."

"I'm going to say it, because one of us has to. Maybe we should call the police," Megan suggested hesitantly.

"I don't think..." Alex began, but Lisa had already started to speak.

"And tell them what?" Lisa said. "That we got drunk and lost our friend? That we woke up in compromising positions? They'll laugh us out of town."

"But Rachel is missing," Jess insisted, her voice cracking. "Like *for real* missing. There are a lot of puzzle pieces here that seem to add up to one thing: Rachel is in trouble. Think about it. Someone put me in that ice bath. Someone handcuffed you. Someone gave you the briefcase. And God knows how you ended up in the showgirl outfit. Someone planned this, and Rachel disappearing is only a part of the mess we're in. The biggest part, but... something is very wrong here."

"I think Lisa's right," Alex said, his voice hoarse. He cleared his throat. "I don't want to make any assumptions about your friend, but... sometimes getting the police involved can create more trouble than it solves."

Lisa's face visibly paled.

"People wander off, sure. But they don't accidentally end up in ice baths. Or handcuffed to strangers." Alex looked pointedly at Lisa. "I don't want to scare you, but..."

"I think you've already done that," Lisa said, her voice breaking.

Alex moved slightly towards her as if impulsively about to reach out with a hug, but he pulled up short.

Jess took over, wrapping Lisa in an embrace.

"We'll figure this out," she said, her voice lost in Lisa's soft hair.

Lisa sucked in air, and Olivia and Megan gathered to join the hug, making Lisa the centre of their circle.

"It's going to be all right," Olivia said.

"We'll find Rachel. We'll find out who did this." Megan's words were just as unconvincing as Olivia's.

"Okay," Jess said, taking charge. "Let's think about this. The message was sent at 11:58 PM. Where were we at midnight? And more importantly, where was Rachel?"

The group fell silent, each trying to piece together their fragmented memories of the night. After a moment, they all looked at each other, their faces blank.

"I... I can't remember," Olivia admitted, frustration clear in her voice.

"Me neither," Lisa added, shaking her head. "It's all just a blur."

Jess settled on one of the sofas and laid the phone back on the table before her.

"Come on, sit down," Jess said. "Let's break this down piece by piece," she said, her voice steady despite the fear churning in her stomach. "We need to connect the dots between the text message, the flash drive, the credit card charges, and this note about the man in the hat that Olivia doesn't remember writing. And most importantly, we need to find Rachel."

The girls took their places, sitting uncomfortably despite the luxury of the sofas.

"Okay," Lisa said with a forced calmness. "Any idea where to start?"

TWELVE
LAST NIGHT

The night was a whirlwind of sensations - pulsing lights, thumping music, and flowing drinks. Jess couldn't remember the last time she'd danced this much, her silver dress sending sparkles across the dance floor with every move. She was surrounded by her best friends, their laughter and conversation nearly drowned out by the pounding beat.

"This is freaking awesome!" Lisa yelled, twirling in her red bodycon dress. "Jess, your bachelorette is off the charts!"

Jess grinned, pulling Lisa in for a hug. "It's perfect!"

Cynthia appeared from nowhere with a tray of colourful shots. "Ladies, it's time to turn it up a notch!"

They gathered in a circle, clinking glasses. "To Jess!" Megan shouted. "May your married life be as exciting as tonight!"

As they took in their drinks, Jess was overwhelmed with affection for her friends. This was the bachelorette she had dreamed of - a night of pure fun and celebration with the women who meant the most to her.

Rachel reappeared at their side, slightly out of breath. Jess hadn't even noticed she was gone, but now she saw a flicker of something cross her friend's face.

"Rach, where have you been? Is everything okay?" Jess shouted over the music.

Rachel's smile was dazzling, if a little forced. "Everything's perfect! Just had to take care of something."

"All sorted now?" Jess asked.

Rachel nodded. "I think so. I want your night to be the absolute best, Jess. Trust me, okay?"

Her expression was serious, despite the wild action around them.

"Of course," Jess smiled. "Always." But as she spoke, she couldn't help but think of her earlier phone conversation with Miles.

Don't let Rachel get you into trouble. Wasn't that what he had said?

She was about to ask what was going on when Cynthia materialised beside them.

"Ladies, are you enjoying yourselves?" Cynthia purred, her eyes scanning the group.

"It's incredible!" Olivia gushed. "I've never been anywhere like this!"

Cynthia's smile widened. "Honey, the night is young, and Vegas has so many secrets to share."

"I want to stay here forever," Lisa gushed. "It's..." Her voice trailed off as though there wasn't a superlative strong enough to describe the night.

"It is," Cynthia nodded.

As Cynthia chatted with the others, Jess noticed her eyes darting towards a group of men in expensive suits gathered in a corner of the VIP section. One man, in particular, stood out - distinguished-looking, with salt-and-pepper hair and an air of authority.

"Who's that?" Jess whispered, nudging Rachel.

Rachel followed her gaze and tensed slightly. "That's Carter Reeves, the casino mogul. He owns half the Strip, or so they say. And what he doesn't own, he controls."

Before Jess could inquire further, the music changed, and Olivia squealed in delight. "Ladies, I love this song! Come on, let's dance!"

Taking her hand, she followed Olivia to the dancefloor and tried to focus on the friends around her, rather than Carter Reeves and his entourage, who seemed to be staring over in their direction.

The Cherry Pop embraced the girls: the atmosphere was electric, the bass line incessant, and the free drinks seemingly never ending.

As Jess sank back down into their booth, Cynthia presented the group with a tray laden with rainbow-coloured cocktails. Jess waved her hand.

"I'm going to have to slow down," she said, "or I'm not going to remember anything about tonight."

Megan laughed and scooped up one of the small glasses.

"They're so small," she said. "How could it possibly hurt to have one more?"

"That's the spirit," Cynthia said. As Jess sipped her cocktail, she watched Rachel. Something was troubling her. The light seemed to have gone out in her eyes, and her smile was forced. When she excused herself to go to the restroom, Jess followed.

Rachel was standing at the mirror, reapplying her lipstick. As Jess approached, her friend seemed not to see her.

"Hey," Jess said.

Rachel jumped. "Oh, hey."

"What's wrong?"

Rachel sighed. "Nothing."

"Come on," Jess said. "You can tell me. We've known each other forever."

"I know," Rachel said.

"It's supposed to be a fun night, but you seem kind of... distant..."

"No," Rachel said. "I'm fine, really. Don't worry about me."

"You're my maid of honour," Jess said. "Worrying about you is part of my job description."

"I think that's supposed to be the other way round," Rachel said with a small smile.

"Then consider me a role-breaker," Jess said.

"Fine," Rachel said. "It's just... I saw someone tonight that I wasn't expecting to see. I guess it just threw me."

"Anyone I know?"

Rachel looked at her, then shook her head. "It's nothing," she said. "Let's get back to the party."

But Jess wasn't satisfied. She grabbed Rachel's arm as her friend turned to leave. "Hey," she said. "If something's bothering you, you can tell me. No matter what it is."

Rachel's face was impassive, unreadable. Then, finally, she spoke. "I saw my ex tonight."

"Oh," Jess said. She felt a knot of tension release inside her.

"Yeah," Rachel said. "And he brought his new

girlfriend with him. They were, uh... dancing."

"Are you still in love with him?"

"No," Rachel said. "Not in the slightest. I don't care about him anymore. It's just... seeing them together reminded me of how he hurt me."

"He was an idiot," Jess said. "You deserve so much better than him."

"Thanks," Rachel said.

"I mean it," Jess said. "And you will find someone. Someone who loves you and treats you like the amazing woman you are."

"You're going to make me cry," Rachel said.

Jess smiled. "Come on," she said. "We're here to celebrate, not cry over past heartbreaks. Let's go have some fun."

"I'm so glad you're marrying Miles," Rachel said.

"Me too," Jess said. "And I'm glad you're my best friend."

Rachel smiled, and the sadness seemed to fade from her eyes. "Let's go," she said. "There are more cocktails with our name on them."

Jess linked arms with Rachel. "I don't know if I can manage much more, but everyone seems to be having a great time. Thanks so much for this. For everything."

The next hour was a blur of dancing and laughing. Jess found herself swept up in the moment, pushing aside her earlier concerns about Rachel's behaviour. This was her bachelorette party, after all. She deserved to let loose and have fun.

Megan, usually the reserved one, was chatting animatedly with a group of finance bros, her eyes sparkling with interest. Lisa, still recovering from her divorce, seemed to be coming out of her shell, flirting confidently with a bartender. Olivia was in her element. She moved gracefully to the music, attracting admiring glances from all around. Jess was mindful in the moment, grateful for the presence of her best friends.

And there was no sign of Carter Reeves and his crew.

Jess sat in the booth, watching her friends on the dance floor. Rachel seemed lost in the groove, holding Olivia's hands as they followed the music together. Whatever had been distracting her seemed to have passed.

Carter Reeves had gone, and Rachel's focus had returned to the party. There was so little Jess knew about the time spent in Las Vegas without her and their friends. It was as though Rachel had an entire second life she wasn't part of.

Jess shook her head. No. She trusted Rachel.

She trusted all of her friends. And she would not let anyone or anything spoil her perfect night.

As she took a sip of her cocktail, a deep, smooth voice spoke from beside her.

"Excuse me. Do you mind if I join you?"

Jess turned and looked up. A man was standing beside her, tall and well-built, with striking blue eyes and dark hair that was almost hidden beneath a smart fedora. He was wearing an expensive-looking suit, and he carried himself with an air of confidence.

"Uh, sure," Jess said, not sure what else to say.

"I'm sorry," he said. "I didn't mean to startle you."

"You didn't," Jess said, trying to recover herself.

"My name is Jack," the man said, holding out his hand. "Taking a break from the partying?"

Jess smiled, her initial surprise fading. "Something like that," she said. "My friends are the real party animals."

Jack glanced over at the dance floor, where the others were still lost in the music.

"They look like they're having a good time," he said.

"They are," Jess said. "This is, after all, my bachelorette party."

"Congratulations," Jack said, unflustered. "Your husband to be is a lucky man."

Miles. At the mention of her husband to be, Jess realised she had barely thought about him all night. She felt a pang of guilt, but quickly pushed it aside. This was her bachelorette, after all, and she had a right to enjoy it.

"Thank you," she said.

"Is this man bothering you?" Cynthia stood by the side of the booth, looking down at Jess.

"Sorry, ma'am," Jack said, raising his hands and sliding back out of the booth. "No offence intended."

"And none was taken," Jess said, almost irritated at the party planner's interruption. "It's fine, Cynthia."

"I should leave," Jack said, tipping the brim of his hat. "Wouldn't want to get on the wrong side of this lovely lady." He spoke the last two words as though he meant the opposite.

"Sorry," the man said. "Maybe we'll catch up again later tonight."

Jess laughed again, but Cynthia was almost glaring at the man.

As he left, Jess turned to the blonde woman.

"You didn't need to do that," she said. "He..."

Cynthia raised a hand. "You don't want to get involved with the likes of him," she said.

Jess thought for a split second that Jack seemed to feel the same about Cynthia. Las Vegas culture was a mystery she didn't want to dig into.

"He's bad news," the planner added.

Jess nodded, although she didn't agree. "Got it."

Cynthia smiled.

"Can you believe it's almost midnight?" she said. "Time flies so quickly when you're partying."

"What?" Jess said, pulling her phone out of her clutch. "How can it be so late already?"

"Lots of drinking, lots of fun," Cynthia laughed.

Jess checked the time. It was five minutes to twelve.

"Don't look so worried, my dear. You're hardly going to turn into a pumpkin. And there are so many more places for us to visit tonight. The Cherry Pop is just the beginning." Cynthia smiled like a hungry wolf, sending a shiver down Jess's spine.

Oblivious, Rachel slid into the booth, and took a sip of Jess's drink.

"Delicious," she said, and as she settled in, Cynthia slipped away.

"There's something about her..." Jess began, but Rachel appeared calm and happy, and she decided not to pursue the matter. She wasn't ready to spoil her own night.

Jess leaned against the booth and watched the club,

the lights pulsing, the music thumping. Beside her, Rachel flinched slightly and pulled her phone out of her purse. It had vibrated with a text message.

"Excuse me a minute," she said. "I'll be right back."

As Rachel slipped away, Jess felt a growing unease. She watched her friend disappear into the crowd, her gold dress shimmering under the club lights. The nagging feeling that something was off intensified, but before she could dwell on it, Lisa danced her way over, slightly out of breath and flushed from exertion.

"Where's Rachel going?" Lisa asked, noticing the empty spot beside Jess. She leaned in close to be heard over the pulsing music, the scent of her perfume mingling with the smell of sweat and alcohol that permeated the club.

"I don't know," Jess replied, a knot forming in her stomach. She scanned the crowd again, hoping to catch a glimpse of Rachel's gold dress. "She said she'd be right back, but..."

Lisa followed Jess's gaze. "Want to go look for her?"

Jess hesitated for a moment, then nodded. "Yeah, I think I should check on her."

As they pushed their way through the throng of dancers, Jess realised she couldn't see Cynthia anywhere, either. The VIP section where Carter Reeves and his entourage had been holding court earlier was now empty, the velvet ropes swaying slightly as if they'd left in a hurry.

Just as Jess was about to suggest they return to their friends, she caught sight of a familiar flash of gold disappearing through a door marked "Staff Only".

"There!" Jess shouted to Lisa, pointing. But when she turned to her friend, Lisa was already being pulled back onto the dance floor by Olivia.

"I'll be right back," Jess called, but the music swallowed her words. Lisa gave her a thumbs up before turning back to Olivia, already laughing at something she'd said.

Alone now, Jess hesitated for a moment, torn between following Rachel and respecting her privacy. But the nagging feeling that something wasn't right won out. Taking a deep breath, she pushed through the door, stepping into a dimly lit passage.

The music from the club became muffled, replaced by the sound of hushed voices coming from further down the corridor. Jess crept forward, her heart pounding in her chest. As she neared the end of the hallway, she could make out Rachel's voice, tense and urgent.

"I told you; I can get them all together. I'll be there. We'll be there."

A male voice responded, low and hoarse. "He's a very busy man. Don't keep him waiting."

Jess froze, her mind racing. What had Rachel got herself into? And who was she talking to?

Before she could decide whether to confront Rachel or slip away unnoticed, a hand clamped down on her shoulder. Jess spun around, coming face to face with Cynthia.

"You shouldn't be back here, honey," Cynthia said, her voice sickly sweet but her eyes hard. "Let's get you back to your friends, shall we?"

As Cynthia steered her back towards the public area of the club, Jess's mind was reeling. What was Rachel involved in? And how did Cynthia fit into all of this?

They emerged from the hallway just as Rachel slipped out of the back room, her face composed but her eyes wild. When she saw Jess with Cynthia, a flash of panic crossed her features before she smoothed it away with a bright smile.

"There you are!" Rachel exclaimed, her voice a little too high. "I was just looking for you. Come on, let's get back to the others. I've got a surprise for our next stop!"

THIRTEEN
THIS MORNING

In the morning sun, the room fell silent as they all considered their options. Jess caught Alex's eye, silently acknowledging their shared secret. There was no need to reveal Alex's history to the others; at least not yet. They all had enough to worry about without bringing up the stranger's past. Jess thought herself an excellent judge of character, and regardless of what Alex had shared with her, she believed what he had said, that he was trying to move on with his life and put it behind him.

Finally, Megan spoke up, her voice hesitant. "Well, we could start with the flash drive," she suggested, turning the small device over in her hand. "If we can access what's on it, it might give us some clues."

Jess nodded, latching onto the idea. "Good thinking, Meg. Do you think you can open it on your phone?"

Megan shook her head. "It's not that kind of drive. We'd need a computer."

"Does anyone have a laptop with them?" Jess asked, looking around the room hopefully.

Lisa and Olivia shook their heads, while Alex shrugged helplessly.

After a moment of uncomfortable silence, Megan cleared her throat. "I, uh... I have mine," she mumbled, not meeting anyone's eyes.

Jess turned to her, surprise clear on her face. "You brought your laptop on a bachelorette weekend?"

Megan's cheeks flushed. "I was planning to do some work in my downtime. My boss has been breathing down my neck about this project and —"

"Oh, Meg," Olivia interrupted, her voice a mixture of concern and something else - perhaps envy or frustration. "You've got to start setting some boundaries with work. This is supposed to be your time off."

Jess noticed a flash of emotion cross Olivia's face, quickly masked. There was more to her friend's reaction than simple concern, but now wasn't the time to pry.

Lisa nodded in agreement. "Yeah, you can't keep letting them walk all over you like this. It's not healthy."

"I know, I know," Megan said, looking almost embarrassed. "I just... I didn't want to fall behind. You know how it is."

Olivia opened her mouth as if to say something more, then closed it, shaking her head slightly.

Jess, sensing the underlying tension, decided to move things along. "Well, looks like your dedication might just save the day. Can you go grab that laptop, Meg?"

Megan nodded, already heading for the door. "I'll be right back."

As she left, Jess caught Olivia's eye, raising an eyebrow in silent question. Olivia just shrugged, her expression unreadable.

The anticipation in the room was palpable as they waited for Megan's return, each of them wondering what clues the flash drive might hold about their missing night. But Jess couldn't shake the feeling that there was more going on with Olivia than she was telling them.

Megan returned to the suite, laptop tucked under her arm. She made her way to the coffee table, carefully stepping over a discarded shoe and pushing aside an empty champagne bottle. The room's disarray was a stark reminder of their wild, forgotten night.

As Megan knelt on the floor and opened her laptop, the others gathered on the surrounding sofas. Jess absently straightened a crooked lampshade, her mind already racing ahead to what they might discover.

"All right," Jess said, turning back to the group. "Let's see what secrets this little drive is hiding."

Just as Megan was about to insert the flash drive, Alex shouted, "Wait!"

Everyone froze, tension thick in the air.

"What?" Jess asked, her heart pounding.

Alex looked sheepish. "I just... shouldn't we check for viruses first? You shouldn't put an unknown drive into your computer."

Megan chuckled, relieved. "Don't worry. This work laptop is so protected, it's like it's wearing three condoms."

The room erupted in laughter, the tension breaking. Lisa and Alex inadvertently caught each other's eyes and shared an awkward glance before quickly looking away, both blushing slightly.

Still managing to hold her grin, Megan inserted the

flash drive and began typing. After a moment, she nodded, unsurprised. "As expected, there's a passcode required to access the data."

"Can you crack it?" Olivia asked, leaning forward.

Megan let out a short laugh. "I'm a data analyst, not a CIA hacker. This isn't exactly in my job description."

"So... that's a no?" Lisa asked, her hope deflating.

Megan shrugged helplessly. "Unless the password is 'password123', we're out of luck. Whatever's on here, someone clearly wanted to keep it secure."

Just in case, Megan tapped **password123** into the prompt box

"No dice," she said.

Jess shuddered as Megan said the words, so noticeably that Olivia shot a look in her direction.

"What? Someone walk over your grave?"

"Dice," she said. "It's like the word triggered something. A memory. No, not a memory. I don't... I can't quite bring it to mind." Jess shook herself and shrugged.

"Did you play craps, maybe?" Alex asked. "It's pretty popular in the Bellagio."

"I... don't know. I just don't know," Jess said.

"What we *do* know is that we can't get into this flash drive," Megan sighed.

The group exchanged worried glances. What could be so important that it needed such protection? And how were they going to access it without specialised skills?

Jess leaned back on the sofa, her mind racing. "Wait a second," she said, sitting up straight again. "We're forgetting something important. Megan, how did you end up with that briefcase in the first place?"

Megan looked down at the briefcase, still clutched tightly in her hands. "I... I don't know. I just woke up holding it."

"Okay, so either you took it from someone," Lisa suggested, "or someone gave it to you. Or..."

"Or someone left it with you," Alex finished.

Olivia leaned forward. "But where? At the club? Or back here in the suite? Did we go anywhere else?"

"And why Megan?" Jess asked, looking at her friend. "No offence, Meg, but why would someone choose you specifically to hold on to something so important?"

Megan shook her head, looking as confused as the rest of them. "I have no idea. Maybe because I seemed the most... responsible?"

"Or the least likely to be suspected of anything," Alex muttered, earning him sharp looks from the others.

Jess sighed, running a hand through her hair. "This just adds another layer to the mystery. Not only do we need to figure out what's on the flash drive, but we also need to understand how and why Megan ended up with it. If someone left it with her, maybe they *wanted* us to have it."

"Like a way to help us find Rachel?" Olivia said, almost dreamlike in thought.

"Exactly," Jess said. "And if Megan took it from someone..."

"Then there must have been a reason," Megan said, catching on to Jess's train of thought. "The briefcase didn't have any markings, no name or anything. It was plain, leather, kind of expensive looking. That's all I know."

The group fell silent, each contemplating the implications of this new angle.

"Okay," Jess said. "Right now, we can't access the flash drive and we don't know how Megan got it. We can come back to it later. What's our next move?"

Megan suddenly leaned forward, animated by an idea.

"Guys, I think we're missing something. Or rather, someone." She turned to Alex. "No offence, but you're the odd man out here. We've been so focused on our own memories, we haven't really asked you much about last night."

All eyes turned to the man in their midst, who shifted uncomfortably under their collective gaze.

"That's a good point," Jess said, leaning forward. "Alex, how long have you worked at the Bellagio? That's where you said you work, right? In the casino here. Maybe you saw us earlier in the night?"

Alex hesitated for a moment. "Yes. Uh, not too long. I'm still pretty new."

Lisa perked up. "And you work the blackjack tables, you said?"

"Blackjack?" Olivia's head snapped up, a faint blush colouring her cheeks.

Megan grinned. "That's right, Olivia's quite the card shark. She could probably go pro if she wanted."

Olivia waved her hand dismissively, but her eyes sparkled at the compliment. "I'm not that good. Just lucky sometimes. But maybe that's a new career opportunity."

She smiled, but the smile didn't reach her eyes.

Jess turned back to Alex. "Is that where we met you? At the blackjack tables?"

Alex's discomfort was palpable. "No, I don't think so." He paused, then quickly added, "I mean, I doubt it. We're not really supposed to get chatty with customers. A few wisecracks or polite conversation depending on the vibe, but that's all. Too many cameras, you know?"

The girls exchanged glances, picking up on Alex's unease.

"But you *did* meet us last night, right? Obviously," Lisa pressed. "How *exactly* did that happen?"

Alex shifted slightly on the sofa. "It's all a bit fuzzy, to be honest. I have flashes of being in a club, maybe more than one club. Dancing. Drinking. Sitting in a booth. It's like fragments of a night; the details are... hazy."

Jess narrowed her eyes. "That's convenient. You're the only one who is an outsider to this group, and yet you can't remember how you met us?"

The tension in the room grew as Alex struggled to find a response.

"I... I" Alex shook his head, unable to give the girls what they wanted. "I honestly don't know. I'm so sorry."

Megan stood up, pacing the room. "Okay, let's think about this. We have a mysterious man who claims to work at the casino but gets uncomfortable talking about it. He somehow ended up with us last night, but can't explain how. And he's handcuffed to Lisa when we wake up." She turned to face the group.

"Does anyone else think this is more than a little suspicious?"

The others nodded slowly, their gazes fixed on Alex.

"Look," Alex said, raising his hands defensively, "I know how this looks, but I swear I'm not involved in whatever happened to your friend. I'm just as confused as you are. If it was up to me, I would have left as soon as I was unshackled from Lisa. Jess asked me to stay to help you all out, and I agreed. I would much rather be at home, in bed, sleeping off this hangover, rather than being here in your firing line."

Jess stood up, her expression determined. "And we appreciate that, Alex, but I think it's time you told us everything you know. And I mean everything. Because right now, you're looking less like a helpful stranger and more like our prime suspect."

Alex's shoulders slumped. He looked around the room, his gaze lingering on each face before settling on Lisa. "I swear, I know no more than you do. It's all a blur."

Lisa, who had been quiet during the interrogation, suddenly spoke up. Her voice was soft, almost vulnerable. "But... do you remember me? Us?" She gestured between herself and Alex. "I thought we had... I don't know, some kind of connection."

The room fell silent, all eyes now on Alex and Lisa as they waited for his response.

Alex's expression softened as he looked at Lisa. "I... I remember being close to you. That feeling is clear, even if the details aren't." He paused, seeming to choose his words carefully. "I remember thinking how gorgeous you were, how your laugh made me smile. But the specifics of what happened, where we met, what we talked about... it's all hazy, like I said." He coughed slightly as though suddenly realising that the two of them were not alone.

Lisa's cheeks flushed, a mix of embarrassment and pleasure at his words. But Jess wasn't so easily swayed.

"That's convenient," Jess said, her voice sharp. "You remember just enough to keep Lisa interested, but not enough to actually help us figure out what happened."

Megan nodded in agreement. "It seems a bit too perfect, doesn't it? Just the right balance of romantic and mysterious."

Olivia, however, seemed torn. "But guys, what if he's telling the truth? What if whatever wiped our memories affected him, too?"

The group fell into an uneasy silence, each wrestling with their own thoughts and suspicions. Lisa looked between Alex and her friends, clearly conflicted.

Finally, Jess spoke again, her voice softer, but no less determined. "Okay, Alex. Let's try this another way. Instead of telling us what you remember, why don't you tell us what you were doing before you met us? Let's think about what you *do* remember. Start with yesterday afternoon and walk us through it step by step. Maybe that will jog your memory."

Alex nodded slowly. "All right. Yesterday afternoon, I was..." He paused, his face contracting in concentration. "I was getting ready for my shift at the casino. I remember ironing my uniform, making sure everything was perfect."

"What time was your shift supposed to start?" Megan asked.

"Four pm," Alex replied quickly, then hesitated. "That's standard for the evening shift."

Jess exchanged a glance with Megan. "Go on," she urged.

"I arrived at the Bellagio around half-past three. Clocked in, got my station assignment..." Alex trailed off, his eyes narrowing as if trying to pierce through a fog. "But after that, it gets... confusing. I remember the lights, the noise of the casino floor, but it's all jumbled up with memories of the club... clubs... and you girls."

Lisa leaned forward, her voice gentle. "What's the first clear memory you have of us?"

Alex's gaze softened as he looked at her. "Your laugh. I remember hearing your laugh and thinking it was the most beautiful sound I'd ever heard." His cheeks reddened slightly. "But I can't remember where we were or what was so funny."

"That's very sweet," Jess said, her tone measured, "but it doesn't really help us figure out what happened to Rachel or how we all ended up in this mess."

"If I think of anything, of course I will tell you," Alex said. "Really, I'm sorry. And I'm here, okay? You asked me to stay, and here I am."

Jess nodded, relenting.

"Okay," she said, addressing the group. "We've hit a dead end with the flash drive, and Alex's story isn't giving us much to go on. What's our next move?"

FOURTEEN
LAST NIGHT

The pulsing beat of the music enveloped Jess as she stepped back onto the main floor of the club, her mind still reeling from what she'd just overheard. The fragments of Rachel's conversation echoed in her head, competing with the thunderous bass that seemed to vibrate through her very bones.

"I told you, I can get them all together. I'll be there. We'll be there."

The man's response, low and hoarse, sent a chill down her spine. "He's a very busy man. Don't keep him waiting."

The opulent surroundings of the club, which had seemed so magical just moments ago, now felt oppressive. The flashing lights cast eerie shadows across the faces of the dancing crowd, and the air felt thick with secrets and unspoken tensions. The sweet scent of spilled cocktails mixed with expensive perfumes, creating an intoxicating yet somehow menacing aroma.

Jess scanned the room for her friends, finally spotting them near their VIP booth. Rachel was there, laughing at something Lisa had said, her gold dress catching the light and throwing off tiny starbursts with every movement. To anyone else, Rachel looked completely at ease; the life of the party. But Jess knew her best friend better than anyone. She could see the tension in Rachel's shoulders, the way her eyes darted around the club as if looking for someone.

For a moment, Jess considered pulling Rachel aside and demanding answers. The secrets between them felt suffocating, pressing down on her chest like a physical thing. But as she watched her friends - Lisa finally letting loose after her divorce, her red dress swirling as she danced with abandon; Olivia embracing the night with her characteristic enthusiasm, her blue eyes sparkling with excitement; Megan even relaxing her usual reserved demeanour, a rare smile gracing her features - Jess made a conscious decision to push her concerns aside. This was her bachelorette party, after all. Rachel had put so much effort into making this night special. Whatever was going on, surely Rachel would tell her if it was truly important.

"Trust her," Jess told herself, forcing a smile as Megan handed her another drink. The cool glass was a welcome sensation against her palm, grounding her in the present moment. Condensation trickled down her fingers, almost soothing against the heat of the club. "She's your best friend. She wouldn't keep secrets unless she had a good reason."

Jess took a sip of her drink, the sharp tang of alcohol cutting through her muddled thoughts. She let the atmosphere of the club wash over her - the heat of bodies moving on the dance floor, the array of vibrant hues from the light show above, the intoxicating mix of perfumes and colognes in the air. The bass thrummed through her body, making her heart beat in time with the music.

"There you are!" Olivia's voice cut through Jess's reverie. Her friend grabbed her hand, pulling her towards the dance floor. "Come on, bride-to-be! It's time to show Vegas what you've got!"

Jess laughed, allowing herself to be swept along. As they danced, Olivia leaned in close, her breath tickling Jess's ear. "So, how does it feel? Celebrating the end of freedom and all that?"

"Honestly?" Jess shouted back over the music. "It feels amazing. But also... a little scary?"

Olivia nodded knowingly. "Big changes ahead. But hey, that's what we're here for, right? To remind you that no matter what, you've got us."

The sincerity in Olivia's eyes made Jess's heart swell. She pulled her friend into a tight hug, overcome with emotion.

"We haven't had enough times like this," Jess said. "I know we haven't known each other long, but...you're as much a part of this group as anyone, and I'm so glad you're here."

Olivia squeezed even harder. "You've all made me feel so welcome. I love all of you, and that's not just the champagne and cocktails talking."

As they broke apart, Jess caught sight of Lisa, who was chatting animatedly with a tall, dark-haired stranger at the bar. The spark in Lisa's eyes, something Jess hadn't seen since before the divorce, made her smile.

"Looks like someone's enjoying the night," Jess commented to Olivia, nodding towards Lisa.

Olivia grinned. "About time, too. She deserves

some fun after everything she's been through."

Just then, Megan appeared at their side, her cheeks flushed from dancing. "Ladies, I hate to be the voice of reason, but maybe we should slow down on the drinks? We've got a long night ahead."

Jess and Olivia exchanged amused glances. "Always the responsible one," Jess teased, throwing an arm around Megan's shoulders. "Come on, Meg. Live a little!"

Megan rolled her eyes, but Jess could see the smile tugging at her lips. "Someone has to make sure we all make it back to the hotel in one piece."

As they laughed together, Jess felt a wave of affection for her friends. Each of them was so different, yet together they formed a perfect balance. Olivia with her boundless enthusiasm, Megan with her steady practicality, Lisa rediscovering her confidence, and Rachel...

Jess's eyes again sought her best friend. Rachel was now deep in conversation with a woman Jess didn't recognise. As if sensing Jess's gaze, Rachel looked up, flashing a quick smile before turning back to her companion.

"Everything okay?" Megan asked, following Jess's line of sight.

Jess hesitated for a moment before answering. "Yeah, it's just... have you noticed Rachel acting strange lately?"

Megan considered this. "Strange how?"

"I don't know. Secretive, maybe? And Miles said something weird before we left..."

"Miles?" Olivia cut in, her eyebrows raised. "What did he say?"

Jess bit her lip, unsure how much to reveal. "He told me to be careful around Rachel. Said I shouldn't trust her completely."

Her friends exchanged concerned glances. "That's... odd," Megan said carefully. "Did he say why?"

Jess shook her head. "No, and that's what's driving me crazy. I mean, Rachel's been my best friend since college. She's the one who introduced me to Miles in the first place!"

"Maybe he's just being overprotective?" Olivia suggested. "You know how he gets sometimes. Remember the fit he threw when Rachel planned that surprise weekend trip for your birthday?"

Jess nodded, remembering. Miles had been furious that Rachel had "kidnapped" Jess without telling him first, even though it had been a wonderful surprise.

"I guess," Jess said, not entirely convinced. "It's just... Rachel's been acting off tonight too. Disappearing, having hushed conversations. Something has to be going on, and I'm not sure I like it one bit."

Before her friends could respond, Rachel appeared at their side, slinging an arm around Jess's waist. "What are we all looking so serious about? This is a party, remember?"

Jess studied her friend's face, searching for any sign of the tension she'd seen earlier. But Rachel's smile was wide and genuine, her eyes sparkling with excitement.

"You're right," Jess said, pushing her doubts aside once more. "This is our night. Let's make it count!"

As they moved back to the dance floor as a group, the energy around them electric, Jess tried to lose herself in the moment. This was what Rachel had planned - a night of freedom, of celebration, of the four of them together like old times, now five with their newest addition Olivia.

Yet as the night wore on, Jess couldn't completely shake the nagging feeling in the pit of her stomach. The fragments of conversation she'd overheard, Miles's warning, Rachel's strange behaviour - it all swirled in her mind, a puzzle she couldn't quite solve.

But for now, surrounded by the friends who had stood by her through everything, Jess decided to embrace the magic of the night. Whatever secrets tomorrow might bring, tonight was for the here and now, for dancing until their feet ached, for laughing until their sides hurt.

FIFTEEN
THIS MORNING

The room fell silent for a moment as everyone pondered the question. None of them could remember anything. The flash drive had been no help. Alex didn't seem to know any more than any of the girls. What *was* their next move?

Megan spoke up first. "We should try to establish a timeline of last night based on what we *do* know. Maybe if we piece together where we were, we can figure out where Rachel might have gone."

Olivia nodded. "That's a good idea, but how? Our memories are so fuzzy."

"Your shift finished at what time?" Lisa looked at Alex.

"Midnight," the man said with a nod.

"And you must have met us some time after that?"

"Not that it means a lot, but I'm not wearing my nasty blue waistcoat and uniform shirt, so I got changed out of my work gear before I ended up with you. I'm pretty sure I finished my shift," he said.

"Unless someone dressed you to make you think that," said Olivia. Her face suddenly paled. "Guys, what if someone *und*ressed me? What if...?"

"Hey." Megan put her arm around her friend's shoulder. "Hey, it's okay. Let's try not to think the worst until we can piece things together."

Olivia nodded rapidly, but didn't appear reassured.

"We don't seem to have many pieces to... piece," she moaned.

Lisa's eyes suddenly lit up. "Wait, what about my credit card charges? I checked them earlier, but we didn't really analyse them. They could show us exactly where we went and when."

Jess snapped her fingers. "Lisa, that's brilliant! Those charges could give us something solid to work with."

"I'll pull them up now," Lisa said, already reaching for her phone.

As Lisa opened her banking app, the others gathered around her, a mix of anticipation and apprehension on their faces.

"All right," Lisa said, her finger hovering over the screen. "Let's see what story these charges tell about our night..."

The group leaned in, knowing that what they were about to discover could change everything in their search for Rachel. As the screen loaded, a collective gasp filled the room.

"Wow," Lisa whispered, her eyes widening at the list of charges. "I didn't realise it was this bad. What was I thinking?"

Jess leaned in closer. "What is it? What do you see?"

"There's a charge here for over a thousand dollars from somewhere called the 'Enigma Nightclub'," Lisa said, her voice shaky.

As Lisa continued scrolling through her credit card charges, she paused, her eyebrows knitting together in confusion.

"There's a payment here to 'Glamour and Grace' for... quite a bit of money," Lisa said, her voice tinged with disbelief.

"Glamour and Grace?" Megan repeated. "Isn't that a super expensive boutique?"

Olivia nodded. "I'd never have the guts to go in there. Or the money."

"Well, apparently we did last night," Lisa said, her eyes still fixed on the screen. "But what on earth did we buy? It's not like we needed new clothes for the trip." Suddenly, she gasped. "Oh no. No, no, no."

"What now?" Jess asked, feeling a knot form in her stomach.

Lisa looked up, her face pale. "Look! Just after 4am. There's a charge here for over five thousand dollars from 'The High Roller Suites'. What the hell did we *do* last night?"

"Wow, you must have good credit," Alex blurted before turning bright red and slapping his hand over his mouth.

The room fell silent as the magnitude of their forgotten escapades began to sink in. Jess was the first to speak up.

"Okay, let's think about this logically. Does anyone remember going to *any* of these places?"

The others shook their heads, their expressions blank.

Megan, ever the organised one, suggested, "Why don't we try to create a timeline based on these charges? It might help jog our memories."

They huddled around Lisa's phone, noting the times

of each transaction. As they did, a pattern emerged.

"Look," Jess said, pointing at the screen. "There's a gap here between just after 1am and 3:30am where there are no charges. Does that mean anything to anyone? We hit The Enigma club hard until around one and then there's nothing until Glamour and Grace at half-past three."

"It's open at that time?" Olivia said with more than a hint of doubt in her voice.

"My credit card thinks it is." Lisa was shaking her head, her voice trembling. "I might have good credit, but I don't have the kind of money to pay this off. What with the divorce and..."

Suddenly, Lisa's composure crumbled. She let out a choked sob, her hands shaking as she gripped her phone. "Oh shit, what have I done? I can't afford this. I can't..." Tears started streaming down her face, smearing what was left of her makeup.

The others exchanged worried glances. Jess immediately put an arm around Lisa's shoulders, pulling her close. "Hey, hey, it's okay. We'll figure this out, I promise."

Megan knelt in front of Lisa, comforting her friend. "Lisa, look at me. This isn't your fault. We're all in this together, okay? Whatever you spent, it was for all of us."

Olivia, despite her own dishevelled state, moved to Lisa's other side, rubbing her back soothingly. "That's right. We've got your back, no matter what."

Even Alex, still somewhat of an outsider, looked concerned. He shifted uncomfortably before speaking up. "Um, I know I'm not really part of your group, but... maybe there's been some kind of mistake with the charges? We could try contacting the credit card company."

Lisa looked up at him, her tear-streaked face a mix of gratitude and lingering worry. She nodded, unable to speak through her tears.

Jess squeezed Lisa's shoulder reassuringly. "That's a good idea, Alex. We'll get this sorted out, Lisa. Right now, let's focus on piecing together what happened. The money... we'll deal with that later, okay?"

Lisa took a shaky breath, trying to compose herself. "Okay," she whispered, wiping at her eyes. "Okay. You're right. One thing at a time. I hope I didn't pay for these handcuffs," she said with a faint smile.

The group's swift rally around Lisa seemed to strengthen their resolve. Despite their own confusion and worries, they had come together to support one of their own. It was a reminder of the bond they shared, a glimmer of hope amid their chaotic situation.

"All right," Jess said, her voice gentle but determined. "We're going to work this out, Lisa. Let's get back to this timeline."

"I left work at midnight," Alex reminded them.

"Then Rachel gets the text just before midnight and possibly goes to meet someone. We're in The Enigma Nightclub at around 1am. I phone Rachel at just after 3:15 and then we end up in Glamour and Grace not long afterwards. And the last definite location we know is The High Roller Suites at around 4am."

"Somewhere along the way there's a man in a hat," Olivia shrugged.

"And maybe dice," Lisa offered.

Megan picked up a pen and page of Bellagio headed paper from the room's stately desk and wrote down what they knew of the timings.

23:58 – Rachel gets the text to meet someone

00:00 – Rachel meets someone in a back room ?where

01:07 – Credit card charge at The Enigma Nightclub

03:17 – Jess leaves a voicemail for Rachel

03:30 – Credit card charge at Glamour and Grace

04:12 – Credit card charge at The High Roller Suites

Excitement built as they felt they were finally making progress. Jess stood up, addressing the group.

"Okay, so now we have some solid leads. Should we try visiting these places? Maybe someone there remembers us."

Alex shifted uncomfortably. "I don't know if that's a good idea. If we were involved in something... complicated... going back to the scene might be dangerous."

The others fell silent, considering his words.

Lisa stared at the charge from Enigma Nightclub. "I don't understand. We had VIP passes. Why would we have such a large charge?"

"Maybe we bought drinks?" Olivia suggested, but her tone was uncertain.

Jess shook her head. "No, Rachel said those passes included an open bar. Something doesn't add up."

"You remember leaving here to go out then? Getting the passes?" Alex asked, as though no one had thought of this.

"Well, yes," Jess said. "We got here, had drinks and took a limo to..."

They all fell silent for a moment, trying to recall details from the previous night. The atmosphere in the room grew tense as they grappled with their hazy memories.

"A club..." Lisa said, hesitantly.

"But not The Enigma," Olivia added. "It was..." She sat with her mouth slightly open, as if waiting for the name of the club to form on her lips. "Nope. I've no idea. Still, it doesn't look as if the fun started until a few hours later," she said, nodding at Lisa's phone.

Lisa sighed and clicked the screen closed.

"What about our phones, though?" Megan suggested, as Lisa's action triggered an idea. "Maybe we took photos or got someone's number?"

Simultaneously, the girls reached for their devices, scrolling through contacts and recent calls.

Suddenly, Olivia gasped. "Wait a second. I have a number here under 'Cynthia VIP'. Does that ring any bells for anyone?"

The moment she said the name, recognition dawned on their faces.

"Cynthia!" Jess exclaimed. "Tall, blonde woman in a red dress?"

Lisa nodded vigorously. "Yes! That sounds so familiar. Like a dream, but... real somehow."

"How could we forget her?" Megan wondered aloud. "She seemed so... memorable."

Alex, who had been quiet, suddenly spoke up. "That name sounds familiar."

Jess turned to him, curiosity piqued. "What do you mean, Alex?"

He shifted uncomfortably before responding. "It's not a common name, but I've heard it around the casino before. Someone called Cynthia, who fits that description. She's known for entertaining high rollers. Showing them a good time, if you know what I mean."

The group exchanged worried glances, the implications of this information sinking in.

"Do you know anything else about her?" Jess asked.

Alex shook his head. "Like I said, I haven't been at the casino for long. No one shares any juicy gossip with me. It's just something I've heard in passing. I never knew I would need to know any more about this woman."

"Okay," Jess said, trying to hide her disappointment behind a veneer of determination. "It seems like this Cynthia is our link to last night. Olivia, did you call her, or did she call you?"

Olivia checked her call log. "Neither. I just have the number here. And I definitely didn't have it before."

There was a collective silence as the group processed the new information. The fact that Olivia somehow had Cynthia's number, despite not remembering getting it, added another layer to their already complex puzzle.

"Should we... call her?" Lisa asked hesitantly.

Jess bit her lip, considering. "I don't know. If she's involved in whatever happened to Rachel, we might tip her off that we're looking into things."

"Of course you'd be looking into things," Alex said sharply. "Your friend is missing. But... just be careful."

The group looked at each other, the atmosphere electric with tension.

"What if we texted her instead?" Megan suggested. "We could pretend we're still partying, ask her where the next spot is. Maybe she'll reveal something without realising it. If she's innocent in this, she might be able to help."

"And if not?" Lisa asked.

The group mulled over the idea, weighing the risks and potential benefits.

"It's risky," Jess said slowly, "but it might be our best shot at getting more information without raising suspicion. Olivia, are you okay with sending the text?"

Olivia's fingers hovered over her phone's keyboard as the others huddled around her. After a few minutes of brainstorming and debate, they settled on a message:

Hey Cynthia! Last night was EPIC! 🎉 We're ready for round two. Any hot spots we should hit tonight? The crew's getting restless! 😊

"That sounds believable, right?" Olivia asked, her finger hovering over the send button.

Jess nodded. "I think so. It's vague enough that she won't suspect anything, but it might prompt her to reveal something about last night."

"Plus, the emojis add a nice touch," Alex chimed in. "Makes it seem more... party-girl authentic."

With a collective deep breath, Olivia hit send. The message whooshed away, and they all stared at the phone for a moment.

"Okay," Jess said, breaking the silence. "We can't just sit here waiting for a reply. We need to explore other leads. Any ideas?"

SIXTEEN
LAST NIGHT

As the night wore on, Jess found herself relaxing, caught up in the infectious energy of her friends and the club. The worries that had plagued her earlier began to feel distant, like a half-remembered dream. She laughed as Olivia attempted to teach Lisa a new dance move, their bodies moving in sync with the pulsing rhythm. She felt a surge of affection as Rachel pulled her close for a selfie, their faces pressed together, smiles wide and genuine.

The club around them was a swirl of activity. On elevated platforms, dancers in glittering costumes moved with hypnotic grace, their bodies undulating to the beat. Behind the bar, mixologists put on a show, their hands a blur as they deftly manipulated shakers and glasses. With practiced precision, they poured streams of colourful liquids simultaneously from multiple bottles, creating layered cocktails that were as much a feast for the eyes as for the palate. The drinks emerged as miniature works of art, garnished with exotic fruits, edible flowers, and wisps of aromatic smoke that curled enticingly above the rims. In dark corners, people leaned close together, sharing secrets or stealing kisses, the intimacy of their moments a stark contrast to the frenetic energy of the dance floor.

It was then that Cynthia materialised beside them, a

tall man in a glittering jacket at her side. Her sudden appearance startled Jess, bringing back the unease she'd been trying to ignore. Cynthia's red dress seemed to shimmer in the club lights, clinging to her curves in a way that drew admiring glances from those around them. Her smile was as dazzling as ever, but there was something in her eyes that made Jess's skin prickle.

"Ladies," Cynthia purred, her voice somehow carrying over the music. "I want you to meet someone very special. This is Drake Holloway, the hottest new action star in Hollywood!"

A tall, ruggedly handsome man stepped forward, his smile dazzling under the club lights. He was dressed in an impeccably tailored suit that accentuated his muscular frame. His piercing green eyes scanned the group, lingering a fraction too long on each woman.

"It's a pleasure to meet you all," Drake said, his voice a smooth baritone that sent shivers down Jess's spine. "Cynthia tells me you're celebrating a bachelorette party. Congratulations to the bride-to-be."

The girls exchanged excited glances, star-struck by Drake's presence, even though none of them recognised the man before them. Jess, however, felt a knot form in her stomach. There was something about the way Drake looked at them, almost predatory, that set her on edge.

"Thank you," Jess managed, forcing a smile.

Drake's gaze locked on Jess, his smile widening. "You know, I'm hosting a little gathering at The High Roller Suites. Very exclusive, very private. Why don't you ladies join me? It'll be a night you'll never remember... oh, I'm sorry, of course I mean a night you'll never forget."

The invitation hung in the air, tempting and dangerous all at once.

"Heck, yes!" Olivia exclaimed, her eyes wide with excitement. The others nodded enthusiastically, caught up in the allure of celebrity and exclusivity.

Drake stepped closer to Jess, invading her personal space. "What do you say, bride-to-be? Care to live a little dangerously before tying the knot?"

Jess laughed nervously, trying to ignore the way her heart had started racing. "I... I'm not sure. It's very kind of you to offer, but—"

"Nonsense!" Drake insisted, his hand coming to rest on the small of Jess's back. His touch was warm, almost uncomfortably so. "I insist. It wouldn't be a party without the guest of honour."

Before Jess could respond, Rachel quickly interjected, her voice a little too bright. "We'd love to join you, Mr Holloway. Your invitation is too generous to refuse."

As Drake moved away to make arrangements with Cynthia, a feeling of unease settled over Jess. She watched as he disappeared into the crowd, his confident stride and the way people parted for him suggesting a man used to getting what he wanted.

"Did you see how he was looking at us?" Jess whispered to Rachel. "There's something off about him."

Rachel squeezed Jess's hand reassuringly, but her eyes darted nervously around the club. "It's fine, Jess.

He's a celebrity. This is exactly the kind of exclusive experience I wanted for your bachelorette party. Just... stick close to me, okay?"

Jess nodded, but couldn't help but wonder what secrets lay behind Drake's charming smile and what exactly they were getting themselves into.

"Can you believe this night?" Megan gushed, her cheeks flushed with excitement. "VIP treatment, meeting celebrities... Rachel, you've outdone yourself!"

Rachel beamed, throwing an arm around Jess. "Only the best for our bride-to-be!" But Jess felt the slight tremor in Rachel's hand. It was a subtle thing, something only a best friend would notice, but it spoke volumes to Jess.

They made their way back to their VIP booth, the plush velvet seats a welcome respite from the crowded dance floor. Jess sank into the cushions, her mind racing. The night had taken on a surreal quality, events unfolding in a way she couldn't have predicted. She watched as Olivia struck up a conversation with a tattooed bartender, his muscles rippling as he mixed their drinks. Champagne, shots, cocktails... Jess was starting to feel her head spin.

As Olivia made her way back over, Jess's attention was drawn to Cynthia, deep in conversation with a well-dressed man near their VIP booth.

Suddenly, Cynthia's clutch slipped from her lap, spilling its contents onto the plush carpet. The man she was talking to didn't seem to notice, his attention fully on Cynthia's animated gestures.

Jess watched as Olivia hesitated for a moment. She crouched down, ostensibly to help gather Cynthia's things. Jess couldn't quite see what happened next, but she noticed Olivia slip something into her own purse before standing up with a lipstick and compact mirror.

"I think you dropped these," Olivia said, handing them to Cynthia with a smile.

Cynthia looked surprised for a moment, then flashed a dazzling grin. "Oh, aren't you a dear? Thank you so much."

As Olivia rejoined them, Jess glimpsed something like triumph in her friend's eyes. Before she could ask about it, Megan nudged her, nodding towards a corner of the club.

"Isn't that Carter Reeves? He looks upset."

Jess followed her gaze. Indeed, the distinguished man was engaged in what appeared to be a heated discussion with another suit-clad individual. Their body language spoke of barely contained anger.

"I thought he'd gone," Jess said, failing to hide the disappointment in her voice.

A movement caught Jess's eye. Rachel had stepped away again, phone pressed to her ear. Despite the noise, Jess caught fragments of her conversation.

"...yes, I've got them all here. It's your move."

Jess felt a chill run down her spine. What was Rachel up to?

Before she could dwell on it, Cynthia's voice cut through her thoughts. "Ladies, the night is young, and Vegas has so much more to offer. Who's ready for the next stop on our adventure?"

The other girls erupted in excited cheers, their

enthusiasm infectious. Jess forced a smile, trying not to let her concern show. As they gathered, preparing to follow Cynthia into the Vegas night, Jess took a moment to look at her friends. Lisa was glowing, her recent divorce troubles forgotten for the night. Olivia's eyes sparkled with mischief, no doubt thinking of the mysterious item in her purse. Megan, usually so reserved, was laughing freely, caught up in the excitement. And Rachel... Rachel was trying so hard to make this night perfect.

Jess made a silent promise to herself. She would enjoy this night with her friends, but she wouldn't ignore the nagging feeling in her gut. Something was going on beneath the glittering surface of their Vegas adventure, and she was determined to figure it out.

For now, though, she would embrace the moment. Jess raised her glass in one final toast. "To unforgettable nights and unbreakable friendships!"

As they clinked glasses and sipped their drinks, Jess felt both excitement and apprehension. The night was far from over, and Vegas, she was learning, was full of surprises.

SEVENTEEN
THIS MORNING

Back in the cold light of the morning, the girls were suddenly interrupted by the ping of Olivia's phone. She glanced at the screen, her brow furrowing in confusion.

"It's... it's from Cynthia," she said. "That was quick."

"Maybe she was expecting us," Jess said, almost allowing herself to feel relieved. "Quick, what did she say?"

Olivia read from the screen: "**How did you get this number?**"

The group exchanged bewildered looks.

"What? What does she mean?" Lisa asked, leaning over to look at the message. "Didn't she give you her number?"

Olivia shook her head slowly, looking increasingly confused. "I... I thought she must have. It was stored in my phone, obviously. But I don't actually remember her giving it to me. And if she's asking this..."

"Maybe it's a joke?" Megan suggested, but her tone lacked conviction.

"Is there any way Rachel could have given you Cynthia's number?" Alex asked, already knowing the answer.

"Anything is possible, and none of us would know

133

either way," Lisa sighed. "Shit, shit, shit. This hasn't helped at all."

The hair on the back of Jess's neck stood up, a cold unease settling in her stomach. "What do we do? Should we be honest or try to get more information from her by playing innocent?"

"I wish I knew..." Olivia said, her voice faint and reedy. "I wish I knew anything."

"What if we've just made things worse?" Lisa said.

Alex reached out and put a hand on her shoulder, and pulled away again, as if not knowing what to do.

Jess suddenly straightened, her face a mix of frustration and fear. "I can't do this anymore. I just want Rachel back. I want to know she's safe." Her voice cracked slightly. "This weekend was meant to be fun, and it's turned into... into this."

They fell silent, the truth of their predicament sinking in. Olivia, being the newest to the group, hesitantly voiced the question the others had all been avoiding.

"Is there... is there any reason Rachel would disappear on her own? Or..." she paused, swallowing hard, "is there anyone that might want to hurt her?"

The words loomed, heavy and ominous. None of them wanted to consider the implications, but now that they had been spoken aloud, they couldn't ignore the possibility.

The luxurious room suddenly felt colder than the air conditioning could account for. The girls huddled closer, seeking comfort in each other's presence as they grappled with the shocking direction the bachelorette party had taken.

Jess gazed at her friends, recognising her own anxiety mirrored in their faces. The glittering lights and pulsing music of Vegas seemed far away now, overshadowed by the mystery of Rachel's disappearance and the growing realisation that they might be in over their heads.

Suddenly, Megan blurted out, "What if... what if Rachel's family has the wrong sort of connections? Maybe she's—"

"Stop right there," Jess cut her off, her voice sharp. "I've known Rachel since college. There's no way she or her family are involved in anything shady."

Lisa nodded vigorously in agreement. "Jess is right. We've both known Rachel for years. This isn't like her at all."

A tense silence fell over the group. Jess's mind raced, trying to piece together the puzzle. Suddenly, her eyes widened. "Wait. The text Rachel got last night. 'Meet at midnight.' Who was that from?"

Olivia fumbled with her phone. "You think it was from Cynthia?"

"There's no name stored on Rachel's phone, but... we have Cynthia's number now. Check if it matches," Jess urged.

With trembling fingers, Olivia pulled up the mysterious text and compared it to Cynthia's contact. "It... it's the same number," she confirmed.

The weighty implications of the revelation permeated the air, causing a tangible sense of tension.

Alex, who had been quiet until now, spoke up. "Maybe the meeting was about party plans? Couldn't it be innocent?"

Jess shook her head, frustration evident in her voice. "Then why text? Why meet out of sight? None of this makes sense. Why would there be any reason to hide?"

"We don't remember," Megan said. "Maybe we were split up for some reason? We could have lost Cynthia, and she was helping us to regroup."

"I feel like we're clutching at straws. But you're right. We don't remember. We don't remember any of it," Jess said, sounding more troubled with every word.

"We need to find Rachel," Lisa said, her voice trembling. "Now."

Megan glanced at her watch, her practical nature asserting itself even amid their panic. "We've got another problem. We have to check out in two and a half hours. Trying to search for Rachel with our luggage in tow is going to be a nightmare. We need to find her before check out."

Alex cut in. "I'd say you need to find her before anything..."

"Before anything happens to her?" Lisa breathed. Her voice was fragile.

"We don't know that anything's going to happen to her." Jess shot a sharp look in Alex's direction. "Let's not think that way. Let's just find Rachel."

The reality of their situation crashed down on them. They were in a race against time, with no idea where to start looking for their missing friend.

Jess paused, a thought suddenly striking her. "Wait a minute. We were at The Enigma club, right? Lisa's credit card was charged there around one am."

Lisa nodded, pulling out her phone to double-check. "That's right. A big fat charge at 01:07, to be exact."

"So, if Rachel and Cynthia were planning something at midnight, wherever we were, it must have included where we went next," Megan reasoned. "The Enigma Nightclub."

"And that was around the same time that Alex left work," Jess said.

All eyes turned to Alex. Jess stepped towards him, her gaze intense. "Alex, you say you don't remember last night, but on a regular night after your shift, where would you go?"

Alex shrugged. "Home to sleep, usually."

"Okay, well, you didn't last night, so..."

"We left the first club before one am," Olivia chimed in. "Whatever we did next, we must have gone to The Enigma Nightclub before one, because that's when Lisa's card was charged."

Alex repeated the name, as though trying to dredge up a memory. *The Enigma Nightclub*? I've never heard of it."

The girls exchanged glances. "But we must have met you there," Lisa said. "How else did you end up with us?"

Alex shook his head, looking perplexed. "There's no way I would be planning to go to a nightclub after work. Maybe... maybe you picked me up somewhere?" Suddenly, his eyes lit up with a spark of realisation. "Wait, get your map out. Did you go back down the strip past the Bellagio?"

Jess pulled up a map on her phone, and they all bent around it. After a moment of searching, they found what they were looking for.

"There," Alex pointed. "The Enigma Nightclub is

down Flamingo. That road passes the side of the Bellagio. That's where I get my bus, the 202. Old unreliable 202."

He looked up at Lisa, their eyes meeting. A moment of understanding passed between them.

"We stopped to give you a lift," Lisa said softly, the shadow of a memory hazily forming.

The room fell silent as they processed this new information. It was a small piece of the puzzle, but it felt significant somehow.

"Okay," Jess said, breaking the silence. "So, we picked up Alex on our way to The Enigma. But that still doesn't explain what happened to Rachel, or why Cynthia is pretending not to know us."

As they considered their next move, the urgency to find Rachel grew even stronger. Whatever had happened at The Enigma, it seemed to be at the heart of their friend's disappearance.

EIGHTEEN
LAST NIGHT

Cynthia escorted the girls as they piled into the waiting limo, the cool leather a relief after the heat of the club. As they settled in, giggles and excited chatter filled the air.

Olivia raised her champagne glass. "To Jess's last night of freedom! Better make it count before you're shackled to Miles forever!"

Everyone laughed, and Jess playfully swatted at Olivia. "Hey, I'll have you know marriage is going to be an adventure!"

Megan sighed dramatically. "I'd settle for a boyfriend at this point. A husband seems like a distant dream."

"Tell me about it," Olivia agreed, her tone suddenly serious. "My love life is as dead as the studio. Actually..." She took a deep breath and let it out slowly before speaking again. "Girls, I need to tell you something. I'm not just taking time off. I lost my job three weeks ago. I'm not a yoga instructor anymore, and I've been too ashamed to tell anyone."

"We were going to start coming again after the wedding," Jess said. "It wasn't because you weren't getting the numbers in, was it? Oh, I feel awful now."

Olivia shook her head. "No, no. Don't feel bad. They're 'redistributing their efforts'. I don't know what it means apart from that I'm out of a job."

The confession hovered for a moment, the others looking at Olivia with a mixture of surprise and concern.

Lisa reached out and squeezed Olivia's hand. "Oh, Liv. I understand how you feel. Don't feel bad though. You'll soon find something else."

Olivia gave a small smile.

"To be honest," Lisa said, "I've been feeling guilty too. Partying like this when I'm literally just divorced... it feels wrong somehow."

The mood in the limo shifted, the excitement of moments ago replaced by a sombre atmosphere. Jess felt a pang of guilt, wondering if she should have been more considerate of her friends' feelings.

But before she could say anything, Rachel spoke up, her voice warm and reassuring. "Ladies, I want you to listen to me. I'm well aware of everyone's situations, and I've taken everything into account. This night is about celebrating Jess, her upcoming nuptials, and our friendship. It's all on me, and I want you to enjoy it without worrying."

She turned to Olivia and Lisa specifically. "Your struggles don't define you, and taking one night to let loose doesn't make you bad people. We're here for each other, through good times and bad." In a low whisper to Olivia, she said, "I've got you. Don't worry."

Olivia looked at her, eyes open in question, and Rachel gave a brief nod of confirmation. The group's shared communication could sometimes pass unspoken, even between the two women who had only

140

known each other a matter of months.

Jess felt a warm glow of affection for Rachel. "Rachel's right," she added, smiling at her friends. "I'm just happy to have you all here with me. That's what matters most."

The tension in the limo dissipated, replaced by a sense of camaraderie and relief.

"You don't need money tonight," Rachel said. "And you certainly don't need a man."

Just then, Lisa's gaze drifted to the window. Her eyes widened, and a small smile played on her lips. "Well, I wouldn't mind a guy like that one, though."

Instantly, the other girls crowded to the window, peering out to see what had caught Lisa's attention. There, standing at a bus stop by the columns at the side of Caesar's Palace, was a handsome young man in a shirt and jeans, looking frustrated as he checked his watch.

Cynthia overheard the conversation and smiled. "Driver, pull up!" she said mischievously. "Let's see if he wants to join our VIP adventure!"

Lisa's face flushed bright red. "No, no, I was just joking!" But her protests were half-hearted, and the glint in her eye betrayed her interest.

Jess chimed in. "Pull over!"

The rest of the group joined in until the chant rang through the limo.

"Pull over! Pull over! Pull over!"

The driver tilted his eyes to the rear-view mirror, smiled and drew up alongside the man.

As the limo stopped, Rachel lowered the window. "Hey there! Waiting for the 202? How about a ride with some VIPs instead?"

The man looked startled.

"No thanks," he said, waving his hand.

"We could drop you off at home," Olivia called from the other window. "Think of it as a free Uber. We have champagne!" She waved her glass out of the window.

The man looked away and then turned back, laughing. He hesitated for a moment, and a grin spread across his face. "You know what? Why not? It's Vegas, right?"

As he climbed into the limo, the energy in the vehicle shifted. The addition of this handsome stranger added an extra layer of excitement to their already thrilling night.

"What's your name?" Rachel asked, passing him a glass.

"I'm Alex," he said with a wide smile. "And I thought I was going home to sleep off my shift."

Olivia poured the champagne, and Jess raised her glass in a toast. "To new friends and unexpected adventures!"

The limo erupted in cheers, and as they clinked glasses, Jess wondered if this chance encounter was going to change the course of their night in ways she couldn't begin to imagine. This was so unlike them, and yet somehow it felt completely normal.

As the limo merged back into traffic, the glittering spectacle of the Las Vegas Strip flashed by outside, a blur of neon and LED brilliance that painted ever-changing patterns across the limo's tinted windows.

Inside, the excitement was palpable, mirroring the electric atmosphere of the city beyond.

"So, Alex," Lisa said, her earlier shyness giving way to curiosity, "what do you do?"

Alex took a sip of champagne before answering. "I work at the Bellagio, actually. Blackjack dealer."

"Ooh, a man of mystery," Olivia teased, her eyes sparkling. "I love blackjack. Any insider secrets you can share?"

Alex laughed, shaking his head. "Sorry, ladies. What happens at the table stays at the table."

As they chatted, Jess noticed the familiar sights of the Strip beginning to fade

"Where exactly are we going?" Megan asked, a hint of concern in her voice as she peered out the window.

Cynthia's smile was enigmatic. "Somewhere special. Trust me, it's worth the trip."

Jess felt a flutter of unease in her stomach. She glanced at Rachel, hoping for reassurance, but her friend was engrossed in her phone.

The limo cruised past the Gold Coast casino, its retro neon sign a bright beacon in the growing darkness. Jess realised with a start that they were heading away from the Strip, towards the outskirts of the city, where the desert began to encroach.

"Um, guys?" Jess said, her voice barely above a whisper. "Is it just me, or are we heading into the middle of nowhere?"

Alex, who had been laughing at something Olivia said, suddenly looked alert. "You're right," he said, his eyes scanning the unfamiliar landscape outside. "We're definitely off the beaten path now."

The mood in the limo shifted, the earlier excitement tinged with a hint of apprehension. Even Lisa, who had been flirting shamelessly with Alex, now looked uncertain.

"Rachel," Jess said, turning to her friend. "What's going on? Where are we really going?"

Rachel finally looked up from her phone, her expression unreadable. "It's a surprise, Jess. I told you, tonight is going to be unforgettable."

There was something in Rachel's tone that made Jess's skin prickle. She was about to press further when Cynthia's voice cut through the tension.

"Ladies - and gentleman," she said, nodding at Alex, "we're almost there. I promise you, what awaits you is unlike anything you've ever experienced in Vegas."

As if on cue, the limo slowed down. Outside, the last vestiges of the city had given way to an expanse of desert, dark and mysterious under the starlit sky. Jess felt her heart racing, a mix of fear and excitement coursing through her veins.

The limo pulled up to a nondescript building. It was nothing like the casinos they had passed on the Strip, but somehow, that was refreshing. As they stumbled out, the cool night air a shock after the warmth of the limo, Jess felt a cocktail of anticipation and slight unease. This didn't look like any club she'd ever seen.

Cynthia, seemingly unfazed, led them to an unmarked door. "Welcome to The Enigma, ladies. The night is just getting started."

As Cynthia reached for the door handle, Jess caught Rachel's eye. Her best friend gave her a reassuring smile, but Jess couldn't shake the feeling that they were about to step into something far bigger — and potentially more dangerous — than a simple night out in Vegas.

NINETEEN
THIS MORNING

Jess sat on the edge of the plush sofa, her head in her hands, trying to piece together the fragments of their wild night. Around her, her friends were in various states of disarray. Lisa was curled up in an armchair, nursing a glass of water; Olivia was now pacing restlessly; Megan was hunched over her laptop, fingers flying across the keyboard as she scoured social media and local news sites for any mention of unusual events from the previous night. There was nothing.

The room bore silent witness to their predicament - empty champagne bottles, scattered shoes, and the faint lingering scent of expensive perfume mixed with the staleness of the morning after. Outside, the Las Vegas Strip buzzed with its usual energy, oblivious to the drama unfolding in their suite.

"Listen," Jess said, standing up. "We're not getting anywhere. We need to get out there and start actively looking for Rachel."

Her voice cut through the heavy silence, causing the others to look up. The determination in her tone was even more noticeable after the uncertainty that had permeated the room moments before.

Megan nodded, already pulling up her phone's map app. "The Enigma Nightclub seems like our best lead. We know we were there around 1am. I have no idea where we were before that, and there's nothing to give us any clues."

Jess agreed. "The Enigma is the first location we know for sure we were at, and when we were there."

The soft blue glow of Megan's phone screen illuminated her face, casting shadows that accentuated the worry lines around her eyes.

"But it's barely past 10:30am now," Lisa pointed out, glancing at the ornate clock on the wall. Its golden hands seemed to mock them, a reminder of how much time had passed since they'd last seen Rachel. "The club's bound to be closed."

"Looks like it's attached to The Enigma Hotel," Megan said, looking up from her phone. "That will be open, at least."

Olivia's face lit up with an idea, the sparkle in her eyes a glimpse of her usual vivacious self. "What about the hotel staff? Housekeeping, bartenders, security - someone must have seen us last night."

"Good thinking," Jess agreed, feeling a small surge of hope. "And even if the club's closed, maybe we can find the manager or someone who works there during the day."

Alex had been sitting quietly by the window; the morning sun silhouetted him, giving him an almost ethereal appearance. His voice was clear and firm. "I might be able to help. I know some of the staff at different hotels. Comes with working in the industry. I don't know The Enigma, but I do have a few contacts around town."

The group exchanged glances. The weight of Rachel's absence hung heavy in the air, an invisible presence that couldn't be ignored.

"All right," Jess said, taking charge. Her voice was steady, but her friends could see the worry in her eyes. "Let's head to The Enigma. We'll start with the hotel staff and see if we can work our way to someone from the nightclub. Maybe we can even get security footage if we explain the situation."

As they got to their feet, the shrill ring of Jess's phone cut through the room. She fished it out of her purse, her heart skipping a beat when she saw the caller ID.

"It's Miles," she said, her voice a mixture of relief and apprehension.

The others paused, watching as Jess answered the call. Her fiancé's voice came through, tinny and distant on the speakerphone.

"Hey, babe! How's the head this morning? Wild night?"

Jess hesitated, her eyes meeting those of her friends. She could see the question in their gazes - should she tell him about Rachel?

"Uh, yeah, it was... quite a night," she replied, her voice carefully neutral.

"I didn't want to call too early. Figured you'd be nursing some epic hangovers," Miles chuckled. "Everything okay? You sound a bit off."

Jess's mind raced. This was her chance to tell Miles everything, to ask for his help. But something held her back. She remembered his strange behaviour the night before, his cryptic warning about Rachel. And then there was the complicated history between Miles and Rachel, the tension that had always simmered beneath the surface of their interactions.

"Everything's fine," she lied, ignoring the looks of surprise from her friends. "We're just... heading out for some breakfast. Hair of the Dog, you know?"

"All right, well, have fun. Don't do anything I wouldn't do!" Miles's laugh sounded forced, even through the phone. "Try the biscuits and gravy at Hash House a Go Go if you get a chance. Love you, babe."

"Ok, hon. Love you too," Jess replied, ending the call. The thought of food almost made her gag.

The silence that followed the phone conversation was deafening. It was Lisa who broke it.

"Jess, why didn't you tell him about Rachel?"

Jess flopped back onto the sofa. "I... I don't know. It's just... Miles and Rachel have never really gotten along. And he was acting weird last night before we went out. To be honest, I just don't want to get him involved in this right now."

Megan raised an eyebrow. "Weird how?"

Jess shook her head, remembering Miles's cryptic warning. "He said something about being careful around Rachel. It didn't make sense at the time, but now..."

Lisa gulped visibly, letting out a sharp squeak of a sound.

Jess looked over at her, and Lisa immediately turned away.

"He worries about you," Lisa said quietly.

"*I* worry about us," Jess sighed.

The implications of her words lingered.

Olivia, ever the optimist, broke the tension. "Let's not jump to conclusions. We need to focus on finding

Rachel first. We can deal with your future husband and his weirdness later. You know how much he loves you. I'm sure he's only looking out for your best interests."

Jess nodded, grateful for Olivia's pragmatism. "You're right. Okay, let's get moving."

As they gathered their things, preparing to leave, Jess felt a surge of determination. They had a plan, a direction. It wasn't much, but it was a start.

"Remember," she said as they headed for the door, "we're looking for *any* clues about Rachel or what happened last night. Anything at all. Keep your eyes and ears open for *anything* that might help."

As they gathered their things, Megan spotted the flash drive on the table. She scooped it up and pocketed it. "Just in case we find a way to access it," she explained.

Lisa's eyes fell on the discarded handcuffs. "I am definitely not taking those," she said with a grimace.

With everything settled, they moved towards the door. Jess took one last look around the room, hoping they weren't missing anything important.

"All right, let's go," she said, leading the group out.

With a shared nod of understanding, the group set out, stepping into the hallway. Jess pressed the elevator button, her heart racing as they waited.

"Remember," she whispered as they entered the elevator, "we need to avoid the lobby. We can't risk running into the hotel manager. We're in enough trouble with him already."

They all nodded, recalling Mr Chen's stern warning about checking out. Megan glanced at her watch.

"We've got just over two hours left before we're supposed to be out. We need to find Rachel and be back before one."

The elevator began its descent, the tension palpable in the small space. Lisa fidgeted with her hair, still damp from her hasty shower. "I can't believe this is happening," she muttered. "What if we can't find Rachel in time?"

Olivia, looking like her normal self now she was out of her showgirl costume, tried to lighten the mood. "Hey, at least we're all in this together, right? It's like our own little 'Hangover' movie."

Alex chuckled nervously. "Yeah, except we're not exactly the Wolf Pack, are we?"

"Speak for yourself," Megan quipped, surprising everyone with her attempt at humour. "I could totally be the responsible one like Ed Helms."

"And who would I be?" Alex smiled, aiming the question at Lisa.

"Well, not Zach Galifianakis," Lisa smiled.

Olivia tilted her head. "I quite like him," she said with a wink.

Jess appreciated their attempts to ease the tension, but her mind was racing with worry. As the elevator continued its descent, she couldn't help but wonder what they might find when they stepped out into the casino.

The ding of the elevator reaching the casino floor snapped them all back to attention. As the doors opened, they were immediately engulfed in the cacophony of slot machines and the murmur of early morning gamblers. The group weaved their way through the maze of blinking lights and ringing bells, past the baccarat tables where serious-faced players barely glanced up from their cards.

"This way," Alex murmured, guiding them towards a less conspicuous exit.

They slipped through the door, emerging into a quieter hallway that led to the parking garage. The contrast between the vibrant casino and the stark concrete structure was jarring.

The view of The Strip beyond was different in the daylight - less magical, more real. The glaring lights on the casinos now looked gaudy and worn. The sidewalks, which had been filled with revellers just hours ago, were now populated by weary-looking tourists and hurried locals on their way to work.

"Uber or taxi?" Lisa asked as they descended the ramp to the pickup area.

"Uber," Jess decided. "Quicker and we can avoid small talk."

Lisa typed their details into the Uber app.

"On its way," she said, triumphantly.

As they huddled in the parking lot, waiting for their ride, the reality of their situation sank in. They were racing against time, not just to find Rachel, but to solve this mystery before they were forced to check out and leave Vegas altogether. Their weekend had been cut short, but they weren't leaving without their friend.

Their Uber, a nondescript sedan, pulled up a smooth five minutes later, and the group piled inside. The air conditioning was a relief as they set off towards The

Enigma.

Jess stared out the window, watching the Vegas Strip slide by. A line of palm trees marched down the centre of the boulevard, their fronds barely stirring in the heavy air. As they drove, they passed under several pedestrian bridges crowded with tourists snapping photos of the iconic skyline. Even in the bright daylight, the casino lights glowed defiantly.

The inside of the car was silent, each of the group lost in thought. As they turned away from the Strip, Alex suddenly perked up, pointing out the window.

"Hey, that's my bus stop! Right by the back of the Bellagio."

The group craned their necks to look. None of them showed any signs of recognition.

"Do you think that's where we picked you up last night?" Jess asked.

Alex shrugged, his expression a swirl of confusion and frustration. "I think it must have been. It's all so hazy."

They passed the Rio, its massive towers looking dull in the harsh daylight. The Palms loomed next, its distinctive architecture a stark contrast to the more traditional casinos they'd left behind.

"This feels familiar," Megan murmured. "But there's nothing I can put a finger on. You know what I mean?"

Lisa nodded, her eyes scanning the landscape. "I remember seeing that sign," she said, pointing at the retro neon of the Gold Coast casino as they drove past. "Or maybe I've seen it on the internet."

Olivia leaned forward, her face pressed against the

window. "Guys, we're heading away from the Strip. Does anyone remember going this far out last night?"

The car fell silent as they all tried to recall their journey from the previous evening. The effort was futile; their memories remained stubbornly blank.

As the last vestiges of the city gave way to an expanse of desert, Jess felt her heart racing. The landscape outside was both familiar and alien, stirring a sense of unease in her gut.

"This is definitely the way we came," Alex said, his voice tinged with certainty despite the gaps in his memory. "I remember thinking how strange it was to be heading out into the desert."

The Uber driver, sensing the tension in the car, glanced at them through the rearview mirror. "You folks okay back there?"

"We're fine," Jess replied quickly, forcing a smile. "Just trying to retrace our steps from last night."

As they approached their destination, the group fell into an anticipatory silence. The nondescript building of The Enigma Hotel came into view, its plain exterior a stark contrast to the opulent casinos they'd left behind.

The Uber pulled to a stop, and as they climbed out, the heat of the desert sun hit them like a physical force. Jess squinted against the glare, her eyes fixed on the unmarked door that led into The Enigma.

"Well," she said, her voice barely above a whisper, "here we are again. I guess."

The group exchanged nervous glances, each of them acutely aware that beyond that door lay answers to the mystery that had consumed their morning. With a collective deep breath, they stepped forward, ready to uncover the secrets of their lost night and, hopefully, find Rachel.

TWENTY
LAST NIGHT

Walking towards the vast façade of The Enigma, Cynthia ushered the group to a doorway at the side of the building.

"I know a few little secrets," she said with a smile.

"You're going to love it here," Rachel said, squeezing Jess's hand.

At the end of a thin, dark corridor was the silver door of an elevator, a red light glowing beside it. Cynthia pressed the button, and the elevator slid open to let them in.

"After you, ladies," Cynthia said, stepping to the side. "There's just enough room for us and our plus one."

"He'll be able to get in?" Lisa asked.

"It's fine," Cynthia reassured, smiling at Alex. "I know everybody here, and everybody knows me."

As they stepped out of the elevator on the penthouse floor, the pounding rhythm of The Enigma nightclub enveloped Jess. The scent of expensive perfume, spilled cocktails, and the faint tang of sweat was overwhelming as they walked into the club. Neon lights in deep purples and electric blues swirled across the dance floor, casting an otherworldly glow on the sea of writhing bodies.

"This is you," Cynthia said, guiding them towards a

roped off area. Their booth was bordered by lush sapphire coloured velvet. The table was already set up with champagne on ice and glasses for each of them. A sign proclaimed: JESSICA PARKER'S BACHELORETTE. In smaller letters below was handwritten in swirling silver cursive: What happens in Vegas stays in Vegas.

A rush of excitement coursed through Jess as she took in the scene. This was what Las Vegas was all about - the glitz, the glamour, the promise of a night she'd never forget. The bass throbbed through her chest, matching the rapid beat of her heart. She turned to share a smile with Rachel, but her best friend was already distracted, her fingers flying over her phone screen.

"Rachel, come on," Jess shouted over the music, frustration creeping into her voice. "Put that away. We're here to have fun!"

Rachel looked up, flashing a quick smile that didn't quite reach her eyes. "Just making sure everything's perfect for the night. Don't worry about it!"

Before Jess could respond, Cynthia appeared at Rachel's side, materialising out of the pulsing crowd. Jess felt a twinge of unease as she watched the woman whisper something in Rachel's ear.

With a quick "Be right back!" Rachel disappeared into the throng, leaving Jess feeling oddly abandoned.

Lisa sidled up to Jess, her red dress shimmering under the club lights. "Is everything okay?" she asked.

Jess forced a smile, pushing down the knot of worry forming in her stomach. "Yeah, of course. Let's dance!" She hoped the enthusiasm in her voice sounded more genuine than it felt.

As they made their way to the dance floor, Jess noticed Alex hanging back, looking slightly out of place in his trousers and shirt. Their eyes met, and he shrugged, a sheepish grin on his face. Jess felt a pang of guilt; she hadn't meant for him to get caught up in whatever Rachel was up to.

"I can't believe I'm actually here," he shouted over the music. "I should be halfway home by now!"

Lisa laughed, the sound bright even amidst the club's cacophony. "Well, we're glad you joined us!" She held out her hand. "Come on, let's show these Vegas regulars how it's done!"

Jess watched as Alex hesitated for a moment, then took Lisa's hand. As the two of them danced, Jess saw something spark between them - a connection that seemed to surprise them both. Jess temporarily forgot her worries, losing herself in the infectious energy of her friends. Maybe Alex's presence was going to be exactly what they needed after all.

The club was a blur of flashing lights, pounding music, and flowing drinks. Jess laughed more freely than she had in months, her pre-wedding jitters momentarily forgotten as she danced with her friends. But when she looked for Rachel, she found her best friend on the fringes of the group, phone in hand.

The joy of the night was souring, a growing knot of frustration forming in Jess's stomach. Rachel was hiding something. She just didn't know what. The club seemed to close in around Jess, the music suddenly too loud, the lights too bright. Jess fought to catch her breath, feeling overwhelmed by the sensory assault and the growing unease inside her. She needed to sit down before she fell.

Jess made her way back to the table with her name on it and almost slumped onto the soft seat.

She wasn't alone for long.

"Hey," Lisa's voice came as she sidled up to Jess in the booth. "Not dancing?"

Jess shrugged, forcing a small smile.

"I can't have you sitting here with an empty glass and a sad face on your bachelorette," Lisa said. "It should be me who's sad. You have a gorgeous future husband. All I have is..."

Before she could continue, Alex slipped into the booth beside Lisa, sliding a garish cocktail towards Jess.

"Thought you could make use of this," he said with a grin.

Jess lifted her eyes.

"I think you're going to be just fine, Lisa," Jess said, picking up the cocktail and removing the garnish. "This looks great, Alex, thanks."

Alex bowed, banging the table as he did so and making the cocktail slosh over the side of the glass.

"Oopsie," he laughed.

Lisa patted his arm, and a look passed between them that made Jess's smile widen.

"So, tell," Lisa said. "What's up?"

Jess rolled her eyes. "It's nothing, really. This is such a great bachelorette party. Rachel has gone above and beyond."

"For sure," Lisa nodded.

"But..."

"But..."

"She's hardly spent a moment with us. I mean, I understand she's sorting everything out with that Cynthia, but..."

"But..." Lisa said again.

"I just want to have my girls together." Jess's eyes flicked to Alex. "You can be an honorary girl tonight. You know what I mean."

"Well, if I'd been maid of honour we wouldn't have been anywhere nearly as flash as this, but I guarantee I would have been right by your side," Lisa said.

"Thanks, Lis," Jess said, her eyes locking with her friend's.

"Rachel probably thinks she's doing the right thing, I'm sure, but she must have paid that Cynthia a LOT for all this. Surely, she can leave her to deal with it and come and have fun?"

Jess nodded. "I would never say a bad word about any of you girls, you know that, and especially not Rachel, but... I need her here, not over there."

Jess gestured across the room to where Rachel and Cynthia were huddled in a quiet corner. Lisa followed her gaze and shook her head.

"I'm going to sort this," she said resolutely. "Shuffle up," she said to Alex, waving him out of the booth and out of her way.

Alex stood to let her pass, and as Lisa moved away, Jess put her hand on her arm.

"Don't..." she said.

"She should be with us. She should be with you. For all we know, she might need rescuing from Cynthia."

160

Lisa winked, and Jess relaxed back into the velvet seat.

Jess watched as Lisa marched over to Rachel.

"I can't let her do this," Jess said. "Sorry, Alex."

Alex stood again and Jess hurried across the dancefloor after Lisa, her heart racing with a mix of anticipation and dread.

"Rachel, what's going on?" Lisa demanded, her words slightly slurred from the countless cocktails she'd consumed. "This is supposed to be Jess's bachelorette party, but you've barely spent any time with us!"

Jess winced as she heard the pain in Lisa's voice, feeling a surge of guilt. Had she been too caught up in her own doubts to notice how her other friends were feeling?

Rachel's eyes widened, a flash of guilt crossing her face. "Lisa, I'm sorry. I'm just trying to make sure everything is perfect-"

"It would be more perfect if you were actually spending time with us!" Lisa interrupted, tears welling up in her eyes.

Jess watched the exchange, her stomach churning. This wasn't how the night was supposed to go. She wanted to step in, to smooth things over, but the words stuck in her throat.

Rachel reached out to Lisa, but Lisa stepped back, nearly stumbling into a nearby table. The glasses on it rattled, drawing curious glances from nearby patrons.

"I got us VIP access to every exclusive venue in Vegas," Rachel said, her voice pleading. "I wanted this night to be special for all of us."

"VIP access?" Lisa's voice cracked. "Is that what

this is all about? The money and the connections?"

Jess felt her heart sink. She'd been so focused on Rachel's strange behaviour that she hadn't considered how it might look to the others.

Lisa reached down and, with more effort than she had apparently expected, she ripped the VIP pass down the middle. The sound of tearing plastic seemed to echo in the suddenly quiet corner of the club, and Jess flinched.

Rachel opened her mouth to respond, but Cynthia interrupted. "Rachel, we need to go over the details for the next venue," she said, either oblivious to or ignoring the emotional storm brewing around her.

As Rachel moved to walk away, Jess finally found her voice. "Maybe we should call it a night," she suggested, suddenly feeling exhausted. The tornado of an evening, the alcohol, and the swirling emotions threatened to overwhelm her.

Cynthia, overhearing this, gently pulled Jess aside. Her touch was light, but Jess felt an inexplicable chill run down her spine. "Honey, can we talk for a moment?"

Jess hesitated, eyeing Cynthia warily. The woman exuded an aura of mystery that both intrigued and unsettled her. In the pulsing lights of the club, Cynthia's features seemed to shift: one moment warm and inviting, the next sharp and calculating.

"Look," Cynthia began, her voice softening, "I know things seem a bit... off right now. But Rachel? She's only distracted because she's trying her damnedest to give you the best bachelorette party ever. She's been planning this for months."

Jess sighed, running a hand through her hair. "I appreciate that, but it feels like she's barely been present all night. This isn't what I wanted."

Cynthia's eyes sparkled with understanding, a knowing look that made Jess feel exposed. "Sometimes, the people who love us most show it in ways we don't always understand. Trust is a delicate thing, Jess. It's like a house of cards - takes forever to build, but can topple in an instant."

The words hit Jess like a punch to the gut. She thought of Miles's warning about Rachel, of her own growing suspicions. The club's pulsing lights and writhing bodies seemed to melt together, creating a disorienting whirlpool of colour and motion that made Jess's head swim. Faces became indistinct, merging into a dizzying blur as the room appeared to tilt and sway around her.

"How do you know who to trust?" she asked, her voice barely audible.

Cynthia smiled, a hint of sadness in her eyes. "That's the million-dollar question, isn't it? In my experience, trust your gut. But also remember that love - true love, whether it's romantic or friendship - it's messy. It's imperfect. Sometimes it's about having faith, even when your head is telling you to run."

Jess nodded slowly, processing Cynthia's words. There was wisdom there, but also something else - a hint of personal experience that made Jess wonder about Cynthia's own story. Who was this woman, really? And how had she become so entwined in their night?

"The night is young," Cynthia continued. "And

Rachel has something truly special planned next. Give her a chance to explain. After all, Vegas is a city of second chances and unexpected miracles."

As Cynthia walked away, Jess found herself torn. On one hand, Cynthia's words had struck a chord. On the other, she had a gnawing feeling that there was more going on than met the eye. Miles's warning echoed in her mind, along with Rachel's strange behaviour.

The club suddenly felt claustrophobic, the air heavy with secrets and unspoken tensions. Jess scanned the crowd, her eyes settling on her friends scattered throughout the venue. Lisa was now laughing with Alex at the bar, her earlier distress seemingly forgotten. Olivia and Megan were chatting animatedly nearby, their faces flushed with excitement and alcohol. And there was Rachel, tapping away at her phone near the VIP area. As if sensing Jess's gaze, Rachel looked up, their eyes meeting across the crowded room. For a moment, Jess saw a flicker of something in her best friend's eyes - fear? Guilt? Determination? It was gone in an instant, replaced by Rachel's characteristic smile.

Jess made a decision. This was her bachelorette party, a celebration of friendship and new beginnings. Whatever was going on with Rachel, whatever secrets were swirling around them, they would face it together.

She had to trust Rachel. Rachel had never let her down. Why would she tonight?

TWENTY-ONE
THIS MORNING

Making their way towards The Enigma, Jess's jeans felt uncomfortably tight, a stark reminder of the indulgences from the night before. Olivia had managed to find an oversized t-shirt that barely covered the hem of her shorts, while Megan looked starkly casual in yoga pants and tank top. Lisa was the only one who looked as though she had made an effort. She was wearing red shorts and a white crop top that emphasised her best assets. Her blonde hair was impeccable, and Jess was pretty sure that although Lisa was going to a natural look, she was wearing makeup.

Jess smiled internally, wondering if the effort was for Alex's benefit. Even with Lisa's contribution, they were a very different group from the polished, excited group that had arrived in Vegas just a day before.

The heat of the desert sun was already intense. Jess clicked open her phone: it was nearly 11am. They had barely two hours to find Rachel. The air shimmered above the pavement, creating mirages that seemed to embody the illusive nature of their search. Jess could feel sweat beading on her forehead, and she wished she'd thought to bring her sunglasses.

They entered the hotel lobby, the blast of air

165

conditioning a welcome relief from the outdoor heat. The hotel and casino was so plain on the outside, but the interior was a feast for the eyes - lush tropical plants, gurgling water features, and intricate mosaics covering every surface. Under different circumstances, Jess would have been awestruck. Now, she barely noticed the opulence, her eyes scanning for anyone who might help them.

Alex took the lead, approaching the front desk with a confidence that surprised the others. His amiable smile and familiar manner as he chatted with the receptionist spoke of someone used to navigating the complex social dynamics of the Vegas hospitality scene.

The girls hung back, trying to blend in. As they waited, Jess found her mind wandering back to her conversation with Miles. Had she made the right decision in keeping him in the dark? The doubt must have shown on her face, because Lisa gently squeezed her arm.

"Hey," Lisa said softly, "Thinking about Miles? You did what you thought was best. We'll figure this out together, okay?"

Jess nodded, grateful for the support. She looked around at her friends - Megan's determined focus as she tapped away at her phone, likely researching something relevant to their search; Olivia's restless energy; Lisa's steady presence at her side. And Alex, this near-stranger who had seemingly become an integral part of their mission.

They could see him leaning over the desk, looking at a monitor, talking to the receptionist, nodding,

166

smiling.

When Alex returned, his expression was a mix of triumph and confusion. The group gathered around him, eager for news.

"I've got something, but I'm not sure if it helps," he said. "I saw the CCTV footage. You all arrived with Rachel, and you left with her, too. Or more to the point, WE did."

"What? Are you sure?" Jess asked.

Alex nodded. "Positive. The timestamp shows you leaving at around 1:30am. The five of us," he gestured to Jess, Lisa, Megan, Olivia, and himself, "came out together. Rachel and Cynthia followed about five minutes later."

Lisa's eyes widened. "Can we see the footage ourselves?"

Alex's expression hardened slightly. "You wanted me to come along and help you, right? I don't have to be here. You can trust me, or I can go."

The girls exchanged glances, uncertainty clear on their faces.

Jess spoke up, her voice careful. "We have no reason to trust or not trust you, Alex. We're just trying to be thorough."

Alex's eyes met Jess's, a hint of challenge in his gaze. "Trust doesn't seem to be your strong suit, does it?" He paused for a moment before he continued, his tone softening. "Look, I get it. But I'm here to help, remember?"

The tension in the group was palpable.

Finally, Megan broke the silence. "So, The Enigma is a dead end, then? We've only proved that we were here, and that we left."

Jess nodded slowly, processing the information and letting the disappointment sink in. "But now we know Rachel was with us when we left, and that Cynthia was still in the picture. That's something, right?"

Olivia chimed in, her voice hopeful. "Maybe we can track down Cynthia? She might know what happened after we all left The Enigma."

The group considered this, a new sense of purpose emerging from their dismay.

"All right," Jess said, taking charge once again. "The Enigma might be a dead end, but we've got a new lead. Let's see if we can find out anything about Cynthia. And Alex," she turned to him, her expression softening, "thank you for your help. We do appreciate it."

Alex nodded. "No problem."

The group stood in a corner of The Enigma's lavish lobby. Jess leaned against a marble pillar, its surface cool against the warmth of her skin. She watched as tourists streamed past, their faces alight with the promise of Vegas fortune, oblivious to the drama unfolding in their midst. Even out here, far from the main stretch of casinos on the strip, the slot machines were almost all in use. There were signs for blackjack, poker, and roulette, but she couldn't see a single one for a nightclub.

"So. Cynthia," Jess said, raising her voice to be heard over the constant din.

"Do you think we should just phone her?" Olivia said hesitantly.

The group fell silent, exchanging uncertain glances. The idea of calling Cynthia was a last resort they'd been avoiding.

"I don't know," Jess said. "I mean, I feel like we have to, but... Can we trust her? We don't even know how we got her number."

"We don't know if Rachel gave it to us in case of an emergency..."

"You don't know *anything*," Alex interjected. "For all we know, Rachel could be with Cynthia right now, having breakfast at Eggslut or something."

"Egg what?" Lisa asked, momentarily distracted from her worry.

"It's a breakfast place in the Cosmopolitan," Alex explained, a hint of a smile playing on his lips despite the tense situation. "The point is, they could be together, safe and sound."

Jess turned to Alex, her eyes narrowing. "You said earlier that you'd heard of a Cynthia who was friendly with VIPs, moving in high roller circles. If this is the same woman... is she likely to be casually having breakfast, or could Rachel be in serious trouble?"

The implications of her words hung heavy in the air, punctuated by the distant cheers of a slot machine winner.

"The point is, Jess, you just don't *know*," Alex said. "But you have to find Rachel, and, well, I think you should find out what this woman knows. You're right that I've heard of her, but if there was anything terrible about her, I'm sure I would have heard that too."

After a moment of tense silence, Megan spoke up. "I think we have to risk it. Calling Cynthia is our best shot at finding out what happened after we left."

Reluctantly, the others nodded in agreement. Olivia took out her phone, her hand trembling slightly as she pulled up Cynthia's number.

"Here goes nothing," she murmured, putting the phone on speaker and placing it on a nearby cocktail table.

The group gathered in, heads bent together as they strained to hear over the ambient noise. The phone rang once, twice, three times. Each ring seemed to stretch on for an eternity.

Finally, Cynthia's voice came through, smooth and controlled despite the less-than-perfect connection. "Hello?"

"Cynthia, it's Olivia. From last night? We're trying to find Rachel. When did you last see her?"

There was a pause on the other end of the line, during which the group held their collective breath. A burst of laughter from a nearby group of tourists made them lean in even closer, desperate not to miss Cynthia's response.

"Olivia? How did you...?" The sentence trailed off and Cynthia sighed. "Never mind." Cynthia took a breath and then spoke. "I last saw Rachel at The High Roller Suites. Then you girls left."

Jess nudged Olivia, mouthing, 'Ask if Rachel left with us.' Olivia nodded, swallowing hard before speaking again.

"Was Rachel with us when we left?"

Cynthia's reply was difficult to hear over the sudden burst of a slot machine's musical jingle. "The night was quite... eventful. It's hard to keep track of

170

everyone's comings and goings."

"Cynthia," Jess cut in, unable to contain herself, "please. We're worried about Rachel. Was she with us or not?"

Another pause, longer this time. When Cynthia spoke again, her voice was low, almost reluctant. "Well, Rachel... disappeared."

The girls exchanged alarmed glances, the bright lights of the casino suddenly seeming garish and overwhelming.

"What do you mean, disappeared?" Jess pressed, her knuckles white as she gripped the edge of the table.

"Have you called the police?" Cynthia asked abruptly, her tone shifting.

The group exchanged nervous glances. "No, not yet," Megan replied hesitantly. "We were hoping to track her down ourselves first. We didn't want to cause a panic if she's just... taking some time to herself."

"Do you think it's a police matter?" Olivia asked, her voice trembling slightly.

There was a long pause before Cynthia responded. "No, you should definitely not involve the police," she said, her voice barely audible but filled with urgency. "Keep following her trail. She'll probably reappear when you least expect it."

The cryptic nature of Cynthia's response made the group shiver.

"What are you trying to say? Do you know something we don't?" Jess demanded.

"I'm afraid that's all I can say," Cynthia replied, her tone final. "This is one you're going to have to work out on your own. And girls? I'm pretty busy, so I'd appreciate if you didn't call this number again, however you got it. Good luck."

The line went dead, leaving the group staring at the phone in stunned silence. For a moment, the chaos of the casino faded into the background as they processed Cynthia's words.

"What the hell does that mean?" Lisa exclaimed, voicing what they were all thinking.

Jess ran her hands through her hair, frustration evident on her face. "It means we're in deeper than we thought. Why would Cynthia warn us against calling the police?"

"The High Roller Suites," Alex said quietly. "That's where we need to go next. Whatever happened to Rachel, it started there."

As the group began to plan their next move, Cynthia's words hung heavy in the air. Rachel had disappeared – but where? And why? The mystery was deepening, and with each new piece of information, the stakes seemed to get higher.

TWENTY-TWO
LAST NIGHT

The pulsing beat of The Enigma club throbbed through Jess's body as she watched her friends dancing. Rachel appeared at her side, her gold dress shimmering under the club lights. Her eyes were bright with excitement.

"Ladies, gather round!" Rachel called out, her voice carrying over the music. As the group huddled together, Rachel's smile widened. "You won't believe this, but I just got a text from Drake Holloway!"

Olivia squealed with delight. "Drake? Oh wow, I thought he was just being polite earlier. Are we really going to hang out with him?"

Rachel nodded. "He wants us to join him at The High Roller Suites as soon as we can. It sounds like there's going to be quite the performance."

Jess felt a mixture of unease and resignation wash over her. She hadn't been impressed by Drake's slick charm earlier, but her friends seemed enamoured with the action star.

"Performance?" she asked, careful to hide her uncertainty. "I thought it was a party?"

"I guess we'll find out. If you're up for it, of course." Rachel posed the statement as a question, waiting for Jess's acceptance of the idea.

Jess looked around at the excited faces of her

friends. "Is this what you've been working on all evening?" she asked.

Rachel hesitated momentarily before smiling. "This is part of it, yes. Shall we...?"

"A real celebrity," Olivia said. "This is so cool."

Jess forced a smile, not wanting to dampen her friends' enthusiasm. But she couldn't shake the feeling that Drake's invitation was leading them into something she wasn't sure she wanted to be part of.

"I'm sure it will top the night off perfectly," Jess said. "How many brides-to-be can say they went to an exclusive celebrity party on their bachelorette?"

"Well, what are we waiting for?" Lisa exclaimed, her earlier melancholy forgotten. "Let's go see what Drake has in store for us!"

"I hope Miles won't be too jealous," Megan laughed.

As the group erupted in excited chatter, Jess couldn't help but notice a look pass between Rachel and Cynthia. It was quick, almost imperceptible, but it sent a shiver down her spine.

Olivia and Megan linked arms for a last trip to the restroom before their next adventure. Jess, however, found her attention drawn to Lisa, who was making her way to the bar. The club's flashing lights, once enchanting, now seemed harsh and accusatory, highlighting the tear in Lisa's VIP pass—a stark reminder of her earlier outburst.

Concerned, Jess followed Lisa, watching as she signalled the bartender. Jess approached just as he asked Lisa, "Closing out?"

Lisa nodded, retrieving her credit card from her clutch. As they waited for the transaction, Jess caught their reflections in the mirrored backsplash. Lisa's once-perfect makeup had smudged, dark smears under her eyes, aging her beyond her years. Jess realised her own appearance wasn't much better—both a far cry from the excited women who had started this bachelorette celebration.

"We might need a freshen up before we party with the stars," Jess said, putting her arm around Lisa.

"You could be right," Lisa smiled. "How long is it since we left The Bellagio? I feel like we have partied hard tonight... and apparently, the night isn't over yet."

"It's just after one," Jess said, checking her phone screen. "Tired?"

"Not too tired to see what The High Roller Suites has in store," Lisa said.

"What about the guy?" Jess asked, with a small grin. "Alex. You like him?"

The blush on Lisa's cheeks answered the question as the bartender handed the cheque over to her.

A familiar presence interrupted their banter. Rachel, still resplendent in her gold dress that shimmered under the club lights, stood next to them at the bar. Despite the night's drama, and the hours of partying, she remained effortlessly glamorous. Her makeup had somehow remained impeccable.

"You don't need to pay, you know," Rachel said softly to Lisa, her jasmine-infused perfume wafting over them. "It's all taken care of."

Lisa shook her head, a rueful smile playing on her lips. "I'd feel better if I did. Besides," she gestured to

175

her torn pass, "I'm not exactly VIP material anymore."

Rachel dismissed the concern with a wave, her bracelets jingling melodically. "It's not a problem, really."

As the bartender returned Lisa's card, Jess observed the interaction, acutely aware of the unspoken tension between her friends. The weight of the night's events seemed to press down on them, heavier than the club's humid air. Jess couldn't shake the growing concern that both Lisa and Rachel were carrying burdens they weren't fully sharing.

Jess and her friends headed back to the elevator, to make their way out of The Enigma. As they stood waiting for it to arrive, Jess's phone began to vibrate in her clutch. She pulled it out, frowning at the screen.

"It's Miles," she said with uncertainty. "What does he want at this time in the morning?"

"I guess he knows you're still painting Las Vegas red," Lisa smiled.

"Maybe he wants to check you're back at the hotel, all tucked up," Rachel said, with the slightest hint of sarcasm.

"Ignore it!" Olivia called out. "It's your bachelorette party, girl! No husband allowed!"

The others chimed in with agreement, and after a moment's hesitation, Jess declined the call. Almost immediately, a text message appeared on her screen.

Vegas can be a dangerous place. People aren't always who they seem to be. Watch out for yourself and your friends.

Jess stared at the message, a mixture of confusion and unease settling in her stomach. She glanced up at her friends, all caught up in the night's excitement, and decided to keep the message to herself. No need to dampen the mood with Miles's cryptic warnings.

"What is it?" Lisa asked. "What did he say?"

"Rachel was right," Jess lied. "He wanted to check we were all back at the hotel in our PJs."

"How sweet!" Rachel laughed, and the others joined in.

The elevator pinged, and the door opened.

As they prepared to move on to the next venue, Jess caught Rachel's eye. For a moment, the tension between them seemed to dissipate, replaced by the warmth of their years-long friendship. Jess gave her a small nod, a silent promise to trust, to believe.

"Watch out for your friends," the message had said.

That was exactly what Jess intended to do: Rachel was her best friend, and nothing was going to change that.

"Ladies first," Alex said, standing aside.

Jess, Megan, Olivia, and Lisa stepped into the lift.

"You girls go ahead," Rachel called out, her voice overly bright. "Cynthia and I just need to sort out some details for The High Roller Suites. We'll be right behind you!"

After the conversations that had already taken place, Jess felt a rush of annoyance.

"One last time," Rachel said, her eyes pleading. "When we leave here, I promise I won't be checking my phone anymore."

"I'll take it off her, if it makes you all feel better," Cynthia smiled. "I know you've felt a little ignored, Jess, but this night has been months in the planning. None of us wants anything to go wrong."

Rachel dipped her eyes downwards. Her face was tight-lipped.

"Rach, I know you've done your best," Jess said. "Don't think I don't appreciate it. Things have been said, but... at the end of the day... or night... I'm so happy that you're all here with me, and so very grateful to you for tonight."

Whatever Miles was trying to warn her about, there was no way it could be the kind, gentle, giving woman who had put so much effort into the night that she had barely left herself any time to enjoy it.

"When we get to The High Roller Suites, I'm not leaving your side," Rachel said.

This time, it was Cynthia's turn to raise her eyebrows and tighten her lips.

Whatever was going on between the two women, Rachel had given Jess her word that it would no longer affect their night, and Jess believed her.

"Come on," Megan urged, linking arms with Jess. "Let's wait in the limo. They won't be long."

Jess nodded to Alex, and he stepped into the elevator, giving Cynthia a long look as he did so.

The luxurious limo stood by the curb waiting for the group. They all piled inside, the plush leather a welcome respite. Despite being an exclusive venue, the dancefloor in The Enigma Club had left them as hot and sweaty as any nightclub they had ever visited.

178

"Let's sort this makeup out while we wait," Lisa said, opening her purse.

"I need to brush my hair," Olivia sighed. "I'm a sticky mess."

"No way," Megan smiled. "You look amazing."

"Meg, we are going to party with Drake Holloway!" Olivia said, as though this were explanation enough for her need to be picture perfect.

Megan pulled a small comb from her clutch, smoothing out her own hair before passing it on to her friend.

Alex sank back against the side window as the girls chattered and reapplied mascara and lip gloss.

"Rachel seemed to..." Lisa started speaking, but stopped, letting her sentence trail off. "Don't worry about it."

Jess nodded. "I think she's with us now. I trust her."

Lisa looked at Jess for a couple of seconds and nodded back.

"And Miles?" Lisa asked. "What did his message really say?"

Jess flicked a gaze over to Megan and Olivia before answering.

"He told me to look out for us all," she said. "You know what he's like."

"Yeah," Lisa said. "He worries about you, but..." She looked at the other two girls, who were using their phones as makeshift mirrors, and then leaned in close to Jess to whisper, "...I think he's worried about Rachel."

Jess's eyes widened. "Well, you know what it's like between them," she breathed.

Lisa patted Jess gently on the thigh. "I've got your back," she said. "Always."

Jess put her hand on Lisa's. "Thanks," she said.

In that moment, something passed between them that Jess couldn't quite articulate. Before either of them could say anything else, Rachel and Cynthia emerged from the club, both wearing expressions of barely contained excitement.

"Sorry for the wait, ladies!" Rachel exclaimed as they climbed into the limo. "But trust me, it'll be worth it. The High Roller Suites are going to blow your minds!"

"Everything okay?" Jess whispered to Rachel, searching her friend's face for any sign of trouble.

Rachel's smile was dazzling. "Everything's perfect. Just you wait and see."

TWENTY-THREE
THIS MORNING

The neon lights of The Enigma club seemed to envelope the group as Jess, Megan, Lisa, Olivia, and Alex stood in the lobby. Their search had turned up empty, to all intents, leaving them with more questions than answers.

"Well, that was a bust," Lisa sighed, fidgeting with the strap of her purse. Her fingers traced the intricate pattern of the leather. "At least we know Rachel was with us at The High Roller Suites."

"Guys, does anyone else think it's weird how Cynthia said Rachel 'disappeared'? Like, is that something Rachel does often when she's with her?" Jess said.

Alex raised an eyebrow. "You think there's something this Cynthia isn't telling us?"

"Maybe," Jess shrugged. "I mean, it could be nothing, but the way she said it... I don't know. It felt off."

Lisa nodded. "I know one thing for sure. Rachel wouldn't just abandon us."

Jess nodded. As the bride-to-be, she felt responsible for the whole situation. "She wouldn't, but that doesn't explain much. We still don't know where she *disappeared* to – or what happened after we left The High Roller Suites. And..." She paused, her face greying. "This isn't just about Rachel disappearing. I woke up in an ice bath. You two..." She gestured towards Alex and Lisa. "...were handcuffed together. You, in the closet with that briefcase. We still don't know what's on the flash drive. You.... where the hell did the showgirl costume come from? And more importantly, why, why why?"

Olivia fished the crumpled note from her pocket. "Guys, remember this too: 'The man in the hat knows'. We still have no clue what it means."

"And we've still got no way to access that flash drive," Megan added, frustration in her voice. "Maybe she left us a message..."

"There are easier ways she could have done that," Olivia said, shaking her head. "An encrypted flash drive seems too complex."

"That doesn't explain why I had it. Or who gave it to me," Megan frowned.

"And how did Rachel's phone end up back in the suite?" Jess said. "It's not like she could call us if we had her cell. It doesn't make sense. None of it does."

Jess leaned heavily against a gaudy slot machine, its cheerful jingles out of sync with the pit of dread in her stomach. The flashing lights of The Enigma casino blurred in her vision as she stared blankly ahead, her mind racing with worries about Rachel.

"Where are you, Rach?" she whispered, her voice almost inaudible amidst the commotion of the casino floor.

The situation could not have been more serious. Her maid of honour, her best friend since college, was missing. And Jess had a gut feeling that it was somehow her fault. If she hadn't agreed on this lavish bachelorette weekend in Vegas, if she'd kept a closer eye on Rachel last night...

The others - Megan, Lisa, Olivia, and their unexpected companion Alex - huddled nearby, discussing their next move. But their voices grew faint as Jess's mind conjured increasingly dire scenarios.

Was Rachel hurt? Lost? Or worse? In a city like Las Vegas, anything could happen. The thought made Jess's stomach churn.

She quickly checked her watch – an hour and a half left before they had to check out of their Bellagio suites. The ticking clock seemed to mock her, each passing second a reminder of their failure to find Rachel.

"Jess?" Megan's voice cut through her spiralling thoughts. "We need to decide what to do next."

Jess blinked, forcing herself back to the present. She straightened up, trying to compose herself. As Rachel's best friend, she needed to hold it together. But the facade cracked as she met Megan's concerned gaze.

"What if something terrible has happened to her, Meg?" Jess's voice quivered. "What will we do if we can't find her?"

"Then we call the police. No matter what Cynthia said. If we don't find her before we have to check out..." Lisa began.

"There must be a reason for what Cynthia said, though. She sounded serious. No police.... why? I... I don't know what to do." Jess broke down into a gentle sob.

The rest of the group fell silent, the gravity of Jess's fears settling over them. Even Alex, who barely knew them, looked troubled.

Lisa stepped forward, placing a comforting hand on Jess's arm. "Hey, this is Rachel we're talking about. She's smart, she's resourceful. I'm sure she's fine."

"But why would she disappear like this?" Jess countered, her frustration bubbling to the surface. "It's not like her to just vanish without a word."

Olivia, ever the optimist, chimed in. "Maybe it's part of some elaborate surprise? You know how Rachel loves to go all out."

Jess wanted to believe it, but the knot of worry in her chest wouldn't ease. She tried to centre herself, inhaling and letting the breath out slowly, just like Olivia had taught them in her yoga class.

"Okay," she said finally, her voice steadier. "You're right. We need to focus. What are our options?"

As the group discussed their limited clues - the mysterious note about the man in the hat, the inaccessible flash drive, the credit card charges - Jess tried to push aside her fears. But her eyes kept darting to the crowds around them, searching for a familiar face that wasn't there.

'Hang on, Rachel,' she thought, a silent plea to her missing friend. 'We're coming for you. Just please, please be okay.'

With renewed determination, Jess turned back to her friends. Time was ticking, but they weren't giving up. Not when Rachel was counting on them.

"Okay," she said, wiping her eyes. "Let's find her."

The group fell silent, each lost in thought. The High Roller Suites seemed like a logical next step, given the charges on Lisa's credit card, but none of them had any idea where to find it.

As they debated, Megan's phone rang. She glanced at the screen and groaned. "It's my boss. I should probably take this."

The others watched as Megan answered the call, her posture immediately stiffening.

"Hello, Mr Thompson. No, I'm not at my computer right now. I'm sorry, but I can't look that up for you at the moment." There was a pause as she listened, her face growing increasingly uncomfortable. "I understand it's urgent, but I'm not sure when I'll be back at my laptop. No, I can't drop everything and go to work right now. I'm in the middle of something important."

The group exchanged concerned glances as they overheard the muffled sound of Mr Thompson's raised voice through the phone. Megan winced, holding the device away from her ear.

"Yes, sir. I understand. I'll get to it as soon as I can. Goodbye." Megan hung up, her shoulders sagging with relief.

"Megan, wasn't this supposed to be your weekend off?" Jess asked gently, concern etched on her face.

Megan looked surprised, as if the thought hadn't occurred to her. "I... yeah, I guess it is."

Lisa put a comforting hand on her friend's shoulder. "Your boss shouldn't be calling you like that during Jess's bachelorette weekend. You're allowed to have a life outside of work, you know."

Megan nodded, but her expression was conflicted. "I know, it's just... I've always been available. It's expected."

Alex, who had been quietly observing, spoke up. "Look, I may be new to your group, but even I can see that's not healthy. You're in Vegas for your friend's bachelorette party, for crying out loud."

Megan's phone rang again, and instead of answering, she looked at it, and then at her friends.

Jess nodded, and Megan slipped her phone into her pocket.

"You don't know how hard it is to do that," she said, almost breathless.

"And you don't know how easy," Jess smiled, reassuringly.

The opulent lobby of The Enigma seemed to mock the exhausted group with its grandeur. Crystal chandeliers cast a soft glow over marble floors and plush velvet seating. Jess paced back and forth, her sneakers sinking into the thick carpet with each step.

Megan seemed to be itching to retrieve her phone from her pocket. Her shoulders were tense, her fingers jittery.

Lisa shook her head, her eyes red-rimmed from lack of sleep and worry. "It's like there's a black hole in my memory. One minute we're all together, having the time of our lives, and the next..." She trailed off, gesturing helplessly.

Olivia leaned forward, head resting against a flashing slot machine. The glow lit up her exhausted face.

A shrill ring cut through the air. They all jumped, startled by the sudden noise. Megan touched her pocket, checking whether it was her own phone ringing again, and pulled her hand back.

"Not me," she said with thinly veiled relief.

It took a moment for Jess to realise the sound was coming from her bag.

With trembling hands, she reached in and pulled out Rachel's phone. The screen was lit up, displaying an incoming call. The name flashing on the screen made her blood run cold: Cyn.

"Oh no," Jess whispered, her eyes wide with panic. "It's Cynthia. She's calling Rachel's phone."

"Don't answer it!" Megan hissed, reaching out to grab Jess's wrist. "She can't know we have Rachel's phone. She must think it's with Rachel."

They watched in tense silence as the phone continued to ring. After what felt like an eternity, it stopped. A moment later, a notification popped up: New Voicemail.

The group exchanged nervous glances. "Should we... should we listen to it?" Olivia asked, her voice hardly louder than a murmur.

Jess nodded slowly. "We have to. It might give us a clue about what's going on."

With shaking fingers, she navigated to the voicemail and put the phone on speaker. Cynthia's voice, now sharp with anger, filled the air around them.

"Rachel, what the hell is going on? How did your friends get my number? This wasn't part of the deal. We had an agreement, and you owe me. If you think this vanishing act is going to work, you have another think coming. Your friends know better than to involve the law now, but if you're not at The High Roller Suites by noon, there will be consequences. And don't forget what you're supposed to bring. No games."

The message ended abruptly, leaving behind a deafening silence. The group stared at each other, shock and confusion written across their faces.

"What deal?" Lisa whispered, her face pale. "What does Rachel owe her?"

"And what is she supposed to bring?" Megan added.

"Guys," Alex interrupted, his voice tight with urgency. "We can figure out the details later. Right now, our major priority is the deadline. Cynthia said noon at The High Roller Suites, wherever that is."

Jess glanced at her watch, her stomach dropping. It's already almost eleven thirty. We have barely half an hour to find this place.

"Well, we can't exactly ask Cynthia for directions," Lisa added, her voice strained with frustration. She crossed her arms over her chest, her manicured nails digging slightly into her skin. Her foot tapped an impatient rhythm on the polished floor as her eyes scanned the crowded lobby, looking for any hint that might help them.

Megan was already opening the maps app on her phone, her fingers moving frantically across the screen. "Okay, let's see where The High Roller Suites is..."

The others crowded around her, their eyes fixed on the small screen. Megan zoomed in and out of the Las Vegas Strip map, searching for any mention of The High Roller Suites.

"I'm not seeing anything," she muttered, her voice filled with annoyance.

Lisa pulled out her own phone. "Let me try a web search."

For a few moments, the only sound was their fingers tapping on screens, punctuated by the ambient noise of the casino - the soft music, the murmur of shoppers, the constant chime of slot machines.

"Wait," Olivia said suddenly. "I found something called the High Roller, but... it's the Ferris wheel at the LINQ. That can't be right, can it?"

Jess shook her head. "No, that's definitely not it. The only two things I've ever been afraid of are heights and commitment. I'm pretty sure I can only face one of my fears at a time. Keep looking."

Their tense expressions and huddled postures drew curious glances from passersby, but they were too focused on their task to notice.

After several more minutes of fruitless searching, Lisa let out a defeated sigh. "Guys, I've tried every combination I can think of - High Roller Suites, High Roller Room, VIP High Roller... nothing's coming up except that Ferris wheel."

"Shit," Megan muttered, her voice low but intense. "What are we going to do? We can't find it anywhere on the map or online."

The realisation that they couldn't locate The High Roller Suites began to sink in, adding another layer of complexity to their already daunting task.

The weight of their predicament settled over the group like a heavy blanket. They were racing against time to find a place they'd never heard of, to meet a

189

deadline for a friend who had vanished under mysterious circumstances. And looming over it all was the threat of "consequences" if they failed.

TWENTY-FOUR
LAST NIGHT

The limousine drove smoothly through the neon-lit streets of Las Vegas, carrying its passengers from The Enigma Nightclub towards the exclusive High Roller Suites. The tinted windows offered a dreamlike view of the city, its lights blurring into a kaleidoscope of colours as they sped past.

Jess sat back in the plush leather seat, the cool material a welcome relief from the warmth of the Nevada night. She glanced around at her friends, their faces illuminated by the passing lights. Lisa and Alex were deep in conversation, their heads bent close together. Olivia was practically bouncing in her seat, her enthusiasm infectious. Megan, ever the practical one, was studying a map on her phone, no doubt trying to figure out exactly where they were headed.

And then there was Rachel, her best friend and maid of honour, looking radiant in her gold dress. Rachel caught Jess's eye and winked, raising her champagne flute in a silent toast.

"To the bride-to-be," Rachel said, her voice carrying over the hum of the limo. "I hope this is a night you'll never forget!"

The others joined in the toast, the clink of glasses filling the air.

191

As they cruised down the Strip, Jess marvelled at the spectacle outside. The shimmering majesty of The Cosmopolitan hotel, reflecting the nearby lights on its facade. The replica Eiffel Tower at Paris Las Vegas loomed overhead, its iron latticework adorned with twinkling lights. Crowds of tourists and revellers thronged the sidewalks, their faces a mixture of wonder, excitement, and that particular brand of hopeful desperation unique to Vegas. It was approaching half-past one in the morning, and it looked as though the Strip was just warming up.

"I can't believe we're really here," Olivia exclaimed, her face pressed against the window. "It's like being in a movie!"

"A very expensive movie," Megan quipped, but her smile betrayed her own excitement.

Jess felt her phone vibrate in her clutch. She pulled it out, seeing another message from Miles. With a sigh, she typed a response.

Rachel leaned over, her curiosity piqued. "Everything okay with the hubby-to-be?"

Jess hesitated, then showed Rachel the earlier message from Miles. Trusting Rachel meant sharing Miles's concerns with her too.

"Like you said earlier, he's being overprotective," Jess said.

Rachel's eyebrows shot up as she read it.

"People aren't always who they seem to be? What's that supposed to mean?" Rachel asked, her voice tinged with annoyance. "What's Miles's problem?"

As Rachel spoke, Jess noticed Lisa glance their

way. Lisa's eyes darted between Jess's phone and Rachel, an unreadable expression on her face. For a moment, it seemed like Lisa wanted to say something, but she quickly turned back to her conversation with Alex, her posture noticeably tense.

Jess shrugged, feeling uncomfortable. "I don't know. He's just... worried, I guess."

Rachel snorted. "Worried about what? That you're having too much fun?"

"I think he's just looking out for me," Jess said defensively. "You know how he is."

Rachel's expression softened. "Yeah, I do. Look, Jess, I know Miles and I have never been best buddies, but I introduced you two because I thought you'd be good together. And you are. But sometimes... I don't know. Sometimes I feel like he doesn't trust me."

Jess looked at her friend, surprised by the vulnerability in her voice. "What do you mean?"

Rachel sighed, her voice dropping to a near whisper. "Miles and I... we are colleagues, associates really. We've never been friends. But I saw how perfect you two would be together. I just wanted you to be happy."

"And I am happy," Jess assured her, squeezing her hand. "But why do you think Miles doesn't trust you?"

Throughout the exchange, Jess couldn't help but notice Lisa's occasional furtive glances in their direction. Each time Jess caught her eye, Lisa would quickly look away, an odd mix of concern and guilt flashing across her face.

Rachel's eyes darted around the limo, as if checking to see if anyone else was listening, but if she saw Lisa's interest, it didn't deter her.

"It's complicated, Jess," she said. "Our work... it isn't always straightforward. Sometimes we have to bend the rules a little. And Miles... he doesn't really like that."

Before Jess could press for more details, Cynthia's voice cut through the conversation. "You never really know how well you can trust someone, or how well you really know them," she said, her tone relaxed but her eyes sharp. "Even the people closest to us can surprise us."

The words seemed to hang in the air. Jess felt a shiver travel down her back, despite the warmth of the limo. Lisa visibly stiffened. Her eyes met Jess's for a moment, a silent question in them that Jess couldn't quite decipher.

The other two girls, who had been trying not to eavesdrop, now looked uncomfortable. Olivia, in an attempt to lighten the mood, pointed out the window. "Hey you guys; look at Circus Circus! I've always wanted to see the trapeze acts there!"

As they passed the whimsical big top outside the hotel, Jess pondered how out of place it looked among the sleeker, more modern casinos. It served as a reminder of Vegas's constant reinvention, the old giving way to the new.

"So, Rachel," Cynthia chimed in, "You introduced Jess to her fiancé? How did you and Miles meet? I don't think I've heard the full story."

Rachel hesitated for a moment, her eyes meeting Jess's. "We work for the same company," she said finally.

"Her family basically own the company," Lisa said, causing Rachel to flash a sharp look in her direction.

"My family does own the company, yes," Rachel said. "But I had to apply for a job just the same as everyone else."

As if ignoring this exchange, Cynthia continued with her line of questioning. "And you thought Miles would be perfect for Jess?" Cynthia asked. There was something in her expression that Jess couldn't read.

Rachel nodded, a small smile playing on her lips. "Pretty much," she said.

Jess felt a warmth spread through her chest at the memory. "I remember that day," she said softly. "It was at the company Christmas party. I was your plus one," she laughed. "You practically shoved me into Miles."

The group joined in with the laughter, the tension from earlier dissipating slightly.

"But with Jess in common, why didn't you and Miles ever become friends?" Olivia asked, her natural curiosity getting the better of her. Jess realised how little of the group's backstory she had shared with the most recent addition. She had known Lisa and Rachel for so long that everything was taken for granted between them. Even Megan had been their friend for so long that their shared understanding was deeply embedded in their friendship.

Rachel's smile momentarily faltered. She paused, as if carefully choosing her words. "You know, it's funny how some connections just don't click, even when you have someone in common. Miles and I... we are more like distant colleagues than friends."

Cynthia leaned forward, her interest piqued. A knowing glint flickered in her eyes, though her face remained neutral. "Distant colleagues? That sounds intriguing. Surely there must be more to the story?"

Rachel shrugged, but Jess noticed a tightness around her eyes. "It's not that exciting, really. We just have different priorities at work. Miles is all about climbing the corporate ladder, while I am more focused on... let's say, building relationships."

"You don't have to worry about climbing the ladder when your parents can shoot you straight up in the elevator, though, do you?" Cynthia purred. Her eyebrow arched slightly at Rachel's words, as if she knew more than she was letting on.

Rachel let out a sharp laugh.

"If only it was that easy," she said. "Anyway... Cynthia, why don't we stop talking about work now? It must be terribly boring for the girls."

"And Alex," Lisa said.

"And Alex," Rachel acknowledged.

"Of course," Cynthia said. "We could talk about Drake Holloway instead."

"Yes!" Olivia said with a happy squeak in her voice. "I've never actually met anyone famous before."

Lisa had turned her focus down to her phone, seeming less interested in the conversation about the movie star, but both Megan and Olivia were literally on the edge of their seats.

The limo turned off the main strip, the pizazz giving way to a more subdued, exclusive atmosphere. The buildings here were sleeker, more modern, with none of the kitschy charm of the big casinos. This was clearly where the real money played, far from the chaos of the penny slots and all-you-can-eat buffets.

"Sorry ladies, no time for that. We're getting close," Cynthia announced. "The High Roller Suites are just ahead."

As they neared their destination, Jess felt her heart rate quicken. The anticipation in the limo was palpable, an electric current tinged with a hint of apprehension. She studied her friends' faces, illuminated by the soft interior lights of the vehicle. Olivia's eyes were wide with wonder, Megan's expression a mix of curiosity and calculation, Lisa's features betraying a blend of eagerness and unease. Rachel, however, wore a smile of confident anticipation, as if she knew exactly what awaited them.

The limo slowed to a stop in front of a nondescript building, its exterior a study in understated luxury. No gaudy signs or flashing lights here; just smooth, dark glass reflecting the city lights like a mirror. As the engine's purr faded to silence, a moment of stillness fell over the group. They exchanged glances, a silent acknowledgment passing between them that they were about to step into a world few ever saw.

With a mixture of thrill, nerves, and curiosity, they filed out of the car, the warm night air enveloping them as they stepped onto the sidewalk. The next chapter of their Vegas adventure was about to begin, and Jess couldn't shake the feeling that it would be unlike anything they had experienced before.

TWENTY-FIVE
THIS MORNING

Jess looked around the group, desperately trying to work out their next move. Coming to The Enigma had been a waste of time. None of them knew where The High Roller Suites was. Worst of all, they were running out of time.

Megan pulled out the scrap of notepaper that she had written their timeline on, back in the Bellagio.

"Well, we also know that we left The Enigma at half-past one," Megan said, writing that into the list.

23:58 - Rachel gets the text to meet someone

00:00 - Rachel meets someone in a back room ?where

01:07 - Credit card charge at The Enigma Nightclub

01:30 - We left The Enigma Nightclub

03:17 - Jess leaves a voicemail for Rachel

03:30 - Credit card charge at Glamour and Grace

04:12 - Credit card charge at The High Roller Suites

Suddenly, Olivia's eyes lit up. "We're in Las Vegas," she said, a hint of excitement in her voice, "so let's gamble."

The others looked at her in confusion.

"What do you mean?" Alex asked, voicing the

question on everyone's mind.

Olivia leaned in, lowering her voice conspiratorially. "We don't know where we were when Jess called Rachel," she said, pointing at the list. "Our only other lead is that we were at Glamour and Grace at a ridiculous hour. Maybe if we go there, we might find some answers."

Jess felt a spark of hope ignite in her chest. It wasn't much, but it was something. She looked around at her friends, saw the same mixture of hope and determination reflected in their eyes.

"It's worth a shot," she said, straightening up and squaring her shoulders. "Let's go."

"Okay," Jess said, "does anyone remember how to get to Glamour and Grace?"

"No..." Megan said, already pulling out her phone. "But I think that's something we *will* be able to find on Google."

As Megan tapped away on her phone, the others huddled around her, their faces a mixture of hope and anxiety. After a few moments, Megan's eyes widened in surprise.

"Guys," she said, her voice a mix of excitement and frustration, "you're not going to believe this. Glamour and Grace is in the Via Bellagio Arcade... in the Bellagio hotel."

A collective groan went up from the group. The irony wasn't lost on any of them - they had been running in circles, only to end up back where they started.

"Are you kidding me?" Olivia exclaimed, throwing her hands up in exasperation. "We've wasted all this time, and it was right under our noses? Didn't you know where it was?" She turned to Alex.

He shrugged. "I've probably walked past it a hundred times on my way to Starbucks, but clothes shops aren't really my thing."

Jess felt a moment of despair, but quickly pushed it aside. "Hey, at least we know where it is now," she said, trying to inject some optimism into her voice. "And we're getting closer to finding Rachel. This is all we have to go on."

Lisa nodded in agreement. "Jess is right. We can't give up now. Let's get back there and see what we can find out."

Alex was already pulling up the Uber app on his phone. "I'll call us a ride," he said. "There's no way we could walk in this heat, even if time wasn't against us."

"Us..." Lisa said with a hint of a smile.

"It looks like I'm in this until you find your friend," Alex said.

"And we will. We will," Jess said.

They made their way through the crowded casino floor towards the exit. Jess felt a sense of the surreal as they walked. Just yesterday, they had been excited tourists, ready for a fun bachelorette weekend. Now, they were on a desperate hunt for their missing friend, navigating a world of secrets and dangers they barely understood.

They pushed through the revolving doors, stepping out into the bright Las Vegas morning. The heat hit them like a wall, after the air-conditioned interior of the casino.

Waiting for their Uber to arrive, Jess's emotions ran riot. They were no closer to finding Rachel or understanding what had happened last night, but at least they had a direction. It wasn't much, but it was something to hold on to.

The Uber pulled up, and as they piled in, Jess made a silent wish that Glamour and Grace would provide the answers they so desperately needed. The clock was ticking, and Rachel's fate hung in the balance. Whatever secrets the boutique held, they were about to find out.

The car set off, and Jess looked at her friends in earnest.

"We can't afford to waste any more time. We need to find The High Roller Suites and be there for noon. That's only twenty-five minutes from now. If we can't find any help at Glamour and Grace..." She stopped speaking, as though she hadn't considered the ramifications.

"We will," Olivia said, reaching out to her. "I have a feeling about this."

"Well," Jess said. "We need to use our time wisely. Let's try to think of any other leads we can while we are on the way."

The group fell silent, the severity of their situation settling over them once again. Jess watched her friends, desperation etched on their faces as they struggled to come up with anything of use. Rachel's disappearance and Cynthia's threats pressed down on her, making each passing second feel like an eternity.

"Wait," Megan said suddenly, her eyes lighting up.

"What about the VIP passes? The ones Rachel gave us last night. They might have some information on them."

Jess's heart leaped. How could they have forgotten about the passes? She fumbled through her purse, her fingers trembling as she searched for the pass.

"I've got mine," Lisa said, pulling out a slightly crumpled pass from her bag. As she smoothed it out, her face fell. "Oh no..."

"What is it?" Jess asked, leaning in to look.

Lisa held up her pass, revealing a jagged tear across its surface. "It's ripped," she said, her voice quivering. "Why would anyone rip my pass? Did I... did I have an argument with Rachel or something?"

The group fell silent, exchanging uneasy glances. Jess felt a chill run down her spine. "Lisa, do you *remember* having any disagreement with Rachel last night?"

Lisa shook her head, her eyes welling with tears. "I don't know. I can't remember *anything* clearly. But..." she hesitated, glancing nervously at Jess.

"But what?" Jess prompted, sensing there was more to the story.

Lisa spoke shakily. "I... I've been talking to Miles. Your Miles. He... he didn't trust Rachel. He was suspicious of her even before last night."

Jess felt as if the floor had dropped out from under her. "What? You've been talking to Miles behind my back? About Rachel?"

"I'm sorry, Jess," Lisa said, quietly. "He reached out to me, said he was worried about you and Rachel. He thought she might be involved in something dangerous."

Jess's mind raced, trying to reconcile this new information with everything else that had happened.

"He..." Jess was about to snap at Lisa when a memory hit her. She gulped in air and looked at Lisa solemnly. "He.... tried to warn me." Lisa pulled out her phone and scrolled to her text messages.

"'Vegas is a dangerous place'," she read from her screen. "He knew something. He knows something."

"But the voicemail you left for Rachel," Megan cut in. "You seemed worried about all of us. Including Rachel." She looked at the others for support. "Didn't you?"

Jess dug in her bag for Rachel's phone and replayed the message.

"Rachel, it's Jess. I don't know what's going on, but something's not right. If you get this, be careful. I think we're in trouble. Don't trust—"

Jess's voice came again from Rachel's phone.

"We?" Lisa said. "*We* as in all of us, including Rachel, or *we* as in those of us left behind after she *disappeared*?"

"I.... I just don't know," Jess sighed.

"You should call Miles," Megan said. "If he knows something about Rachel, it might help us find her."

Jess sighed. "I didn't... I didn't want to worry him. I know he's already so paranoid. He didn't want me to come to Vegas in the first place. I just wanted to be with you girls and have a good time."

"Well, it's certainly been something," Lisa deadpanned. "You need to call him."

Jess nodded numbly.

"Okay," she said. "Okay."

She switched phones and dialled Miles's number; she couldn't help but wonder how many more secrets would come to light before this ordeal was over.

The phone rang once, twice, three times. Jess held her breath, silently willing Miles to pick up. On the fourth ring, there was a click.

"Jess?" Miles's voice came through, tense and worried. "Are you okay? What's going on?"

Jess asked a question that she had never thought she needed to ask before: "Miles, we need to talk about Rachel. What do you know?"

TWENTY-SIX
LAST NIGHT

As they filed out of the limo, Lisa caught Jess's eye. Her friend looked equal parts thrilled and nervous, clearly picking up on the shift in atmosphere. Lisa gave her what she hoped was a reassuring smile.

Standing there on the sidewalk, the warm Vegas night enveloping them, Jess felt as though they were on the precipice of something monumental. The High Roller Suites loomed before them, an enigma wrapped in luxury and secrecy.

"Ladies," Cynthia purred, her voice carrying a promise of decadence and intrigue, "welcome to where the real Vegas comes out to play."

The entrance to The High Roller Suites was deceptively understated - a sleek, obsidian doorway framed by two towering marble columns. As they approached, the doors swung open silently, revealing a world that took their breath away.

The foyer was a study in opulence. The floor was a mesmerising mosaic of black and gold, each tile catching and reflecting the light from the crystal chandeliers that hung overhead like constellations. The walls were draped in deep burgundy velvet, occasionally parting to reveal alcoves housing paintings that were no doubt ridiculously valuable.

Stepping inside, a surge of adrenaline rushed through Jess, causing her heart to race. The air carried a heady fragrance of expensive perfume and aged whiskey, accompanied by a subtle undertone of lingering cigar smoke. The sounds of distant laughter, clinking glasses, and the soft murmur of hushed conversations created an intoxicating ambiance.

Jess noticed Rachel scanning the room, her eyes darting anxiously from face to face, her lips pressed into a thin line of concern.

"Where's Drake?" Rachel whispered to Cynthia, her voice tight with anxiety.

Cynthia's smile faltered for a moment before she regained her composure. "I'm afraid Mr *Holloway* had to leave unexpectedly. An urgent matter came up."

Rachel's face paled, and Jess caught a flash of panic in her eyes before she quickly masked it.

"But ladies," Cynthia continued smoothly, addressing the group, "don't worry. The entertainment Drake arranged will still go ahead. I promise you're going to love it."

"You..." Rachel hissed at Cynthia and snapped her lips closed before unleashing the rest of her sentence.

Jess felt a ripple of disappointment run through the group. Olivia's face fell, and even Megan looked crestfallen.

"That's too bad," Lisa said, voicing what they were all thinking. "I was looking forward to meeting him properly."

Alex shrugged, seeming less bothered by the actor's absence. "Hey, at least we're still getting the VIP treatment, right?"

Cynthia led them deeper into the establishment. Jess couldn't help but notice Rachel's unease. Her friend kept glancing around nervously, as if expecting Drake to materialise at any moment. Jess wondered what could be causing such anxiety. The rest of the group's eyes darted around, trying to take in every detail. They passed by numerous side rooms, each one offering a tantalising glimpse of the activities within. In one, a high-stakes poker game was in progress, the players' faces masks of concentration. In another, a roulette wheel spun lazily, the ball dancing across the numbers as elegantly dressed patrons held their breath in anticipation.

The clientele was as diverse as it was intriguing. Some were dressed in outfits that could have graced the cover of fashion magazines - all glitter and glamour. Others opted for understated luxury, their wealth evident in the cut of their suits and the glint of their watches. And then there were those who seemed almost out of place in their simplicity, yet carried themselves with an air of quiet confidence that spoke of true power.

Showgirls in elaborate costumes that defied gravity and logic milled about, their presence adding a theatrical flair to the already surreal atmosphere. Their feathers and sequins caught the light, creating miniature light shows with every movement.

"This way, darlings," Cynthia said, guiding them towards a set of intricately carved double doors. "Your private room awaits."

The doors swung open, and Jess felt her jaw drop.

The room before them was nothing short of spectacular. It was easily the size of her entire apartment back home, with ceilings so high they seemed to disappear into shadows.

One entire wall was dominated by a bar that seemed to stretch on forever. Behind it, shelves upon shelves of bottles glimmered like jewels - every type of spirit imaginable, and probably some that weren't. The bartender, a dapper gentleman in a crisp white jacket, nodded in greeting as they entered.

In the corner opposite the bar stood a small stage, its red velvet curtains drawn back to reveal a setup that hinted at the performances to come. The lighting was soft and intimate, creating an atmosphere of anticipation.

But it was the seating arrangement that truly took Jess's breath away. Plush, oversized sofas and armchairs in deep, rich jewel colours were artfully arranged around low tables. Each piece looked as if it had been crafted for royalty, with intricate embroidery and gleaming metal accents.

"Please, make yourselves comfortable," Cynthia said, gesturing towards the seating area.

As they settled into the impossibly soft cushions, Jess ran run her hand over the fabric. It felt like silk beneath her fingers, cool and smooth.

Rachel leaned close to Jess, her voice barely above a whisper. "I know I made a promise to you, that I would stay by you for the rest of the night, but..." She put her arm around Jess, so that it would look to the others as though she was giving her a hug, but in reality, Jess could tell that she didn't want any of them to overhear. "Something has happened. I need to make a quick call. Cover for me? And please, believe I wouldn't be doing this unless I really had to."

Jess pulled back enough to see the earnest expression on her friend's face. Before she could respond, Rachel had slipped away, disappearing behind the velvet curtain. Jess's mind raced. Whatever was happening, it must be serious for Rachel to break her promise so soon.

"This is... incredible," Megan breathed, her usual practical demeanour momentarily forgotten as she took in their surroundings.

"It's like we've stepped into another world," Olivia added, her eyes overflowing with awe.

Alex let out a low whistle. "I've worked in Vegas for years, and I've never seen anything like this."

Lisa nodded in agreement. "I feel underdressed here," she sighed.

Alex cast his eyes over her red skintight dress. "No way," he said. "You're even more stunning than this place."

Jess smiled at her friend and looked around, trying to take her mind off Rachel's latest disappearance. The opulence of their surroundings was almost dizzying, making her acutely aware of her own dress, which had seemed so glamorous back at the hotel, but now felt almost plain in comparison, even with its sparkling sequins.

"Is Rachel okay?" Lisa asked.

"Maybe she went to call Drake?" Olivia said. "I can't believe I've been stood up by a celebrity!"

"That's still a pretty cool story," Megan laughed.

Jess frowned slightly. Not only was Drake not there, but they were the only ones in the room. His entire party appeared to have bailed on them.

"Maybe Carter Reeves gave him a better offer," Alex speculated. "They looked chatty earlier."

Olivia shrugged. "His loss," she said with a cheeky grin.

Jess shook her head as though trying to shake out a negative thought.

"What if Carter Reeves did have something to do with it? Rachel looked worried. There could be all kinds of things going on that we don't know about," she said.

Her face was pale, even beneath her refreshed make up.

"Oh honey," Cynthia said, speaking up at last. "I wouldn't worry myself with what any of those boys are doing. If Rachel is worried about Drake, I'm sure she'll straighten things out with him."

The blonde planner didn't seem at all troubled by Rachel's absence, and Jess couldn't help but wonder what the casino boss would think about being called a boy by this woman.

As if on cue, Rachel rejoined the group, her face slightly flushed. Jess wondered what other secrets might be lurking beneath the surface of their night.

Jess perched on the edge of her seat, her eyes searching Rachel's face for any sign of what was going on. Rachel, however, seemed completely at ease. She lounged on one sofa as if she belonged there, her gold dress catching the light and making her look like a modern-day Cleopatra.

"This," Cynthia said, her voice low and full of promise, "is where the magic happens. Speaking of which..." She turned towards the stage, a knowing smile playing on her lips.

Immediately, the stage doors swung open, and a figure stepped into sight. He was tall and imposing, dressed in a tailored suit that seemed to shimmer with an otherworldly quality. His salt-and-pepper hair was slicked back, and his eyes twinkled with mischief and mystery.

"Ladies and sir," Cynthia announced, "allow me to introduce the incomparable Great Marvolo."

The magician bowed with a flourish, his movements graceful and precise. When he spoke, his voice was rich and melodious, carrying an accent that was impossible to place.

"It is my utmost pleasure to make your acquaintance," he said, his gaze sweeping over the group. "I understand we're celebrating a bride-to-be this evening?"

Jess felt herself blush as all eyes turned to her. The Great Marvolo approached, taking her hand and bringing it to his lips in a gallant gesture.

"My dear," he said, his eyes locking with hers, "I promise you a performance of wonders beyond your wildest imagination."

There was something in his gaze that made Jess's heart skip a beat. It wasn't attraction, exactly, but a sort of magnetic pull she couldn't quite explain. She felt as if she were falling into those eyes, glimpsing secrets and mysteries that both thrilled and terrified her.

The spell was broken as a waiter appeared, bearing a tray of cocktails. The drinks were unlike anything Jess had ever seen - swirling, smoking concoctions in glasses that seemed to change colour in the light.

"Ah, perfect timing," the Great Marvolo said, releasing Jess's hand and stepping back. "Please, enjoy these special creations. They're designed to... open your minds to the possibilities of the night."

They each took a glass. Jess noticed how the liquid inside seemed to move of its own accord, like a living thing. She brought it to her lips hesitantly, the smoky aroma filling her nostrils.

The first sip was a revelation. Flavours exploded on her tongue - sweet and bitter, fiery and cool, all at once. It was as if she were tasting colours and hearing flavours. She looked around and saw similar expressions of awe on her friends' faces.

"Now," the Great Marvolo said, "let us begin our journey into the realm of the impossible."

As he spoke, the lights in the room seemed to dim of their own accord. The air grew thick with anticipation, and Jess felt a shiver run down her spine. Whatever was about to happen, she knew it would be unlike anything they had ever experienced.

Jess took another sip of her enigmatic drink; it felt as though they were about to cross a threshold from which there was no return. The real Vegas, the Vegas of secrets and wonders, was about to reveal itself.

TWENTY-SEVEN
THIS MORNING

The sound of the air-con in the Uber and the tyres against the road gave a dull background hum as Jess pressed the phone tightly against her ear, straining to hear Miles's voice. Her friends huddled close, their faces etched with worry and exhaustion.

"Miles," Jess began, her voice trembling slightly, "I need you to tell me everything you know about Rachel. Everything."

As Miles spoke, Jess felt her world tilt on its axis. The world seemed to blur around her. She gripped her phone tighter; her knuckles turned white, as she struggled to process Miles's words.

"Rachel's family," Miles began, his voice low and urgent, "they're not what they seem, Jess. All those businesses they own in Vegas? The Nugget, the Sapphire Lounge, even that little souvenir shop, Lucky Charms? They're all fronts."

Jess's free hand flew to her mouth, stifling a gasp. She felt Lisa's hand on her shoulder, a gesture of silent support.

"Fronts for what?" Jess whispered, though she feared she already knew the answer.

"Money laundering," Miles confirmed, and Jess could hear the tension in his voice. "They've been doing it for years, Jess. I first noticed something was off when I was going through some accounts at work. The numbers... they just didn't add up. Too much cash flowing through businesses that shouldn't have been that profitable."

Jess's mind raced, thinking back to all the times Rachel had casually mentioned her family's businesses, how she always seemed to have inside knowledge about the best places in Vegas. The VIP treatment they'd received last night - had it all been part of this elaborate scheme?

"I'm not involved in any of it, Jess," Miles insisted, his voice earnest. "I swear to you, I've always kept my nose clean. But Rachel... she was in deep. Her family's been doing this for years, and she was groomed to take over. The parties, the connections, the lavish lifestyle – it was all part of her role."

Jess wanted to believe him, she really did. She closed her eyes, leaning against the window for support. The cool surface against her skin grounded her, even as her world seemed to be spinning out of control.

"Hang on," Jess gasped. "You said 'was'. You said she *was* in deep. Has something happened to her? Do you know what happened last night?"

"No," Miles said quickly. "I didn't mean that. I mean, I know she was involved in *The Family Business*. I don't know about now. I... I haven't spoken to her in a few weeks."

"Jess?" Olivia's worried voice broke through her thoughts. "What's he saying? You look like you've seen a ghost."

Jess opened her eyes to find her friends watching

214

her intently, their faces a mix of concern and curiosity. The flashing lights of a casino outside the car window cast alternating shadows across their faces, adding to the surreal atmosphere.

"It's... it's about Rachel," she managed, her voice shaky. "Her family... they're not who we thought they were."

She turned away slightly, trying to focus on Miles's voice.

"Miles," she said, her voice low but intense, "how long have you known about this? And why didn't you tell me sooner?"

The other end of the line was silent, and Jess could almost picture Miles running his hand through his hair, a habit he had when he was stressed.

"Jess, Rachel and I work together a lot more closely than you think. I'm so sorry I didn't tell you, but I didn't want you to think that I'm part of all that, too. I'm not. I never have been. I never would be. I only stayed when I found out because, well, I wanted to be sure you were safe. I've had suspicions for a while," he admitted. "But I didn't want to believe it at first. And then... I was afraid, Jess. Afraid of what might happen if I spoke up. These people, Rachel's family... they're dangerous. They have connections everywhere in Sin City."

Jess looked out of the car window, suddenly seeing the city in a new light. How many of these bright lights, these glittering facades, were hiding sinister secrets?

Jess wanted to believe Miles; she really did. But doubt niggled at the back of her mind. How could he have known all this and never said anything? And how

215

could she *not* have known? She and Rachel had been friends for seven years, and in all that time she had never known how dark Rachel's hidden depths were.

"What about Cynthia?" Jess asked, her voice quiet and urgent. "Do you know who she is?"

Miles paused before responding. "Cynthia?" Miles's voice was puzzled. "I'm sorry, Jess, but I've never heard that name before. Whatever Rachel's caught up in now, I don't know how this Cynthia fits in. But if Rachel's misdeeds have caught up with her..."

He trailed off, leaving the ominous implication hanging in the air. Jess shuddered.

"How could you let me come down here?" Jess demanded, her voice rising. She noticed her friends exchange worried glances. "If you knew it might be dangerous-"

"I didn't know for sure," Miles interrupted. "I hoped... I hoped I was wrong. That Rachel had got out, that it would just be a normal bachelorette party." He cleared his throat awkwardly. "And I... I did try to take some precautions. I asked one of the girls to keep an eye on you, to let me know if anything seemed off."

"Lisa," Jess said. "She told me. How could you do that? Checking up on me..."

"Jess, I'm sorry," Miles said, his voice pleading. "I was just trying to protect you. Please understand, I was worried about you."

"I have to go," Jess said abruptly. "We need to find Rachel."

"Jess, wait-" Miles began, but she had already ended the call.

216

For a moment, Jess sat, staring out of the window, the phone clutched tightly in her hand. The conversation she had just had swirled around her head. It all felt surreal, like a dream she couldn't wake up from. Finally, she looked at her friends. They were watching her anxiously, clearly waiting for her to speak.

"Okay," she said, her voice barely audible. "I think it's time we all put our cards on the table. No more secrets."

TWENTY-EIGHT
LAST NIGHT

The group's private room in The High Roller Suites had been transformed into an intimate theatre. The lights dimmed, casting a warm glow over the small audience. Plush velvet curtains framed the stage, their deep crimson colour adding to the air of mystery. The air was thick with anticipation. Marvolo's tailcoat sparkled with hidden sequins, catching the light with every movement.

The lights dimmed, and a hush fell over the group. Soft, mystical music played, building in intensity. The air seemed to crackle with electricity, a palpable excitement spreading through the room.

"This is so wonderfully cheesy," Olivia giggled, her eyes sparkling with mirth. "I love it!"

Lisa nodded enthusiastically. "It's like being a kid again, isn't it? All wide-eyed and believing in magic."

Jess turned to Rachel, a grin spreading across her face. "How did you find this guy? He's perfect!"

Rachel shrugged slightly. "Nothing to do with me," she said. "I thought we were coming to party with the stars. This is all her doing." She nodded discreetly towards Cynthia.

With a flourish of his hands, The Great Marvolo took to the stage and began his performance.

"Ladies and gentleman," he announced, his voice rich and theatrical, "Welcome to the magic capital of the world: Las Vegas. Prepare to question everything you think you know about reality."

He produced an ornate box from nowhere. It was a beautiful thing, inlaid with mother-of-pearl. Marvolo opened it to reveal two compartments, separated by a solid divider.

"Observe," he said, placing a large, glittering die in one compartment. He closed the box with a snap, then reopened it moments later. The die had vanished from its original position and appeared in the other compartment.

The group gasped in unison. Marvolo repeated the trick several times, the die seeming to pass through solid wood at his command. For the finale, he opened the box one last time - both compartments were empty. The die had disappeared entirely.

"Where did it go?" Lisa whispered, her eyes wide with wonder.

As if in answer, Marvolo snapped his fingers, and the missing die fell from the ceiling, landing perfectly into his outstretched hands.

The group burst into applause, each of them clapping with genuine amazement.

But Marvolo was only just beginning his act. He moved on to his next illusion, a card trick of unprecedented scale.

"For this next feat," he announced, "I'll need a volunteer." Marvolo's eyes landed on one person. "You, my dear," he said, pointing at Jess. "Would you do me the honour?"

Heart pounding with excitement, Jess made her way to the stage. Marvolo guided her to a large, circular platform at the centre.

"Now," he said, producing a deck of cards, "please select a card, any card. Don't show me, but memorise it and show it to the audience."

Jess drew the Queen of Hearts, displaying it to the group before returning it to the deck.

Marvolo shuffled the cards with incredible dexterity, his hands moving so fast they blurred. Suddenly, he flung the entire deck into the air. The cards exploded outward, swirling around Jess in a tornado of suits and numbers.

The small audience gasped in unison. Jess stood at the centre of the maelstrom, her hair whipping around her face, laughing with pure joy.

As quickly as it had begun, the card tornado subsided. The cards floated gently to the ground - all except one, which remained suspended in mid-air before Jess's face.

"Is this your card?" Marvolo asked with a knowing smile.

It was indeed the Queen of Hearts. The group erupted in cheers and applause once more.

But the trick wasn't over. Marvolo snapped his fingers, and the Queen of Hearts burst into flames. As the ashes fell, they transformed into a flock of white doves, which circled the room before disappearing in puffs of smoke.

The group cheered and whooped. Jess returned to her seat, her cheeks flushed with excitement.

"That was incredible!" Olivia exclaimed, squeezing

Jess's arm.

"How did he do that?" Lisa wondered aloud, her eyes still wide with amazement.

Even Megan was shaking her head in disbelief. "I have to admit, that was... extraordinary."

Rachel smiled and patted Jess's arm. "You were a great volunteer," she mouthed.

As Marvolo prepared for his next trick, the girls exchanged thrilled glances. For a moment, all their worries were forgotten, swept away by the sheer wonder of the performance.

A waitress appeared beside them, balancing a tray of elegant, gold-rimmed glasses. Inside each glass, deep rose-pink cocktails swirled, catching the light and creating mesmerising patterns.

"Ooh, what are these?" Jess asked, her eyes widening with curiosity.

The waitress smiled, her voice soft and secretive. "These are our signature 'Eternal Love' cocktails, ladies. The perfect accompaniment to tonight's magical performance."

The girls shared eager glances before each taking a glass. The liquid continued to swirl as they raised their drinks in a toast.

"To magic, mystery, and an unforgettable night!" Rachel proclaimed, her voice ringing with enthusiasm.

As they sipped at their drinks, Marvolo made a bouquet of roses appear out of thin air, each bloom a different, impossible colour.

"Okay, that was actually pretty cool," Megan admitted.

Jess savoured her drink, the heavy liquid leaving a tingling sensation on her tongue. It tasted like nothing she'd ever experienced before - a blend of sweet and bitter, with undertones of exotic spices and a hint of something she couldn't quite place. As the liquid warmed her from the inside, she felt her senses heightening, the colours in the room becoming more vivid, the sounds crisper.

As she watched Marvolo perform increasingly spectacular illusions, Jess felt a sense of childlike wonder. For all the glitz and glamour of Vegas, there was something special about this intimate, magical show. It reminded her of birthday parties long past, of a time when the world still held infinite possibilities and mysteries.

Then Marvolo's voice cut through the excitement. "And now, for my final and most spectacular illusion, I will need another volunteer." His eyes scanned the group, again landing on Jess. "Perhaps our lovely bride-to-be would care to step up once more?"

Jess felt her heart skip a beat. The spotlight swung towards her, and she felt all eyes in the room turn her way. Her group, the security guards, the waitresses, and Cynthia, relaxing on a chaise longue next to the stage, all looked at Jess. She opened her mouth to decline, but no words came out. A strange mix of excitement and apprehension washed over her.

Beside her, Rachel seemed to sense her reluctance and squeezed her hand. "I'll do it," she said, her voice carrying across the suddenly quiet room.

Cynthia raised her head slightly, as if she was going

to speak, but instead, she settled back onto the chaise.

"As maid of honour, it's my duty to step in for the bride, right?" Rachel smiled.

"Not on the wedding day, I hope," Lisa laughed.

Before Jess could say anything else, Rachel was making her way to the stage, her gold dress shimmering under the lights. Marvolo's smile widened as he took Rachel's hand, leading her to an ornate cabinet at the centre of the stage.

The cabinet was a work of art in itself, adorned with intricate carvings and inlaid with what looked like gold leaf.

"My dear," he addressed Rachel, but his eyes swept over the audience, "How bold of you to volunteer like this. Standing in for your friend is truly noble. Now, are you ready to disappear?"

Rachel nodded, a mix of excitement and nervousness on her face.

"Then, my sweet girl, disappear you will. Please, enter." With a swing of his arm that made glitter fall towards the stage, The Great Marvolo indicated Rachel should step into the cabinet.

She moved forward, giving a little wave to her friends before Marvolo closed the door.

Jess felt a sudden, inexplicable urge to rush forward, to stop whatever was about to happen. But she remained rooted to her spot, the cocktail seeming to cloud her judgment. It was just a magic trick. The vanishing girl was a staple of all the shows she had seen as a child, and the girl always reappeared.

The tempo of the music increased as Marvolo made a

series of elaborate gestures. Smoke poured from the cabinet, obscuring it from view. The girls and Alex held their breath. The tension in the room was palpable.

With a flourish, Marvolo flung open the cabinet doors. The smoke cleared, revealing... nothing. Rachel was gone.

The girls applauded, but Jess felt a knot forming in her stomach. Something felt off. The magic that had seemed so wondrous just moments ago now took on a sinister edge.

"The girl always reappears," she muttered quietly, as though she herself was enchanted.

Marvolo bowed, basking in the adulation.

"Thank you, ladies and gentleman. It has been a pleasure spending this brief but charming spell with you tonight." His voice was confident and plummy. There was no trace in it that the trick had gone anything other than exactly as he had planned it.

The group's applause died down, replaced by a murmur of confusion. Rachel *hadn't* reappeared.

Olivia looked around.

Megan whispered to her, "She's going to come through the door there, where we came in. That's the real magic."

Lisa and Alex looked at each other in anticipation.

"Um, Mr Marvolo," Jess called out, her voice shaky, "when is Rachel coming back?"

Marvolo raised his arms. "Ladies and gentleman, I'm afraid we must end our show here. Until next time!"

With a loud bang and a puff of smoke, Marvolo

himself vanished, leaving behind a stunned audience.

As the smoke cleared, Jess ran to the empty stage, staring at the spot where Rachel had last been seen. The extravagance of The High Roller Suites now seemed hollow and oppressive. The scent of smoke lingered in the air.

"Rachel?" Jess called out, her voice echoing in the now-silent room. But there was no answer. She looked down at the velvet chaise longue where Cynthia had been reclining, and it, too, was empty. "Rachel!" She shouted her friend's name so loudly it burned against her throat. "Where is she?"

Lisa, Olivia, and Megan rushed to join Jess on the stage. Alex hung back, his face a mask of confusion and worry.

"What do we do now?" Lisa asked, her voice trembling.

Jess inhaled deeply. "We find Rachel," she said. "Whatever it takes, we find her."

TWENTY-NINE
THIS MORNING

As the Uber headed back to the Bellagio, the group of friends prepared to share their hidden secrets.

Lisa was the first to speak up.

"Jess," she began, her voice soft but steady, "The only secret I had was that I was the one talking to Miles. He asked me to keep an eye on Rachel, and I agreed."

Jess felt a pang of hurt, but pushed it aside. "Why couldn't you tell me?"

Lisa's eyes glistened with unshed tears. "I wanted to, Jess. But Miles made me promise. He was so worried about you, about this trip. I thought... I thought I was doing the right thing." Her voice cracked slightly, revealing the toll the secret had taken on her.

Megan stepped in. "Sometimes, even when we're close, it's difficult to share our secrets," she said, sounding thoughtful. "We worry about how others will react, or we think we're protecting them by keeping things to ourselves."

Olivia nodded vigorously, her hair bouncing with the movement. Her usual bubbly energy was subdued, but still present. "Exactly! Like when I..." she trailed off, biting her lip.

"When you what?" Alex prompted gently, his

outsider status making him both curious and cautious.

Olivia sighed, her shoulders slumping. "When I lost my job. I didn't want to tell you all because I was embarrassed. I didn't want to bring down the mood of the trip. But I... I was messing around with a colleague in the yoga studio. A male colleague. And yes, I mean messing around."

The group fell silent for a moment, processing this new information.

"I... I feel like you told us this," Lisa said, uncertainly. "Last night maybe?"

"I don't know. I really don't know," Olivia replied, her voice tinged with frustration. "I just know that I was embarrassed about losing my job, and even more about how it happened. I met you guys through the studio. That job meant a lot to me. I was so stupid."

Jess reached out and squeezed Olivia's hand, her teacher's instinct to comfort kicking in. "Oh, Liv. You should have told us. We're your friends. We're here for you, no matter what."

Olivia managed a watery smile. "I know that now. I'm sorry I kept it from you all."

As the others opened up, Jess's gaze drifted to Alex. Their eyes met, and in that moment, Jess felt the heaviness of the secret she'd been carrying.

She hadn't planned on revealing Alex's past, but with each passing second, the truth pressed more heavily on her conscience. If they were going to figure this out together, they needed all the information. And Alex's history... it might be relevant, given the increasingly shady circumstances they found themselves in.

Jess made a snap decision. "Guys," she said, her voice cutting through the chatter. "There's something you need to know about Alex."

The conversation halted abruptly. All eyes turned to her, curiosity and apprehension mingling in their expressions.

"I have a criminal record," Alex cut in. "It's okay, Jess. Everyone else is coming clean. I should too."

The reaction was immediate. Olivia gasped, Megan's eyes widened in shock, and Lisa instinctively jerked away from the man. Sitting beside each other in the Uber, there wasn't far she could go to put space between them.

"What?" Lisa hissed. "Jess? You knew about this and didn't tell us?"

Alex held up his hands, his face a mask of regret and determination. "Look, it's not what you think. It was a mistake, a long time ago. I've been trying to make a clean start. That's why I took the job at the casino. I've worked in Vegas for years, but, well, it hasn't always been legitimate."

"Oh, that's rich," Megan scoffed. "A former criminal working at a casino. How convenient."

"Hey, back off," Olivia said, surprising everyone. "At least he has a job. Some of us aren't that lucky. Not all of us have the luxury of drowning ourselves in overtime to avoid our problems."

"What's that supposed to mean?" Megan said flatly.

"It means maybe you should climb down from your high horse, Miss Workaholic," Olivia retorted.

"Enough!" Jess said. The driver looked up into the rearview as she raised her voice. "This isn't helping. We're all stressed and scared, but turning on each other isn't going to find Rachel."

Alex sighed. "Look, you all know my secret now," he said. "It doesn't change who I am, okay? I've stayed with you to help you." He cast his eyes from face to face, ending with Lisa.

"No other skeletons?" Lisa asked timidly.

Alex laughed quietly. "Isn't that enough?"

The tension in the group seemed to ease slightly, as if the pressure of their secrets had been lifting. Jess turned back to Lisa, a question burning in her mind.

"Lisa," she said, her voice serious, "I need to ask you something, and I need you to be completely honest with me."

Lisa nodded, her expression solemn.

"Do you trust Rachel?"

The question weighed heavy between them.

Lisa paused, deep in thought. The seconds stretched out, feeling like an eternity.

Finally, Lisa spoke. "Yes," she said firmly. "Whatever she's caught up in, she wouldn't endanger us. I believe that."

"But she may have endangered herself," Jess replied softly.

THIRTY
LAST NIGHT

The spotlight dimmed, leaving the stage of The High Roller Suites in an eerie half-light. Where moments ago the air had buzzed with the excitement of Marvolo's magic show, now an unsettling silence hung heavy. Jess stood frozen, her eyes fixed on the spot where Rachel had vanished. The thunderous applause that had followed the trick faded to murmurs of confusion as the audience realised something was amiss.

Jess's heart pounded in her chest as she scanned the faces of her friends. Lisa's eyes were wide with shock, Olivia's mouth agape, and even Megan's usual composure had cracked, replaced by a look of bewilderment. Alex stood slightly apart, his brow creased in concentration as if trying to work out the mechanics of the illusion.

"This can't be happening," Jess whispered, more to herself than anyone else. She stepped forward, her silver dress catching the remnants of the stage lights. With trembling hands, she reached for the crimson curtains that had swallowed her best friend.

As Jess parted the heavy fabric, she half-expected – half-hoped – to find Rachel grinning on the other side, ready to reveal the trick. Instead, her fingers met only the solid resistance of a dark wall.

"It's just for show," she said, surprised. "There's nothing back there."

"So where did she go? What just happened?" Lisa whispered, her voice trembling. "Where's Rachel?"

Jess shook her head, trying to clear the fog of confusion. "I don't know, but we need to find her. Fast."

She pulled out her mobile phone and tapped in Rachel's number.

"No signal," she cursed. "How can a place as exclusive as this have no signal?!"

Lisa tried her phone, and the other members of the group followed suit.

No signal. No chance of phoning Rachel.

"Maybe it has no signal *because* it's so exclusive," Megan sighed. "The dream of being free from external distractions."

"Well, it doesn't help us much now," Jess sighed.

"Let's think this through," Megan said, always the voice of reason. "Rachel volunteered for the magic trick. Marvolo made her disappear, but he never brought her back. So logically..."

"Logically, she's somewhere," Jess sighed. "People don't *really* disappear."

Lisa stamped on the wooden floorboards of the stage.

"No trapdoor. She didn't go downwards." She cast her eyes up towards the ceiling. It looked completely normal and unremarkable. "That only leaves..." Lisa gestured towards the door to the side of the stage, which was guarded by a man in a black suit and matching fedora.

Jess frowned. "I've seen him somewhere before," she muttered beneath her breath. "But... Ugh, how much have I had to drink tonight?"

"We need to get backstage," Olivia said, nodding in agreement with Lisa. "That's where they must have taken her."

"But how?" Lisa asked, glancing nervously at the man on the door and then at the security guards positioned around the room. "It's not like they're just going to let us waltz back there."

Jess's eyes narrowed with determination. "We'll figure something out. We have to. Rachel would do the same for any of us."

With a collective nod, they made their way to the door leading to the back areas. As expected, the man in the hat stepped in front of them, his expression impassive.

"I'm sorry, ladies," he said, his voice gruff but not unkind. "This area is staff only. I'm going to have to ask you to return to the main floor."

"Do I know you from somewhere?" Jess asked, tilting her head.

The man smiled. "We ran into each other in a club earlier. Somewhere not quite as pleasant as this."

"Pleasant?" Jess said, her voice rising. "We've just lost our friend. I don't call that very pleasant."

Jess tried to peer around him, catching glimpses of showgirls in elaborate costumes and waitresses bustling about in the corridors beyond.

"Please," she pleaded, "our friend was just on stage. She disappeared during the magic act, and we haven't seen her since. We're worried about her. Jack. It's

Jack, isn't it?"

The man's expression softened slightly, but he stood his ground. "That's right. And I understand, miss, but I can't let you through. It's against policy. If you're concerned about your friend, I can alert management for you."

"Yes! I mean no..." Jess stammered, grasping at straws. "Is Cynthia back there? Could you get her for us?"

At the mention of Cynthia's name, Jack's demeanour changed. His eyes narrowed, and he exchanged a look with another security guard nearby.

"I'm sorry, but it's probably time for you ladies to leave," he said, his tone now firm and brooking no argument.

He nodded to the other guard, and the two of them gathered around the girls and Alex, ushering them towards the exit. The girls resisted, not wanting to go anywhere without Rachel.

"Wait, please!" Jess cried out. "We can't just leave her!"

Jack sighed, then spoke in a low voice. "Look, I can't let you stay in here, but..." he glanced around, then winked, "I can leave you in the foyer. What you do after that is your business. But if anyone asks, you didn't hear that from me."

"I can't leave her. Rachel! Rachel!" Jess's voice rose to a shout.

"Hey," Lisa said. "Let's sit downstairs and make a plan? They aren't going to let us back there..." She waved to the backstage area and looked to Jack for confirmation. He shook his head firmly. "So, let's take a breath and work out what we *can* do. Okay?"

"It's not okay. Nothing is okay. This was meant to be the happiest night of my life..."

Olivia, Megan, and Lisa exchanged a sharp glance.

Jess looked at them. "That's my wedding night, isn't it? What the heck is wrong with me?"

"Come on," Olivia said, looping her arm into Jess's. "Lisa's right. We can sit downstairs. Rachel will probably come and find us."

"Yes," Megan smiled. "She's probably trying to let us know where to meet her."

Tears were falling down Jess's face as her friends steadied her and Jack led them from the room. He guided them back past the endless side rooms to the luxurious foyer. As he left them, he threw one last meaningful glance over his shoulder before returning to his post.

The foyer of The High Roller Suites felt claustrophobic, its gilded walls and crystal chandeliers out of sync with the group's growing desperation. They huddled into a booth, their voices low and urgent.

Olivia leaned against a pillar bordering the booth, her fingers drumming an agitated rhythm on its smooth surface. Her eyes darted around the opulent foyer, searching for any sign of Rachel or a clue to her whereabouts.

"This is insane," she muttered, her voice tight with frustration. "We're in one of the most exclusive clubs in Vegas, and we can't even find our own friend. It's not like we have access to anywhere beyond this damn foyer."

The others nodded, their predicament settling heavily on their shoulders. The distant sounds of laughter and clinking glasses from the main room seemed to mock their distress.

"I'm all out of ideas," Lisa said, in exasperation. "We can't get backstage, we can't find Cynthia, and we can't call Rachel."

Jess nodded, running a hand through her dishevelled hair. "It's not just Rachel disappearing. Cynthia vanishing too... it feels like we're in way over our heads."

Olivia sighed. "If we can't phone Rachel, I guess we can't phone Cynthia either."

The others looked at her quizzically. Olivia reached into her purse and pulled out a business card. "I picked this up earlier. It has Cynthia's number on it."

She quickly punched the number into her phone, but there was still no signal. Olivia's shoulders slumped. "I guess Cynthia's not going to be much help, either."

Megan leaned forward. "Okay, let's think this through. We can't stay here indefinitely, but we can't just leave without Rachel, either."

"What if..." Jess began slowly, "what if we left temporarily? Just long enough to regroup and come up with a better plan?"

The others exchanged uncertain glances.

"I know it feels wrong," Jess continued, "but we're not getting anywhere like this. If we could find a way to slip back in unnoticed, maybe we'd have a better chance of finding Rachel.

After a moment of tense silence, Lisa nodded. "Jess is right. We need a new approach."

Megan's eyes widened. "Wait," she said slowly. "What if we *did* have backstage access?"

"What do you mean?" Jess asked, leaning in closer.

"Those showgirls we saw... if we looked like them, maybe we could slip past security."

Lisa let out a humourless chuckle. "Great idea in theory, Meg. But where exactly are we going to get showgirl costumes at 3am in Vegas?"

As they debated in hushed tones, they didn't notice the woman who had drifted closer, engrossed in examining a nearby art piece.

"I might be able to help with that," a voice interjected smoothly.

The group startled, turning to face the newcomer. She was striking - tall and slender, with fiery red hair cascading over her shoulders. Her vintage-inspired dress hugged her curves, and there was an air of old Hollywood glamour about her.

"Vivian Sinclair," she introduced herself, extending a manicured hand. "I couldn't help but overhear your dilemma."

The friends exchanged wary glances. Jess stood up and moved forward slightly, protective instinct kicking in. "I'm Jess," she said cautiously. "These are my friends Lisa, Megan, and Olivia. And this is Alex. You said you could help us?"

Vivian nodded, a smile forming on her crimson lips. "I own a boutique called Glamour and Grace. We specialise in vintage and costume wear... including showgirl outfits." Her eyes sparkled with intrigue. "I can't turn you into showgirls, but I can certainly make you look the part."

Jess blinked, taken aback. "You... what?"

"I think I can help you," Vivian repeated patiently.

The friends exchanged wary glances before Jess spoke up. "That... could actually work. Thank you. But..." She turned her eyes away, not wanting to say the next words. "...how do we know we can trust you?"

Vivian's expression sobered. "You don't, honey. But right now, I might be your best shot at finding your friend. My shop's not far from here. We can be there in ten minutes if you don't mind me putting the pedal to the metal."

She smiled in a way that was reassuring in a motherly manner.

"Uh..." Jess looked back towards the expectant faces of the group. "Can I just...?"

Vivian smiled and gestured towards the companions in the booth.

"I'll just be here, pretending to look at this terrible painting," Vivian said with a dry smile.

Jess shuffled back into the booth.

Lisa pulled her aside, whispering so as not to be overheard. "Are we sure about this? We know nothing about her."

Megan chimed in, "But she's right. We're out of options, and time is running out."

Olivia nodded in agreement. "Plus, if we're going to sneak back in, we need to look the part."

Alex, still feeling like an outsider, added cautiously, "I've heard of Glamour and Grace. It's legit, at least."

After their hushed communication, Jess nodded and turned back to the redhead.

"Okay. We're in," she said. "And really, thank

you."

Sliding out of the booth, Jess felt a knot form in her stomach. "Wait," she said, grabbing Olivia's arm. "What if Rachel comes back while we're gone?"

The group paused, considering the dilemma.

"One last try..." Jess said, pulling out her phone. She frowned at the weak signal. "One bar. Shit. Better than nothing. If I can't get through, maybe I can leave her a voicemail. It's not ideal, but it's something."

The others nodded in agreement. Jess stepped away slightly, holding her phone close to her ear as she dialled Rachel's number. After a few moments, it went to voicemail. Jess thought quickly and began speaking.

"Rachel, it's Jess. I don't know what's going on, but something's not right. If you get this, be careful. I think we're in trouble. Don't trust—"

Suddenly, the call dropped. Jess stared at her phone in frustration. "Damn it," she muttered, rejoining the group. "The signal cut out. I hope at least some of that got through."

"It's better than nothing," Megan reassured her. "At least she'll know we're looking for her if she checks her voicemail."

Jess nodded, trying to shake off her unease. "Okay, let's go."

With that settled, they followed Vivian out into the warm Vegas night.

THIRTY-ONE
THIS MORNING

The Uber dropped the group off in the South Tour lobby, an elevator ride away from the main casino floor. Avoiding the check-in desk area, Megan led the way, her eyes fixed on her phone's map as she navigated the casino floor and corridors of the massive hotel. Jess couldn't help but notice how Alex seemed to shrink into himself, his eyes darting around nervously.

"You okay?" she asked him quietly.

Alex nodded, his jaw tight. "Yeah, just... I work here, you know? Don't want to run into any colleagues."

Jess felt a pang of guilt. In their desperation to find Rachel, they hadn't considered how this might affect Alex's job. She made a mental note to be more careful.

As they wound their way through the back halls, the opulence of the Bellagio revealed itself. Plush carpets muffled their footsteps, and ornate light fixtures cast a warm glow over the richly panelled walls. The air was cool and crisp, a stark contrast to the sweltering heat outside.

"This way," Megan directed, leading them through a set of double doors and into the opulent shopping arcade of The Bellagio.

The change in atmosphere was immediate. The quiet, almost secretive ambiance of the back corridors gave way to a bustling, glittering world of luxury. They passed by the gleaming storefronts of Dior, Chanel, and Louis Vuitton, their windows displaying the latest haute couture and accessories.

On any other day, Jess knew, they would have been pressing their noses against the glass, admiring the exquisite designs and dreaming of owning such luxury items. But today, they barely spared a glance. Their eyes were fixed straight ahead, their minds focused solely on reaching Glamour and Grace and finding Rachel. As they walked, Jess was filled with nervous energy but fuelled by determination.

Jess's eyes darted up to the elegant clock mounted above the Tiffany & Co. storefront, its Roman numerals a bleak reminder of their dwindling time.

"We have twenty minutes before Cynthia is expecting Rachel at The High Roller Suites. We need to move fast."

Around them, unhurried shoppers strolled past, sipping iced lattes and admiring the luxury goods with no sense of the crisis unfolding in their midst.

Lisa suddenly pointed ahead. "There it is," she said, as the sleek storefront of Glamour and Grace came into view. The store's elegant signage and carefully curated window display stood out among the high-end fashion boutiques, promising a different kind of glamour.

The group paused for a moment, gathering their courage. Whatever they were about to discover, they knew it would be a crucial piece in the puzzle of Rachel's disappearance. The reflection of their worried faces in the store's window was a stark reminder of how much their carefree girls' trip had changed.

Jess looked at the others, then pushed open the door, the soft chime of the bell announcing their arrival.

A vibrant woman in her fifties with a shock of red hair, looked up from arranging a display as they entered. Her face broke into a warm smile of recognition.

"Well, hello again, ladies! I didn't expect to see you so soon after our late-night encounter."

Jess stepped forward, relief washing over her. "You remember us from last night?"

The owner nodded, her eyes twinkling as she looked at Olivia. "Of course! How could I forget my impromptu showgirl? I hope the costume worked out for you."

Olivia cleared her throat, her usual confidence faltering. "That's just the thing. We don't remember much about what happened."

"Oh my," the owner chuckled. "Must have been quite a night then." She sounded less surprised than Jess had expected.

Jess shook her head, her expression serious. "Actually, it's bad. We've lost our friend. We have no idea where to find her."

"You really don't remember anything?" the woman said, standing and leaning against her counter. "And you didn't find Rachel?" The woman shook her head, looking genuinely dismayed by the news.

"Nothing," Jess said. "Not even your name."

The woman extended a hand. "Jess, I'm Vivian Sinclair. Pleased to meet you again. If only we could meet under better circumstances next time. Tell me everything you *do* remember, and I'll see how I can help."

The girls quickly filled the store owner in on their situation - the lost memories, Rachel's disappearance, and their desperate search for answers. They recounted waking up in disarray, the mysterious flash drive, the timeline, cryptic messages, and their growing fear for Rachel's safety.

As they spoke, Vivian's expression morphed from confusion to shock, then to deep concern. She listened intently, her eyes widening and her lips pressing into a thin line as the gravity of the situation sank in. With each new detail, the tension in her shoulders visibly increased, her hands clasping and unclasping as she absorbed the gravity of their predicament.

"Oh dear. You mentioned your friend was missing in The High Roller Suites. You still haven't found her?"

"The High Roller Suites?" Lisa echoed, confused.

"Yes, that's where we met," the owner clarified. "You were quite insistent on getting an authentic showgirl costume right away. Said it was urgent."

The girls looked at each other, realisation dawning.

"Why?" Olivia asked, bewildered. "Why did we need a showgirl costume so urgently?"

The owner shrugged. "You said that you needed to..." She lowered her voice. "...get past security." Despite there being no one else in the store or within earshot, the store owner looked around furtively. "Have you called the police?"

Jess shook her head sheepishly. "No, we... we

242

haven't. That seems dumb, I know, but..."

To their surprise, the owner let out a small sigh of relief. "No, no, no. Good. You don't want to get the law involved if The High Roller Suites is a part of this. It's not exactly... well, let's just say it's not somewhere the authorities need to know about."

The owner's words sent a chill through the group. Whatever this High Roller Suites was, it was clearly more than just an exclusive Vegas venue.

Jess stepped closer, her mind racing. "Can you tell us anything else about last night? Anything at all that might help us find our friend?"

The owner thought for a moment. "You wanted a costume each, but apparently my prices are.... a little steep for your means. Still, this one pulled off the look perfectly." She nodded at Olivia and smiled.

Olivia blushed but returned the grin. For a moment, Jess saw a flash of the confident, vivacious friend she knew, before the worry clouded her features again.

Meanwhile, Megan frowned. "You said we wanted to get past security. Security where?" she asked.

"I assumed at The High Roller Suites," Vivian replied. "You were very determined. Said it was your only chance to find your friend. I know there are showgirls in quite a few of the rooms there. It all made perfect sense at the time. To be honest, you were all so tense and worried that I just wanted to help you. Perhaps I should have asked more questions."

"Thank you," Jess said sincerely. "You've been incredibly helpful. But we still don't know where The High Roller Suites are. We can't find it on any map or website."

The owner's expression grew serious. "That's because it's not the kind of place you find on tourist maps, dear. It's for a... different kind of Vegas crowd."

"Can *you* tell us where it is?" Lisa asked, her voice tinged with desperation. "We need to get back there."

Jess looked at the others and decided to share everything they knew with the woman who had seemingly wanted to help them in their time of need. "Look, we are running to an incredibly tight deadline. We are all out of ideas of how to find Rachel, but..." She looked at Lisa, then Olivia, and then Megan before speaking further. They all nodded. "Rach had a voicemail from someone that we think might be involved in her disappearance."

Vivian tilted her head. "And...?"

"Cynthia, the person who phoned her, told Rachel to be at The High Roller Suites at noon."

Vivian's mouth opened and closed.

"We have Rachel's phone," Lisa explained.

Vivian shook her head slightly.

"No," she said. "I understand that. But Cynthia?" She shuddered as though she had just eaten something unpleasant.

"You know her?" Jess asked, barely surprised.

"I know her," Vivian said.

"Please." Lisa pointed at the clock. "We need to get there. Can you tell us the way?"

The owner hesitated, then seemed to make up her mind. "I'll do you one better. I'll take you there myself."

Relief washed over the group, a glimmer of hope in their increasingly complicated situation.

"Thank you," Jess said, her voice thick with emotion. "You don't know how much this means to us."

The owner nodded, a determined look in her eye. "Don't thank me yet, dears. Let's find your friend first. And maybe along the way, we can piece together what happened last night."

As Vivian moved to flip the 'Open' sign to 'Closed', Jess's apprehension spiked. They were one step closer to unravelling the mystery of their lost night and finding Rachel. But what would they discover at The High Roller Suites? And would they make it in time?

THIRTY-TWO

LAST NIGHT

In the early hours of the morning, the pale desert sunrise heated the already stifling air. A layer of golden light blanketed the ground below the deep purple remnants of the night. It was still only a little after quarter past three when Vivian led the group to a parking garage alongside The High Roller Suites.

"They have valet parking, of course," Vivian said. "But I don't trust anyone with my baby."

As they rounded a corner, they saw her car and understood why. Vivian strode over to a cherry-red 1959 Cadillac Eldorado Biarritz convertible. The classic car stood out like a jewel among the modern vehicles, its chrome gleaming even in the dim light of the garage.

"Wow," Alex whispered, clearly impressed, running a hand along the car's sleek fender.

"Hop in, darlings," Vivian said, positioning herself in the driver's seat with the grace of someone who had done it a thousand times before.

They piled in; the girls squeezed into the back, and Alex took the passenger seat. The leather upholstery was butter-soft, the interior impeccably maintained. It was like sliding into a slice of history. The car's vintage elegance still didn't feel out of place in the modern chaos of Las Vegas.

As Vivian pulled out onto the road, the warm night air whipped around them, carrying the scent of desert sage. The neon lights of Vegas blurred into a dizzy flurry of colours in the distance, painting the night in electric hues of red, blue, and gold. Despite the tension of their situation, Jess felt a thrill of excitement.

Vivian expertly manoeuvred through traffic, the powerful engine of the Cadillac purring like a contented cat.

"So," she called over her shoulder, her voice cutting through the rush of wind, "what's the story with your missing friend?"

The group exchanged glances, unsure how much to reveal.

"It's... complicated," Jess finally said, raising her voice to be heard. "She disappeared during a magic show."

Vivian's eyebrows shot up, visible in the rearview mirror. "A magic show, huh? At The High Roller Suites? Let me guess - Marvolo?"

The name sent a jolt through Jess. "You know him?"

Vivian's laugh was sharp and quick, like the crack of a whip. "Honey, I know everyone in this town worth knowing. And some people who aren't."

"And have you heard of anyone going missing like this before?" Jess asked.

"Missing? All the time. Like this? No." Vivian looked at Jess through the rearview mirror. "In Las Vegas, people go missing all the time. Hell, people sometimes come here intending to go missing."

"Rachel didn't," Olivia cut in without thinking. "We're on Jess's bachelorette. Rachel wouldn't..." Her voice trailed off and Vivian made eye contact with her through the mirror.

Jess looked at Lisa, her stomach sinking.

"She wouldn't," Jess repeated, less confidently than Olivia. "Would she?"

The entire night flashed before Jess's eyes. Rachel's phone calls, secret meetings, the family connections she knew so little about.

"She wouldn't set up my bachelorette so she could disappear, would she?"

"Hey," Vivian said, her voice stern. "Don't be thinking like that. I didn't say that's what your friend has done. I should be more careful choosing my words. I'm sorry. Your Rachel is more than likely sleeping off the party somewhere, okay?"

Jess nodded, but the sick feeling didn't leave her.

True to Vivian's word, after ten minutes of speeding down the Strip, they pulled up into the Bellagio parking garage. The girls looked at each other, a mix of familiarity and trepidation in their eyes.

"Here we are, darlings," Vivian said, killing the engine. The sudden silence was almost deafening after the roar of the road.

"Almost back where we started from," Lisa said, her voice tinged with disbelief.

"You're staying here?" Vivian asked, a note of approval in her voice. "How lovely. One of my favourite hotels."

As they stepped out of the car, the reality of their

situation hit Jess anew. They were about to disguise themselves to sneak back into a high-end casino, searching for a missing friend who might be in serious danger. Or who might not want them to find her at all. It was like something out of a movie, but it was all too real.

Vivian led them towards the elevator, her heels clicking on the concrete. As they descended to the casino level, she turned to the group. "Now, we'll need to cross the casino floor to get to the shops. It's only a few minutes away. Try not to get distracted."

The elevator doors opened, and they stepped out into the opulent world of the Bellagio. Even at this late hour, the casino was alive with activity. The constant chime and whir of slot machines created a chaotic symphony, punctuated by the occasional cheer from a winning table.

As they walked through the lobby, Vivian gestured towards a brightly lit area beyond. "Have you had a chance to visit the Conservatory yet? It's quite spectacular, especially at night."

Jess caught a glimpse of an elaborate floral installation, a riot of colour and beauty that seemed almost surreal in the middle of the desert. The conversation seemed out of place under the circumstances, but as Vivian kept her voice light, Jess realised she was trying to calm the group.

"No," Jess replied, playing along, even though she didn't feel the part. "We'll have to come down here in the morning."

They passed the Petrossian Bar, its polished wood

and crystal glasses gleaming in the soft light. "You should visit this wonderful place when it's open," Vivian said. "Their afternoon tea is divine."

"Thanks," Jess said, trying to infuse some enthusiasm in her voice, but falling flat.

As they made their way across the casino floor, Jess couldn't help but observe the late-night patrons. Even at almost half-past three, serious-faced players hunched over their cards at the blackjack tables, eyes locked on the dealer's hands. The three-card poker tables were quieter, but no less intense, with players scrutinising their hands as if their lives depended on it.

Alex turned away from the tables, clearly trying not to catch the eye of any of his coworkers.

The slot machines were a different world entirely. There, a mix of hopeful tourists and hardened gamblers sat, mechanically feeding coins into the machines. Some stared blankly at the spinning reels, while others muttered what sounded like personal lucky charms under their breath.

"It's amazing how many people are still here at this time," Megan whispered, letting her eyes scan the room.

"Honey, in Vegas, three thirty is just getting started for some folks," Vivian replied with a wink.

They finally reached the Via Bellagio shops, startlingly glamorous and sedate compared to the casino floor. Here, high-end boutiques lined the corridor, their windows displaying luxury goods that seemed to mock the desperation they'd just walked through.

At the end of the corridor stood a shop with a

vintage-inspired facade. The sign above the door read "Glamour and Grace" in flowing script.

"Here we are, darlings," Vivian said, pulling out a set of keys. "Let's get you all dolled up and ready to find your friend."

While Vivian unlocked the door, Jess took one last look back at the casino floor. Somewhere out there, Rachel was waiting to be found. With renewed determination, she turned back to Glamour and Grace, ready to take the next step in their increasingly bizarre adventure.

The store was silent and dark until Vivian flipped on the lights, illuminating racks of glittering costumes and vintage dresses. As the lights flickered to life, Jess felt as though they were crossing a threshold into a new chapter of their adventure - one that would change everything.

"Take your pick, ladies," Vivian said, gesturing to the showgirl outfits. "Though I have to warn you, these don't come cheap."

As the girls rifled through the racks, their excitement quickly turned to concern as they caught sight of the price tags.

"Seriously?" Lisa gasped, holding up a sequined number. "This one's more than my monthly rent!"

Megan, ever practical, was already doing mental calculations. "Okay, let's see what we've got. How much cash does everyone have?"

They pooled their resources, counting out crumpled bills and fishing for spare change in the bottoms of their purses.

Jess's face fell as she realised the total. "This... this isn't even close to enough for all of us."

"We could put it on a credit card?" Olivia suggested hesitantly.

Lisa hesitated for a moment, then squared her shoulders. "You know what? Let's do it. I'll put it on my card."

"Are you sure?" Jess asked, her voice filled with concern. "Didn't you say your card was already pretty maxed out from tonight?"

Lisa nodded grimly. "It is. But finding Rachel is more important than my credit score right now. We'll figure out the finances later."

After a moment of tense silence, Jess spoke up. "We can only afford one costume, even with Lisa's card."

The reality of their situation sank in. They exchanged glances, each wondering who should be the one to wear it.

"Olivia should wear it," Megan suggested after a moment. "She's got a dancer's build."

All eyes turned to Olivia, who suddenly looked uncomfortable. "Me? I don't know..."

"Come on, Liv," Lisa encouraged. "You'd look amazing in one of these."

Olivia bit her lip, her eyes darting between her friends and the glittering costumes. "It's just... I've never worn anything like that before. What if I can't pull it off?"

Jess stepped forward, placing a reassuring hand on Olivia's shoulder. "Liv, you can absolutely pull this off. And remember, it's not just about looking good. We need to get back into that club and find Rachel.

This might be our only chance."

Olivia stood in silent contemplation for a moment, then nodded. "Okay. I'll do it. But you guys owe me big time for this."

Lisa nodded, pulling out her credit card with a mix of determination and resignation. "All right, let's do this. For Rachel."

As Olivia slipped into a dazzling sequin and feather costume, her phone began to ring. She glanced at the screen, her face paling slightly.

"Who's calling you at this hour?" Lisa asked, curiosity getting the better of her.

Olivia hesitated, looking down at her body. Something about the glittering outfit seemed to give her courage.

"It's... it's my... Oh, I may as well just tell you. I have... a... uh... someone," she admitted. "And... I... I didn't just quit my job. I was fired."

The others gathered around her, concern etched on their faces.

"What happened, Liv?" Jess asked gently.

Olivia's eyes welled with tears. "There was an incident with another instructor at the studio." She nodded at her phone. "We were caught in a compromising position after hours. It violated studio policy. They had to let me go."

A heavy silence fell over the group.

"Why didn't you tell us?" Lisa asked, hurt evident in her voice.

"I was embarrassed," Olivia said, wiping her eyes carefully to avoid smudging her makeup. "And I didn't want to bring down the mood of the trip. I'm so sorry for lying."

Jess moved to hug Olivia, careful not to wrinkle the costume. "We're your friends, Liv. You can trust us."

The others murmured their agreement, gathering around to offer comfort. The revelation seemed to strengthen their bond, reminding them of the importance of honesty in their friendship.

Vivian, who had been busying herself in the back of the store to give them privacy, returned with a sympathetic smile. "Everything okay, ladies?"

Jess nodded, giving Olivia's hand a squeeze. "Yeah, we're good. Thank you for this, Vivian. You have no idea how much it means to us."

Vivian waved her hand dismissively. "Don't mention it. Now, let's get you all dolled up."

Once Olivia was dressed in her costume, feather headdress and sequinned shoes in place, she twirled in front of the mirror.

"Perfect," Vivian said. "How do you feel?"

"Tired, drunk, confused and pretty much scared out of my mind," Olivia said, her face falling. "But... I feel like a showgirl."

"That's it, Liv," Jess said. "You've got this."

"I wish I could take you girls back to the Suites, but time is passing and we open again at nine," Vivian said with genuine sadness. "I don't know what you girls are mixed up in, and I'm not sure I want to. But be careful out there. Vegas has a way of turning dreams into nightmares if you're not careful."

Jess nodded solemnly. "We will. And thank you again, Vivian. We owe you one."

Vivian nodded, her expression serious. "Listen, darling, there's something you should know," she said in a low voice. "When you call your Uber, the driver isn't likely to know where The High Roller Suites is. It's not exactly a place you'll find on tourist maps."

Jess frowned. "So, how do we get there?"

Vivian's lips curled into a knowing smile. "The address is 777 Sinners Way. Tell the driver it's just off the north end of the Strip, past the Stratosphere." She paused, her eyes twinkling with a hint of mischief. "And no, don't write it down. It's... kind of a secret."

The others had gathered around, listening intently. Alex whistled low. "777 Sinners Way? Sounds like something out of a movie."

"Welcome to Vegas, honey," Vivian chuckled. "Where reality is often stranger than fiction."

THIRTY-THREE
THIS MORNING

The cherry-red 1959 Cadillac convertible purred to life as the red-haired shop owner turned the key, the engine's low rumble a stark contrast to the tinkling slot machines they'd left behind in the Bellagio. The car was a perfect match for its owner - bold, classic, and unapologetically glamorous. The morning sun glinted off the polished chrome bumpers and sleek tail fins, momentarily dazzling Jess as she slid into the butter-soft leather of the backseat.

"You really don't remember me, do you?" the store owner said, flashing them a warm smile in the rearview mirror. Her vibrant red hair, the exact shade of the car's paintwork, was now tucked under a wide-brimmed white sun hat, her eyes hidden behind cat-eye sunglasses that looked like they'd time-travelled straight from the car's era. "I've been dressing Vegas's finest for longer than I care to admit, but I've never been a chauffeur before."

As they pulled out of the Bellagio's parking garage and onto the Las Vegas Strip, Jess was dazzled by how different everything looked in the harsh light of day. The neon signs that had seemed so alluring the night before now appeared garish and tired, like an aging starlet without her stage makeup.

The tension in the car was palpable as they drove, each passenger lost in their own thoughts and worries. Jess fidgeted with the hem of her hastily thrown on t-shirt, a far cry from the glamorous dress she'd worn the night before. Lisa kept glancing at her phone, as if willing it to ring with news from Rachel. Megan's face bore an expression of deep concentration, no doubt trying to piece together their fragmented memories. Olivia stared out the window, her usual bubbly demeanour subdued. Alex, squeezed between Lisa and Olivia, looked both out of place and strangely at home.

As they cruised down the Strip, the iconic sights of Las Vegas unfolded before them. The massive columns of Caesar's Palace loomed to their right, its faux-Roman grandeur an elegant break from the ultra-modern hotels surrounding it.

"Oh, look!" Olivia exclaimed, pointing excitedly. "The Venetian! Didn't we say something about wanting to ride the gondolas?"

Lisa nodded, a strange expression crossing her face. "Yeah, I... I feel like we talked about that. Last night, maybe? It's so frustrating, not being able to remember clearly."

The sense of déjà vu was overwhelming, adding another layer of unease to their already tense journey.

"It's like trying to remember a dream," Megan mused. "There are flashes, moments that seem so clear, but when you try to focus on them, they slip away."

Alex nodded in agreement. "I know what you mean. I have this vague memory of... of cards? A lot of cards. But I can't remember if I was dealing them or playing."

As the vintage car took them along the Strip, they passed by a massive digital billboard. The screen flickered, changing from a casino advertisement to a movie trailer. Suddenly, a face filled the screen – a tall, dark-haired man with a charismatic smile.

Olivia tapped Megan on the arm, her eyes widening. "Oh wow," she exclaimed, pointing at the screen. "That's Drake Holloway! I think we met him last night!"

The conversation in the car came to an abrupt stop, all eyes turning from Olivia to the billboard and back.

"Drake Holloway?" Lisa repeated, her voice tinged with excitement. "That actor? Are you sure?"

Olivia nodded. "Yes! He was at the club, talking to Rachel. Can you believe it? We actually met a celebrity!"

"I don't know," Alex said, bringing Olivia's buzz crashing down. "None of us remember *anything*. Maybe it was a dream?"

Olivia shook her head resolutely. "No. I remember him. I do."

Jess made eye contact with Olivia, and seeing the earnest expression, she gave her a quick nod and a smile of reassurance.

"Hopefully this means more of our memories are going to come back. Memories that might help us find Rachel," she said.

"Drake Holloway," Megan said, dreamily. "He looks like a fine man."

"I'd be happy to even meet him in a dream," Lisa laughed. Her eyes flashed to Alex, who raised an eyebrow and smiled, shaking his head.

258

While Lisa and Megan shared Olivia's enthusiasm for the actor, Jess felt an inexplicable unease wash over her as she looked at Holloway's face on the screen. She couldn't put her finger on why, but something about him made her uncomfortable.

Why did the sight of Drake Holloway bother her so much? Was it just her worry about Rachel colouring her perception, or was there something more to it? And had they really even met him? As they made their way down the Strip, Jess tried to push thoughts of the actor aside. Celebrity encounter or not, finding Rachel was their priority, and time was ticking away.

They continued along, passing the whimsical entrance of Circus Circus, its colourful facade a playful counterpoint to the sleek, modern architecture of the newly opened Fontainebleau next door.

"Did we really come all this way last night?" Megan wondered aloud.

Vivian chuckled, a sound that somehow managed to be both warm and slightly sardonic. "Oh, honey, you'd be surprised how far people can go in a single Vegas night. I've seen folks cover more ground in a few hours than they do in an entire week back home."

"Vivian," Jess said, leaning forward in her seat, "can you tell us anything more about last night? Anything you remember about us or Rachel?"

Vivian's grip tightened on the steering wheel, her knuckles whitening slightly against the candy-apple red of the car's exterior. "I first met you all at The High Roller Suites, actually. You were huddled in a corner, talking in hushed voices about needing to get backstage to look for your friend."

Vivian's words hung in the air for a moment as the group processed this new information. Jess felt a flicker of recognition, like a half-remembered dream suddenly coming into focus.

"I couldn't help but overhear your predicament. It's not every day you see a group of well-dressed folks plotting an infiltration in The High Roller Suites."

Olivia shifted in her seat. "So that's how we ended up at Glamour and Grace in the middle of the night," she mused, more to herself than the others.

"But we could only afford one costume," Megan added, the memory slowly surfacing. She turned to Olivia, a mix of apology and amusement in her eyes. "And we volunteered you. Or...you volunteered yourself?"

Olivia let out a short laugh, equal parts rueful and bewildered. "Well, I guess that explains the costume," she said.

"You seemed quite eager to play dress up, all things considered," Vivian smiled into her rearview, towards the girls.

As the pieces of their fragmented night began to fall into place, a heavy silence settled over the car. Each recovered memory seemed to bring more questions than answers.

Megan was the first to break the silence. "If we wanted to get backstage at The High Roller Suites to look for Rachel, we must have been sure that's where she had gone missing."

Running a hand through his hair, Alex couldn't hide

the frustration on his face. "But why can't we remember any of this?"

"Vegas has a way of making people forget, honey," Vivian said, her voice tinged with a mixture of amusement and warning. "Especially when they're in places they shouldn't be."

The implication of her words sent a shiver down Jess's spine. What kind of trouble had they got into? And more importantly, what kind of danger was Rachel in? There wasn't long left before they would find out.

Alex checked his watch, his face tightening with worry. "It's 11:50 now. We've got less than ten minutes before Cynthia's deadline."

"That name again," Vivian sniffed.

The mood in the car shifted. As they approached the towering spire of The Strat, casting long shadows across the road, Jess felt a mixture of hope and dread churning in her stomach.

"Vivian," Jess said, her voice barely above a whisper, "what kind of place *is* the High Roller Suite?"

Vivian's laugh was sharp and quick. "Oh, darling, it's where Vegas's elite go when they want to indulge in pastimes that aren't exactly... advertised in the tourism brochures. It's not the kind of place where you can just walk in off the street. There are... protocols."

The way she said "protocols" sent a shiver down Jess's spine.

"Are we likely to even get in there now?" Jess said. "I didn't even think.... I mean, if it was so difficult last night?"

"Cynthia is expecting Rachel to meet her,

apparently," Vivian said. "So Cynthia will be there. Let's take you to her, and see what happens next."

Jess gulped instinctively. Even when they got to The High Roller Suites, there was no guarantee that Cynthia would see them, or that she would help them find Rachel.

As they turned onto a narrow side street, the buildings became less ostentatious, the neon signs replaced by subdued, elegant facades. The contrast between the glitzy Strip they'd left behind and this more discreet area was stark, a reminder of the two faces of Las Vegas - the one shown to tourists, and the one reserved for those in the know.

"We're getting close," Vivian announced, her voice tight with tension. "Now, listen carefully. When we get there, let me do the talking. And whatever you do, don't mention the police or anything about last night. I'm going to take you in as a group of high rollers, looking for a good time. Understood?"

They all nodded, the gravity of the situation sinking in.

The Las Vegas sun beat down on them, harsh and unforgiving, as they piled out of the car and approached the building's subtly marked entrance. Just before they reached the door, Vivian turned to face them, her expression deadly serious.

"Remember, let me do the talking. And girls? Alex? Whatever happens in there... stay together. Vegas has a way of swallowing people whole if they're not careful."

THIRTY-FOUR
LAST NIGHT

The Uber pulled up a discreet distance from The High Roller Suites, its headlights dimming as the engine quieted. The driver, a middle-aged man with sandy blonde hair, glanced at his passengers in the rearview mirror, his eyebrows raised in a mixture of curiosity and amusement. He'd seen his fair share of odd requests and unusual fares in Vegas, but this group must have seemed particularly intriguing.

"This is good, thanks," Jess said, her voice a hushed whisper despite the closed windows of the car. "We'll get out here."

The driver nodded, a small smile playing at the corners of his mouth. "You folks sure you don't want me to drop you closer? It's a bit of a walk in those heels."

Jess shook her head. "No, this is perfect. Thank you."

As they clambered out of the car, the driver's eyes widened slightly at the full sight of Olivia in her showgirl costume. The sequins caught the streetlights, sending tiny rainbow reflections dancing across the interior of the car. Olivia clutched the elaborate feathered headdress in her lap, careful not to damage it as she manoeuvred out of the vehicle.

Once they were all on the sidewalk, the Uber pulled away, leaving them standing in the relative darkness of the early morning. The Strip was never truly quiet, but here, a few blocks away from the main drag, the constant hum of the city felt muted and distant.

Jess looked at her friends, taking in their dishevelled appearance. Her own silver dress, which had seemed so glamorous at the start of the night, now looked tame and almost ordinary next to Olivia's full showgirl regalia. Alex stood slightly apart, his posture tense, eyes constantly scanning their surroundings.

"Okay," Jess said, her voice low but firm. "Let's go over the plan one more time."

Olivia nodded, her fingers nervously toying with the feathers of her headdress. "I go in through the back entrance, pretending I'm late for a show if someone approaches me. I'll try to find my way backstage and look for any sign of Rachel."

"And if anyone stops you?" Megan prompted.

"I act confident, like I belong there," Olivia recited. "If they press, I say I'm new and got turned around looking for the dressing rooms."

Lisa put her hand on Olivia's shoulder. "You've got this, Liv. You look amazing, and you're going to nail it."

Olivia attempted a smile. "I don't know, guys. I feel ridiculous. And what if I mess up? What if I can't find Rachel?"

Jess stepped closer, placing her hands on Olivia's shoulders. "Hey, look at me. You are the only one who can pull this off. Play the role. You're Starla the

Showgirl, now. We need you, Liv. Rachel needs you."

Alex nodded in affirmation. "Remember, confidence is key. I've seen countless showgirls come and go at the casino. The ones who never get questioned are the ones who act like they own the place."

Olivia lifted her chin, squaring her shoulders. "Okay. Okay, I can do this."

As Olivia carefully placed the headdress on her head, adjusting it slightly, Jess marvelled at the transformation. Despite the absurdity of their situation, Olivia truly looked the part – glamorous, mysterious, and just a touch otherworldly.

"All right, Starla," Megan said with a wink, using the stage name they'd concocted for Olivia's alter ego. "Show time."

The group made their way towards The High Roller Suites, keeping to the shadows as much as possible. As they neared the building, its imposing façade loomed before them, all sleek lines and tinted glass. The entrance was flanked by two burly security guards, their faces impassive as they surveyed the street.

"There's the staff entrance," Alex murmured, nodding towards a nondescript door off to the side of the building. "That's your best bet, Olivia... I mean Starla."

They paused in the shelter of a nearby alleyway, hidden from the view of the guards. Jess checked her phone – 3:57am. The night was waning, but the Nevada heat still clung to the air, making their palms sweaty and their clothes stick to their skin.

"Okay," Jess said, turning to face her friend. "This is it. Are you ready?"

Olivia nodded, a determined glint in her eye. But as she took a step forward, she suddenly froze. "Wait," she said, her voice barely a whisper. "What if... what if I can't do this? I couldn't even keep my job as a yoga teacher. How am I supposed to fool an entire casino?"

The words were heavy with the tension of Olivia's recent loss and self-doubt. The others exchanged glances, suddenly understanding the depth of their friend's insecurity.

Lisa was the first to respond, her voice gentle but firm. "Hey, listen to me. Losing your job doesn't define you. You are so much more than that. You have an amazing future ahead of you, I promise."

Megan nodded in agreement. "Think about all the times you've pushed us out of our comfort zones in yoga class. Now it's your turn to push yourself."

"Besides," Alex added with a small smile, "you already look more convincing than half the showgirls I've seen. Trust me, you've got this."

Jess stepped forward, taking Olivia's hands in hers. "Liv, do you remember what you told me when I was freaking out about the wedding last month? You said that fear is just excitement without the breath. So, take a deep breath, and turn that fear into excitement. You can do anything you set your mind to."

Olivia closed her eyes for a moment, inhaling deeply. When she opened them again, there was a new resolve in her gaze. "You're right. I can do this. For Rachel."

"For Rachel," the others echoed softly.

With a final nod to her friends, Olivia stepped out of the alleyway. Her entire demeanour seemed to shift as she sashayed towards the staff entrance, her hips swaying with each step, the feathers of her headdress bobbing gently. She looked every inch the confident showgirl, ready to dazzle an audience. She was acting the role of Starla to a tee.

As Olivia reached the door, she paused for just a moment, her hand hovering over the handle. Then, with conviction, she pulled it open and slipped inside, disappearing from view.

The remaining friends huddled closer together in the alleyway, the severity of the moment settling over them. Jess felt her heart racing, a mixture of hope and apprehension coursing through her veins. This was it – their best chance at finding.

"Do you think she'll be okay?" Lisa whispered, her eyes still fixed on the door Olivia had entered.

Megan nodded, although she couldn't hide her look of concern. "She'll be fine. Olivia's smart and resourceful. If anyone can pull this off, it's her."

Alex added, "The key is to act like you belong. As long as she stays confident, most people won't question her."

Jess gulped, trying to calm her nerves. "Now we wait," she said, her voice barely audible over the distant hum of the Strip. "And hope that Olivia can find some answers."

As the minutes ticked by, the group remained hidden in the alleyway, their eyes darting between the staff entrance and the main doors of The High Roller

Suites. The pre-dawn air crackled with tension and possibility. Whatever happened next would change everything.

Jess couldn't help but reflect on the bizarre turn their bachelorette party had taken. Less than twenty-four hours ago, they had been full of excitement, ready to paint the town red. Now, they were embroiled in a mystery, with Rachel missing and their memories of the night frustratingly blank.

As she watched The High Roller Suites, its windows glinting in the faint light of approaching dawn, Jess silently urged Olivia on. "Find her," she whispered into the night. "Find Rachel and come back safely."

The surrounding city began to stir, the quiet of the early morning gradually giving way to the first signs of Vegas waking up. But for Jess and her friends, time seemed to stand still as they waited, their hopes pinned on Olivia and her daring infiltration of The High Roller Suites.

As the group waited for Olivia, the desert heat was oppressive and unyielding even in the pre-dawn hours. Jess, Lisa, Megan, and Alex huddled in the meagre shade provided by a lone Joshua tree, its twisted branches offering little respite from the relentless warmth. The High Roller Suites towered before them, a stark silhouette against the inky sky, its windows glinting with the promise of air-conditioned luxury just out of reach.

From their vantage point on the outskirts of Las

Vegas, the famous Strip was visible only as a distant glow on the horizon, a mirage-like reminder of the glittering world they'd left behind. Here, on the edge of the Mojave Desert, the landscape was a study in contrasts - barren yet beautiful, silent yet teeming with hidden life.

Jess wiped a bead of sweat from her brow, her sequinned dress now feeling like a poor choice for a stakeout in the desert. "I wish we were back in that limo," she muttered, her throat dry. "With the drinks and the AC."

Lisa nodded in agreement, fanning herself with a crumpled napkin she'd found in her purse. "I never thought I'd miss being cold," she said with a rueful laugh.

Megan, ever practical, scanned their surroundings. "We need to find some water. Being drunk in the desert, even at night, is not a great idea."

Alex, who had been keeping watch on the staff entrance of The High Roller Suites, turned to face them. "There's a vending machine around the corner of the building. I could make a run for it if you want."

Jess shook her head. "No, we need to stay together. We can't risk missing Olivia."

As if on cue, a chorus of unseen insects started up, their chirping a rhythmic counterpoint to the muffled thud of bass emanating from inside the club. The juxtaposition of natural and artificial sounds served as a reminder of their liminal position, caught between the wild desert and the manufactured oasis of Las Vegas.

The air was bone-dry, each breath feeling like it was

sapping moisture from their bodies. Despite the late hour, heat radiated from the ground, a tangible reminder of the day's scorching temperatures. In the distance, a coyote's howl pierced the night, a lonesome sound that sent a shiver down Jess's spine despite the warmth.

"Do you think Olivia's okay in there?" Lisa asked, her voice barely above a whisper. "It's been almost half an hour."

Megan checked her watch, squinting to make out the numbers in the dim light. "Twenty-seven minutes," she confirmed. "But she might need time to comb the place."

Alex shifted uncomfortably, his casino experience lending weight to his words. "The longer she's in there, the more likely someone is to notice she doesn't belong."

Jess felt a knot of anxiety tighten in her stomach. What if they'd made a mistake sending Olivia in alone? What if she'd been caught? Or worse, what if she'd found Rachel but couldn't get back out?

The minutes ticked by with agonising slowness. The group fell into an uneasy silence, each lost in their own thoughts and worries. The desert around them seemed to grow more oppressive with each passing moment, the vastness of the landscape a stark reminder of how small and vulnerable they were.

Just as the tension was becoming unbearable, a flicker of movement caught Jess's eye. The staff door of The High Roller Suites swung open, spilling a rectangle of light onto the dusty ground. A figure emerged, the sequins of her costume catching the light and sending tiny rainbows dancing across the desert floor.

"Olivia," Jess breathed, relief flooding through her. But as quickly as it had come, the relief evaporated. Olivia wasn't alone.

A broad man stepped out behind her, his hand firmly gripping her upper arm. Even from a distance, there was something imposing about him. He wore a well-tailored suit that seemed at odds with the desert setting.

The man guided Olivia towards their hiding spot with purposeful strides. Olivia's feathers quivered with each step, but her posture was rigid, her free hand clenched at her side.

As they drew closer, Jess could make out Olivia's face. Her expression was a mixture of fear and frustration, her eyes darting between the man beside her and her friends huddled by the Joshua tree.

The group scrambled to their feet as Olivia and the man approached. Jess stepped forward, her heart racing. "Olivia, are you okay? Did you find—"

The man held up his free hand, cutting her off. When he spoke, his voice was smooth and cultured, with an undercurrent of amusement that made Jess's skin crawl.

"Now, now," he said, "let's not pretend we don't all know what's going on here." He released Olivia's arm with a small push, sending her stumbling towards her friends. Lisa caught her, steadying her on her feet.

The man's eyes swept over the group. "I must say, I'm impressed by your creativity. The showgirl infiltration? Classic. But ultimately futile."

Jess straightened her spine, meeting the man's gaze defiantly. "Where's Rachel? What have you done with her?"

The man chuckled. "Your friend is fine. For now. But this little game of yours? It ends here. If you want to see her again, you'll come in through the front door like civilised people. Pay the entry fee, play by the rules. You have until sunrise to make your decision. Come through the front door, pay your dues, and you'll get your chance to find Rachel. Refuse, and, well..." He shrugged, leaving the threat unspoken but unmistakable.

With that, the man turned and strode back towards The High Roller Suites. Just before he reached the door, he paused and looked back over his shoulder. "Oh, and ladies? Gentleman? Try to clean yourselves up a bit before you come in. We do have standards to maintain."

The door closed behind him with a soft click that seemed to echo in the desert night. For a moment, the group stood in stunned silence, the reality of their situation sinking in.

Olivia was the first to speak, her voice shaky. "I'm so sorry, guys. I tried to find Rachel, but they caught me almost immediately. It's like they were expecting us."

Jess put a comforting arm around her friend's shoulders. "It's not your fault, Liv. You did your best."

"What do we do now?" Lisa asked, her eyes darting between her friends and the imposing structure of The High Roller Suites.

Megan, ever practical, was already pulling out her phone. "We need to figure out exactly how much money we can access between us. If we're going to pay this 'entry fee', we need to know what we're working with."

As the group huddled together, discussing their options, Jess felt they were stepping into something far more dangerous than they'd initially realised.

She looked up at The High Roller Suites, its windows now taking on a sinister gleam in the pre-dawn light. Somewhere inside was Rachel, and answers to questions Jess wasn't sure she wanted to ask. But they had no choice. Time was running out, and with it, their chances of finding Rachel.

THIRTY-FIVE

THIS MORNING

The sleek facade of The High Roller Suites loomed before them, its tinted windows reflecting the harsh Nevada sun like a mirage in the desert. Jess felt her heart pounding against her ribcage, each beat a reminder of the gravity of their mission. She glanced at her companions—Lisa, Megan, Olivia, and Alex— their faces etched with a mixture of determination and apprehension. Vivian led the way, her confident stride parting the very air around her like an invisible force field.

As they approached the entrance, Vivian slowed her pace, turning to address the group again. Her voice was barely above a whisper, but in the tense silence surrounding them, it felt as loud as a thunderclap.

"Okay," she breathed, her eyes scanning each of their faces, "let me do the talking. You're my special guests, understand? One wrong move, one suspicious glance, and your chance to find Cynthia could be blown."

They nodded silently, the weight of her words settling on their shoulders like a physical burden. Jess swallowed hard, her mouth dry with anticipation.

The group resumed their approach, the click of Vivian's heels on the pavement setting a rhythm for their heartbeats. As they reached the door, a burly security guard materialised from the shadows, his massive frame blocking their path. Dark sunglasses concealed his eyes, but Jess could feel his gaze sweeping over them, assessing, judging.

"Vivian," he grunted, his voice gruff but tinged with respect. "Didn't expect to see you here today."

Vivian's transformation was instantaneous and mesmerising. Her smile bloomed like a desert flower, dazzling and disarming. The charm that radiated from her was almost palpable, a shield against suspicion.

"Hello, Bruno," she purred, her voice honey-sweet. "Last-minute appointment. These are my special guests."

Bruno's hidden gaze swept over the group once more, lingering on their dishevelled appearance and determined expressions. For a heart-stopping moment, Jess thought he might turn them away, shattering their chances of finding Rachel.

Jess sent out a silent prayer that the security guard hadn't been on duty in the early hours, and that no one would recognise them. If they did, there was no chance they'd be let in to meet Cynthia.

The seconds stretched into eternity as Bruno deliberated. Finally, he nodded, stepping aside to allow them entry. Jess released a breath she hadn't realised she'd been holding, feeling lightheaded with relief.

Stepping into the cool, dimly lit interior of The High Roller Suites, a surge of adrenaline coursed through Jess's veins.

"It's only four minutes until noon," Megan

whispered, her eyes darting to her watch. The tension in the group intensified, almost tangible in the air around them. Jess felt as if she could reach out and grasp it, a living, breathing entity born of their collective anxiety and determination.

They approached a bank of elevators, guarded by another security officer. This one was leaner than Bruno, but no less intimidating. His eyes narrowed as they approached, hand hovering near the holster at his hip. Vivian stepped forward, exchanging a few quiet words with him. Whatever she said seemed to work its magic; the guard nodded, pressing a button to summon an elevator.

As they waited, Lisa leaned close to Jess, her breath warm against Jess's ear. "Do you think Cynthia will actually be here?" she whispered, her voice tight with anticipation and fear.

Jess nodded, her jaw set with determination. "She'd better be," she murmured back. "We've come too far to leave without answers. We're not leaving until we know what happened to Rachel."

The elevator arrived with a soft ding that seemed to echo in the tense silence surrounding them. Its mirrored interior reflected their resolute faces as they stepped inside, a tableau of determination and barely contained fear. Vivian pressed a button for the top floor, and they began their ascent.

As the levels ticked by, Vivian turned to face them.

"Now listen carefully," she said, her voice low and urgent. "When we get up there, things might get... complicated. No matter what happens, stick together. Trust no one but each other."

The warning sent another surge of adrenaline through Jess. Her mind raced with possibilities, each scenario more terrifying than the last. What did Vivian mean by 'complicated'? What weren't they being told?

Jess wanted to open her mouth to ask Vivian if they could really trust *her*, but the redhead had got them this far. If it was a trap, it almost felt as though it was one they had to walk into to find Rachel.

The elevator continued its relentless climb, each floor bringing them closer to the confrontation they'd been anticipating. Jess's stomach churned with a potent mixture of anger, determination, and fear. She glanced at her friends, seeing her own emotions mirrored in their tense postures and clenched jaws.

She reached out to Megan and Olivia by her sides and gripped hold of their hands. In turn, they joined Lisa and Alex into the circle. Something in the gesture gave Jess renewed courage for whatever was ahead.

Finally, after what felt like an eternity, the elevator slowed to a stop. The doors slid open with a soft hiss, revealing a corridor lined with numbered suites. The thick carpet muffled their footsteps as Vivian led them down the hallway, the tension mounting with each stride.

They stopped in front of a heavy black door. Vivian was more serious than ever.

"This is it," she said softly. "Cynthia's lair."

The word that Vivian used to describe Cynthia's room made Jess feel sick to her stomach, but there was no turning back now. Not after they had come so far.

Vivian moved towards the door, her hand reaching

for the handle. The room seemed to hold its collective breath, the air thick with anticipation. But before Vivian could open the door, she turned back to face the group. Her expression was unreadable, her eyes scanning each of their faces in turn.

"Before I open this door," Vivian said, her voice low and serious, "I need you all to understand something. What's about to happen... it's not what you're expecting. Cynthia is here, yes, but not for the reasons you think."

Jess felt a chill run down her spine at Vivian's words. "What do you mean?" she demanded, her voice tight with confusion and frustration. "We're here to confront her about Rachel. To get answers. That's the whole point of this!"

Vivian shook her head slowly, her expression grave. "You're here because Cynthia wants to meet you. All of you. And believe me when I say, the answers you're about to get may not be the ones you're looking for."

The group exchanged bewildered glances, the tension in the room ratcheting up another notch. Jess felt as if the floor was shifting beneath her feet, her carefully constructed expectations crumbling.

"I don't understand," Lisa said, her voice trembling slightly. "You know Cynthia? You've spoken to her?"

Jess's blood ran cold.

"*Trust only each other*," she said, repeating what Vivian had told them. "Vivian... you.... What's really going on here?"

Vivian's hand remained on the door handle, but she didn't turn it yet. Her gaze swept over the group once more, her expression softening slightly.

"All will be revealed soon," she breathed. "Are you ready?"

Jess looked at her friends, seeing the same mix of determination and apprehension on their faces that she felt herself. They'd come this far, risked so much. They couldn't turn back now, no matter how terrifying the truth might be.

"We're ready," Jess said, speaking for the group. Her voice was steady, belying the turmoil of emotions roiling within her. "Open the door."

Vivian nodded, her expression grave. She turned the handle, the click of the mechanism seeming unnaturally loud in the tense silence of the corridor. As the door swung open, Jess held her breath, her heart pounding so hard she thought it might burst from her chest.

The door opened fully, revealing the figure standing on the other side. Jess's eyes widened, her breath catching in her throat as she came face to face with Cynthia.

She looked immaculate, wearing a crisp white pantsuit that seemed to glow in the natural light of morning.

"Ladies," Cynthia said, her voice smooth and controlled. "I'm so glad you could make it. I knew you had it in you."

Jess stepped forward, her eyes blazing with a mixture of anger and confusion. "Where's Rachel? What have you done with her?"

THIRTY-SIX
LAST NIGHT

The desert heat clung to them like a second skin, even in the pre-dawn hours. The group huddled together in the shadow of the imposing High Roller Suites, their once-glamorous outfits now wrinkled and stained, a far cry from the polished looks they'd set out with hours earlier.

Lisa was the first to break the tense silence. "Whatever it costs, I'll put the charge on my card," she said, her voice filled with determination. "We have no option but to go in and find Rachel."

The others turned to her, surprise and gratitude evident on their faces.

"Are you sure?" Jess asked. "It's a lot of money, Lisa."

Lisa nodded firmly. "Rachel would do anything for us. We have to help her."

Alex looked at Lisa with newfound admiration. Her willingness to take on such a financial burden for her friend spoke volumes about her character. "That's... that's really impressive, Lisa," he said, his voice soft but filled with respect.

Olivia, still wearing the showgirl costume, now minus the headdress, spoke up. "Even though I'm out of work now, I have some savings. I can contribute when we get back."

Megan, her practical nature asserting itself even in this surreal situation, shook her head. "No, Liv. I work enough overtime to cover your share. I won't hear any more about it."

Olivia hesitated, then nodded. "Okay, but only if you agree not to work so much overtime when we get back. Deal?"

Megan's face softened, and she nodded solemnly. "Deal."

Jess nodded. "Then it's agreed: We're going in." Her voice was calm, even though she was not. "Whatever it takes, we're finding Rachel and getting answers."

The others nodded in agreement, a mix of determination and apprehension on their faces.

The contrast between their surroundings and their destination couldn't have been any more polarised. The Mojave Desert stretched out around them, vast and unforgiving, its barren landscape a testament to nature's harsh beauty. Cacti stood like sentinels in the darkness, their silhouettes stark against the gradually lightening sky. In the distance, the jagged outline of mountains was just becoming visible, a reminder of the wild, untamed world beyond the neon-lit oasis of Las Vegas.

The High Roller Suites stood as a monument to human extravagance in this unforgiving environment. Its sleek, modern façade seemed to defy the very essence of the desert, promising luxury and excess in a place defined by scarcity. As they approached the entrance, the girls could feel the first blast of air conditioning escaping through the doors, a tantalising promise of relief from the heat, which was oppressive even in the early hours of the morning.

The group approached the gleaming glass doors of The High Roller Suites, their reflections distorted in the tinted surface. Jess's heart pounded in her chest, each step feeling heavier than the last. She glanced at her friends, noting the tension in their shoulders and the wary looks they exchanged. The air seemed to thicken around them, making it harder to breathe. Despite the knot in her stomach and the voice in her head screaming to turn back, Jess pressed forward. Rachel's face flashed in her mind, spurring her on. They had come too far to back down now, no matter what awaited them on the other side of those doors.

Lisa's hand trembled slightly as she held out her credit card to the impassive bouncer. For a heart-stopping moment, she feared the transaction wouldn't go through. But the doors swung open, inviting them into a world that seemed galaxies away from the harsh desert night.

As they stood there, dishevelled and out of place in the luxurious surroundings, a familiar figure approached. Jack - the man in the hat - his face, still partially obscured by the brim of his fedora, greeted them with a smile that didn't quite reach his eyes.

"Ladies, gentleman," he said, his voice smooth as silk. "Welcome to The High Roller Suites. If you'll follow me, please."

He led them to a private elevator, its interior lined with plush red velvet. As they ascended, Jess felt a growing sense of unease. What awaited them at the top? And more importantly, where was Rachel?

The elevator doors opened directly into a penthouse suite that took their breath away. Floor-to-ceiling windows offered a panoramic view of the surrounding landscape. To one side, the vast expanse of the Mojave stretched out before them, the first rays of dawn painting the sand in hues of gold and pink. On the other side, the Las Vegas Strip glittered in the distance, a man-made constellation slowly fading as the natural light grew stronger.

In the centre of the room, seated on a plush velvet sofa, was Cynthia. Her red dress from earlier in the night had been replaced by a sleek black number that seemed to absorb the surrounding light.

"Welcome, my dears," she purred, gesturing for them to sit. "I trust your little adventure in the desert wasn't too uncomfortable?"

Jess stepped forward, her patience wearing thin. "Where's Rachel?"

Jack chuckled, moving to stand beside Cynthia. "All in good time, my dear. But first, I believe I owe you an apology."

The group exchanged confused glances.

"An apology?" Megan echoed.

"Yes," the man continued. "For the magic show 'gone wrong.' I assure you, it was entirely intentional. The Great Marvolo didn't make any mistakes – he made Rachel disappear exactly as planned."

Jess felt her heart racing, a mix of fear and anger coursing through her veins.

"Where is she?" she demanded, her voice shaking with emotion. "Is she okay?"

Cynthia leaned forward, her eyes glittering with an emotion Jess couldn't quite place. "Rachel is fine, darling. And she'll continue to be fine, on one condition..."

The words were laden with implication. The breathtaking view outside did nothing to assuage the tension in the room. The desert sun was now peeking over the horizon, bathing the room in a warm, golden light that seemed at odds with the icy fear gripping Jess's heart.

She looked at her friends, seeing her own mix of determination and apprehension mirrored in their faces. Lisa, her red dress now wrinkled and stained, stood tall, her jaw set in determination. Olivia, still in the showgirl costume, looked out of place in the resplendent surroundings, but her eyes blazed with a newfound courage. Megan, ever practical, was already analysing the room, looking for clues or potential escape routes. And Alex, the unexpected addition to their group, stood slightly apart, his casino experience lending him an air of wary familiarity with their luxurious surroundings.

As Jess turned back to face Cynthia and the man in the hat, she knew that whatever came next would change everything. The glittering promises of their Vegas getaway had led them here, to this moment of truth. With the desert stretching endlessly in one direction and the fading lights of the Strip in the other, they stood on the precipice of a mystery deeper and more dangerous than they could have imagined.

"What's the condition?" Jess asked, her voice steady despite the fear churning in her stomach.

Jack's smile widened. "It's quite simple, really. All you have to do is..."

THIRTY-SEVEN

THIS MORNING

Cynthia's laughter filled the air. It was light and melodious and contrasted sharply with the tension that crackled through the room. She stepped back, gesturing for the group to enter with a graceful sweep of her arm.

"Please, come in," she said, her voice smooth as silk. "We have so much to discuss."

Jess hesitated for a fraction of a second, her eyes darting to her friends. They exchanged quick glances, a silent communication born of shared experiences and mutual trust. With a barely perceptible nod, Jess led the way into Cynthia's suite.

Their rooms at The Bellagio had dazzled them with opulence when they checked in the previous day; stepping into Cynthia's suite, they realised those rooms were like roadside motels in comparison. This was luxury on another level entirely - a sprawling space where every surface gleamed, every fabric shimmered, and the very air seemed perfumed with wealth. Crystal chandeliers cast a soft glow over custom furniture that looked more like art than functional pieces. The floor-to-ceiling windows framed a view of Las Vegas that made the city below seem like a personal playground. It was the kind of suite that whispered of secrets and power, where the ultra-wealthy played games with lives and fortunes.

Cynthia's smile never wavered. "Come and take a seat. Please." She gestured towards the lavish room beyond.

Jess stood resolutely still.

"Listen, Cynthia. I don't really feel like taking a seat. I know you're probably used to getting people to do whatever you want, whenever you want, but we aren't those people. I'm stressed, tired and frankly sick of all this shit now. I thought I would be sitting in a spa today, but instead I woke up in an ice bath, found my friends in similarly ridiculous situations, and... well... as you know... spent the morning trying to find my best friend, who is still missing... who I'm still worried out of my freaking mind about... and... and..."

Jess fought to hold back tears of frustration and exhaustion. She wasn't going to cry in front of this bitch.

"What the hell is going on?" Lisa said, hugging Jess and looking over her shoulder to address Cynthia.

"And what do you mean by 'you knew we had it in us'?" Megan asked sharply.

"Please," Cynthia said. "Jessica. Take a seat."

"It's Jess," she hissed. "And I just want to find Rachel and get the hell out of here, please. If you know where she is, then just tell us so we can stop worrying, find her, and be on our way. I'm all Vegassed out and I want to be back at home, on my own cheap sofa with an iced coffee and all of my damn friends."

Vivian had entered behind them and was sitting on a cowskin recliner on the sidelines of the room. She was an observer, watching the scene unfold, until Cynthia threw a pleading look her way.

"Viv? Some help, please?" she said.

"So, you *are* in on this together," Jess said, turning to face the redhead. "Why let us go through all of this? You could just have helped us to find Rachel last night."

"This is fudged up," Olivia said, sinking onto one of the sofas and holding her head in her hands. Megan settled next to her, stroking her back, but not taking her eyes off Cynthia for a moment.

"Can someone please start answering some questions?" Jess said, her voice high-pitched with tension, like a kettle about to come to the boil.

"Cynthia," Alex said, stepping towards her. "They've been through enough. Please."

Lisa tipped her head to the side, regarding Alex.

"Not you too?" she said. Her words were quiet and desperate. "Please, no."

Alex held up his hands and sat on a second sofa. "Cynthia?" was all he said.

The tall blonde sighed visibly. "If you'll just take a seat, I'll tell you exactly where Rachel is and answer any questions that you care to ask." Again, she waved her hand towards an empty seat, indicating that Jess should sit.

She and Lisa were the only members of the group still standing. Jess out of stubborn steadfastness and Lisa out of loyalty. Lisa took hold of her friend's hand and led her to the sofa space.

"It's okay," she said. "Let's hear what she has to say. If she can help us find Rachel, we can work

288

everything else out later. However we've been played, we can get through this, all right?"

Jess didn't feel that anything was anywhere near all right, but she nodded and took her place on the sofa.

Immediately, Cynthia pulled out her phone and tapped the screen before holding the handset up to her ear.

"Yes," she said. "They've made it. Bring her in."

The girls looked across at each other, Megan and Olivia on one lush sofa and Lisa and Jess on another.

"Rachel," Jess said faintly, letting her vulnerability show.

Jess heard footsteps coming along the hallway, and her heart lurched.

She was back on her feet, running to the doorway before the others had a chance to stand. She pushed open the door, and there in front of her was a man wearing a sharp suit and a fedora.

Next to him stood Rachel, a huge smile plastered across her face, her body wrapped in a thick, white dressing gown.

The vision didn't make any sense to Jess. Rachel didn't look like someone who had been abducted against her will and mistreated. In fact, she looked just the opposite.

Jess felt as if the air had been sucked out of her lungs. She looked around at her friends, seeing her own shock and confusion mirrored in their faces.

Not knowing what else to do, Jess pulled Rachel into a hug, the girls squeezing tightly, as if they never wanted to let go. The others crowded around them, joining the embrace. It was a long time before they could bear to pull away.

Rachel was the first to break the silence after their long embrace. "Wait, are you guys okay? What happened?" she asked, her voice filled with concern.

"That's what we want to ask you," Jess said. "Where have you *been*?"

Before Rachel could answer, Cynthia stepped over to them. "Perhaps I should explain," she said, gesturing for everyone to sit down. "It was hard enough to get you to take a seat the first time around. Please?"

Jess's face was a picture of sheer confusion.

"She was fine the whole time?" she whispered to Lisa. "Did we over-react that badly?"

Lisa shook her head, quickly and slightly so as not to draw attention. "The ice bath. The handcuffs. Olivia. Megan. Something happened, and this all feels like a cover up."

Jess turned back to Rachel, scanning her for any sign of injury. To all intents, she looked as though she had spent the morning in a luxury spa.

"What's going on?" Jess asked in a loud whisper.

Rachel nodded towards Cynthia.

Once they were all seated, Cynthia began to speak. "First, I want to congratulate you all on your performance. You've exceeded my expectations in every way."

"Performance?" Lisa echoed, incredulous. "What are you talking about?"

Cynthia's smile widened. "The ultimate Vegas experience, of course. That's what Rachel hired me for, after all."

All eyes turned to Rachel, who seemed to shrink under their collective gaze.

"Rachel?" Jess said, her voice barely above a whisper. "Is this true?"

Rachel nodded. "I wanted to give you something unforgettable for your bachelorette party. VIP passes, a celebrity gathering, and then a chill day at the best spa in Nevada."

"Rachel... we... you..." Jess spoke, but Cynthia interrupted.

Cynthia cleared her throat. "To be fair, Rachel didn't exactly sign up for everything that happened. She came to me asking for the ultimate experience, and I... well, I created it. In fact, Rachel doesn't remember what happened last night at all. We only woke her half an hour ago, and she thinks you've come here to join her at the spa."

"Created it?" Olivia repeated, her voice rising. "You call what happened to us a 'created experience'? We woke up scattered around our hotel room like puppets! That was your doing."

Rachel's cheerful expression faded.

"Not to mention the terror of thinking Rachel had been kidnapped, or worse," Megan added.

"What?" Rachel said. "We *are* going to the spa, aren't we? And why on earth would you think I'd been kidnapped? Holy shit, guys. Someone had better fill me in." Her eyes turned from Jess to Cynthia, pure rage in her glare.

Cynthia remained unperturbed. "I understand your anger. But consider this: each of you has gone through a transformative experience tailored specifically to

291

your needs."

"Our needs?" Lisa scoffed. "And how would you know what our needs are?"

"Research, my dear," Cynthia replied smoothly. "Rachel provided me with your backgrounds, and I did my own digging. Everything that happened was designed to help you grow."

"That was to help you plan the evening..." Rachel began, and then stopped talking.

"It was supposed to be my bachelorette party," Jess said. "We were meant to have fun. All I have is a night I can't remember and a day I'd rather forget."

Cynthia's expression softened slightly. "Oh, Jess. You have so much more than that. All of you do."

"I can't believe Rachel would do this to me," Jess continued, turning to her friend. "To any of us."

Rachel looked on the verge of tears. "Jess, I'm so sorry. It's not my fault. I thought... I didn't know she would do this. I honestly just wanted you to have the best bachelorette that money could buy."

Jess's mouth dropped open. There was so much she wanted to say, but she hadn't had time to process what was going on.

Trust Rachel, she thought.

Don't let Rachel get you into any trouble. Miles's words now seemed more ominous than protective.

Cynthia interjected, her tone careful, "There's more to this story than you realise. She's telling the truth. The request for this... experience... didn't come from Rachel alone."

A collective gasp went up from the group. Rachel's eyes widened in shock. "What do you mean? I was the one who contacted you!"

Cynthia held up a hand. "You did, Rachel, but someone else... escalated the plan. Someone who wanted to create a very specific impression."

Jess felt a chill run down her spine. "Who?" she demanded, though a part of her already suspected the answer.

Cynthia's gaze locked with Jess's. "I think you know, Jess. Think about who might benefit from driving a wedge between you and your friends. Especially Rachel."

The room fell silent as the implications of Cynthia's words sank in. Jess's mind raced, connecting dots she hadn't even realised existed. Miles's warnings, his insistence that she be careful around Rachel, his claim of not knowing Cynthia...

"Miles," Jess said. The blood drained from her face.

Turning to Cynthia, Rachel asked, "How does Miles know you? How did he even...?"

Cynthia tilted her head, her soft blonde hair flopping over her eyes. She shook it away casually.

"You both keep asking questions that you already know the answers to. You're smarter than this, ladies."

"He never comes to Vegas," Jess breathed. Again, she looked at Rachel for support. For anything.

"I deal with the businesses here," Rachel nodded. "And, just so everyone is clear, they are legitimate. Whatever Miles told you, it's not true."

Jess's face was a picture of confusion and concentrated thought.

"Where was he last month?" she asked, addressing Rachel. "He told me he was in Dubuque."

Rachel's face was blank.

"He gave me this spiel about how difficult it was to get there," Jess continued.

Rachel looked away, an expression of unmissable sadness on her face.

"He..." Jess shook her head, tears filling her eyes.

"I'm sorry," Cynthia said. "I've seen Miles around town many times over the years. We're not exactly friends, but..." She shrugged slightly. "Nothing untoward," she added hurriedly. "Nothing like that."

"But you do know him." Jess said, wiping her eyes with her sleeve and taking a deep breath.

"I do," Cynthia confirmed.

"Jess, I didn't... I didn't know anything about this. I had no idea that he was involved at all," Rachel said, her voice trembling. "Jess, you have to believe me. I would never do anything to hurt you."

Jess nodded slowly, her mind still reeling from the revelations. "I believe you, Rachel. But I need to understand what's going on here." She turned back to Cynthia, her eyes hard. "Tell me everything. Now."

Cynthia sighed, settling back into her seat. "Miles approached me a few weeks ago. He said he was concerned about your friendship with Rachel, that he felt it was... interfering with your relationship. He wanted to create a scenario that would make you doubt Rachel, make you see her as unreliable, maybe even dangerous."

Lisa gasped. "That's horrible! How could he do that?"

"But why?" Olivia asked, her face showing her confusion. "Why would he want to come between Jess

294

and Rachel?"

Megan, who had been quietly processing everything, spoke up. "Control," she said softly. "It's about control. If Jess doubts her closest friend, who does she have left to turn to?"

Jess felt as if the floor was tilting beneath her. She grabbed the arm of the sofa to steady herself. "Miles... he's always been a bit possessive, but this... this is insane."

Rachel reached out and took Jess's hand. "Jess, I'm so sorry. I had no idea Miles felt this way about our friendship. If I had known..."

Cynthia interrupted, her voice gentle but firm. "There's more, I'm afraid. Miles... he knows things about your family's business, Rachel. Things that I don't think you're aware of."

Rachel's face paled. "What are you talking about?"

Cynthia hesitated, glancing at the others in the room. "Perhaps this is a conversation best had in private."

"No," Jess said firmly. "Whatever it is, we face it together. All of us." She looked around at her friends, who nodded in agreement.

Cynthia took a deep breath. "Your family's businesses, Rachel... they're not all as legitimate as you believe. There's been talk for years about money laundering, among other things. Miles... he's involved somehow. I don't know the details, but he's in deep."

Rachel shook her head vehemently. "No, that's impossible. My family... they wouldn't... What he said... it can't be true..."

"I'm sorry, Rachel," Cynthia said softly. "But it is

true. And Miles... he's been using this knowledge as leverage. I think he saw your friendship with Jess as a threat. If she ever found out what he was involved in..."

Jess stood up abruptly, her face a mask of determination. "I need to talk to Miles. Now."

THIRTY-EIGHT
LAST NIGHT

The man in the hat's voice trailed off, his eyes flickering to something behind the group. Before they could react, a sweet, cloying scent filled the air. Jess felt her head begin to spin, her vision blurring at the edges.

"What's... happening?" she managed to mumble before her knees buckled beneath her.

The last thing she saw before darkness claimed her was Cynthia's smile.

When Jess came to, she found herself seated in a plush armchair. The room was dimly lit, the heavy curtains drawn against the dawning day. Her friends were arranged in a semicircle around her, each looking as dazed and confused as she felt.

The Great Marvolo stood before them, a pendulum swinging gently from his hand. His voice, when he spoke, seemed to come from everywhere and nowhere at once.

"Ladies and gentleman, I want you to focus on the pendulum. Let your eyes follow its gentle swing. Back and forth, back and forth..."

Jess tried to resist, to look away, but found her gaze inexorably drawn to the hypnotic motion of the pendulum. The magician's voice continued, soft and insistent.

"You're feeling very relaxed now. Your eyelids are getting heavy. So very heavy..."

Despite her best efforts, Jess felt her eyes beginning to close. She was vaguely aware of her friends succumbing as well, their heads lolling forward as they slipped into a trance.

"When I count to three, you will fall into a deep sleep. But you will still be able to hear and respond to my voice. One... two... three."

Jess's world went dark.

"You will remember nothing of the events of tonight," the Marvolo intoned. "When you wake, you will believe you had a wild night of partying. You drank too much, did things you can't quite recall. But you will not question these gaps in your memory. You will accept them as a natural consequence of your night out."

In their hypnotised state, the group nodded in unison.

Marvolo stepped back, surveying his handiwork. "You will wake from your sleep naturally, with no memory of this hypnosis or the true events of the night. Do you understand?"

The group nodded again, still deep in their trance.

With a satisfied smile, Marvolo gave a high-pitched whistle. Cynthia emerged from the shadows, a calculating look in her eyes.

"Impressive work," she murmured.

"Anything else?" The Great Marvolo asked, a weary edge to his voice.

"No," Cynthia snapped. "Now, let's get them back to their suite before the effects wear off."

Marvolo gave Cynthia a sharp look and bowed. "As you wish." He stepped back, away from the sleeping group and out of Cynthia's way.

"Speak soon," she said, dismissively as the man in the hat pushed forward, hooking beneath Jess's arms and dragging her away.

"Such sweet girls," Marvolo said, almost sadly.

"They'll be fine," Cynthia said. "If you've done your job properly."

"As always, Cyn. As always," the magician said.

The pre-dawn streets of Las Vegas were eerily quiet as a nondescript van made its way through the city. Inside, Cynthia and the Jack sat in tense silence, their unconscious charges laid out in the back.

They pulled up to the Bellagio, using a service entrance by the North Lobby to avoid the curious eyes of early-morning guests. With practiced efficiency, they began moving the sleeping friends to their suite.

"Start preparing the tub," Cynthia said as she rifled through her backpack, pulling out props.

Jack nodded and did what he was told.

When he emerged, Lisa and Alex were the first to be positioned. Cynthia deftly handcuffed them together, arranging the pair on the balcony with a hint of a smirk on her face.

"Think they'll thank us for this little matchmaking effort?" she asked, her voice laced with dark humour.

Jack merely grunted in response, already moving to position Olivia behind the sofa. He arranged her carefully, making sure she was comfortable even in the chaos.

Megan was next, gently placed in the walk-in closet. Jack checked the combination on the leather briefcase, and rested it in her arms, watching as her fingers instinctively tightened around the handle, even in sleep.

"You really *do* need to work less," Jack muttered.

From across the room, Cynthia called out, "Just a moment."

She ducked out of the suite into the corridor.

"Hold the door, Jack," she said.

The man in the hat did as he was commanded, allowing Cynthia to wheel a room service cart, complete with a leftover meal, into the room.

The man looked at her with a quizzical expression.

"Don't want this one waking up first and spoiling the show," Cynthia smiled, positioning the trolley outside the closet to block Megan's potential exit.

Jack smiled, picked up one of the champagne bottles and placed it almost artistically beside the plate.

"Nice touch," Cynthia said. "You'll be setting these up on your own soon. Now for the leading lady."

Finally, it was Jess's turn. They carried her to the bathroom, where a tub full of ice and poker chips awaited. As they lowered her into the frigid mix, Jess stirred slightly.

"We need to hurry," Cynthia hissed. "The cold will wake her soon."

They quickly arranged the rest of the suite, overturning furniture and scattering personal items to complete the illusion of a wild night. As they worked, the early morning sunlight peeked through the windows, casting long shadows across the room.

Cynthia and Jack made their last sweep of the suite. Their movements were unhurried, almost casual, as if arranging unconscious bodies was just another day at the office.

"Well," Cynthia said, brushing a strand of hair from her face, "I think our sleeping beauties are all tucked in." Her tone was light, but her eyes were sharp, missing nothing.

Jack grunted in agreement, adjusting his fedora. "Just about. Any last touches?"

Cynthia reached into her purse and pulled out Rachel's phone. With a flick of her wrist, she tossed it onto the floor.

"Can't have them thinking Rachel vanished into thin air, can we?" she said.

She stepped on the phone delicately with her heel; the screen cracked with a soft crunch.

"Oops," she said with a smirk.

Jack watched Cynthia at work with quiet admiration. "You've thought of everything, haven't you?"

Cynthia shrugged, a small smile playing on her lips. "It's what I do. Plan parties, create memories... or in this case, the removal of memories."

She paused by the door, taking one last look around the suite. The scene before her was perfect - a tableau of debauchery and confusion that would leave Jess and her friends reeling.

"Think they'll figure it out?" the man in the hat asked, joining her at the door.

Cynthia's smile widened. "Oh, I'm counting on it. And if they don't..." She let the sentence hang in the air.

With a satisfied nod, they slipped out of the suite; the door closed with a soft click. In the silence they left behind, Jess stirred slightly in her ice-filled tub, blissfully unaware of the game that lay ahead of her.

THIRTY-NINE
THIS MORNING

Jess stepped out into the corridor, leaving Cynthia's team and her group of friends in shocked silence. She leaned against the velvet wallpaper and put her hands down on her knees, trying to catch her breath.

Pulling her phone from her pocket, she inhaled deeply and called her fiancé.

It took three rings before Miles's voice sounded out.

"Hi, love," he said. "Everything okay?"

"Great," Jess said. "We're just heading to the spa now."

Miles hesitated.

"Oh... good," he said. "You found Rachel? Everything was okay?"

Jess didn't speak.

"Must have all been a big misunderstanding, eh?" Miles said.

Still, Jess was silent.

"Jess? Love?"

"You had Lisa spying on me. You tried to turn me against Rachel. What next, Miles?" Jess hissed in a loud whisper, not wanting her friends back in the room to hear her. "Are you going to try to poison me against Liv and Megan?"

"Jess, I..."

"Was it just this weekend you didn't want me to be with the girls, or is this how you thought it was going to be when we were married? You didn't want me coming here with them. You didn't want me to have a good time..."

Jess sucked in a breath.

"You knew about Cynthia. You know Cynthia. You never went to damn Dubuque," she said, sinking into a sitting position with her back against the wall. "You did this to us. It was all down to you."

"Jess, please. Let me explain. I'll get a flight. Stay there, I'll..."

Jess pressed her top row of teeth into her bottom lip, trying to hold back her tears.

"Miles, what the hell were you thinking? Did you know how far Cynthia would go? Did you think it was going to be fun? Did you think I would enjoy thinking my best friend had been kidnapped? What that actual...? Shit..." Jess suddenly remembered what Cynthia had said. "*I* was the one that was supposed to disappear. Miles, how could you...?"

"Look, as soon as you told me you were going to Vegas with Rachel, I had my suspicions. When you started calling it the 'Ultimate Vegas Experience' I knew Cynthia was involved. That's what she calls her shitshow. Rachel wanted her to keep it simple and show you girls a good time. I thought you could all do with a wake-up call. Cynthia was meant to explain everything," Miles said flatly. "That was part of the deal. That dumb bitch is going to pay for this."

Jess could picture Miles's expression, even though she couldn't see his face.

"You said you didn't even know Cynthia," Jess said, thinking back to their conversation earlier. "Just how far were you prepared to go?"

"How far was I prepared to go?" Miles asked. "I think you know that. You know nothing about the world I operate in. You know nothing about Rachel's family..."

"But I *do* know Rachel," Jess said. "And I trust her with my life."

As she spoke, she looked up to see her friends peering out of the suite, watching her.

Lisa gave her a smile, and Rachel nodded.

"You weren't checking in with me, you were checking up on me. You knew exactly what was going on and you let it happen."

"Cynthia is an expert," Miles said. "She has her reasons for..."

"Reasons? I don't care, Miles."

"Come inside, Jess," Rachel said. "Cynthia has something to tell us."

Jess raised a hand, as if to tell them to wait a moment, but seemed to think better of it.

"I have to go," she said. "My friends are waiting for me."

"Jess –" Miles's voice was cut off as Jess hung up.

Lisa and Rachel reached a hand out each to pull Jess upright, and helped her to walk back into the suite.

"It's all right," Rachel said. "Everything is going to be all right."

Soon they were back on the lush sofas, Cynthia sitting alongside them. Close up, in the daylight, she looked more human, softer somehow.

"I'm sorry this weekend didn't start off how you expected," she said. "Rachel wanted to make it perfect for you, and I have to take responsibility for distracting her last night. I was told to keep her out of the picture..." Cynthia said.

"Miles..." Jess whispered.

Cynthia nodded. "But I'm not a bad person. My brand of party planning focuses on making sure everyone gets something out of it. Even when it's an unconventional night like yours."

"Well," Jess said. "Whatever it was, it was wasted on me. I can't see there being a wedding anytime soon. At least not to that duplicitous..."

Rachel pressed her finger against Jess's lips. "Let's talk that through later," she said.

"Please, let me explain," Cynthia said.

Jess closed her eyes and exhaled deeply.

"Go ahead," Rachel said.

Cynthia turned to Lisa. "Lisa, you've been struggling to move on after your divorce. Meeting Alex, feeling that spark again, was designed to show you that you're ready to open your heart once more."

Lisa's cheeks flushed, remembering the handcuffs and the unexpected connection she'd felt with Alex.

"But he was acting," she said. "It wasn't real."

"The feelings were real," he said. "I was supposed to play my part, sure, but... Lisa, I hope I can see you again."

The flush in Lisa's cheeks turned to a burning fire beneath her skin. She smiled slightly.

Meanwhile, Cynthia addressed Olivia. "Losing

your job shattered your confidence. But last night, as a showgirl, you rediscovered your strength and sensuality. That costume wasn't just for show – it was armour, rebuilding your self-esteem."

Olivia shifted uncomfortably in her seat, her mind flashing back to the memory of wearing the showgirl costume. A mix of emotions crossed her face - embarrassment, excitement, and a hint of newfound confidence.

"I... I can't believe I actually wore that outfit in public," she murmured, a faint blush colouring her cheeks too.

"And don't worry about your job," Rachel said. "I can set you up with something. That's what friends are for."

Olivia nodded, seeming to sit up straighter and lift her head higher than she had all weekend.

"Megan," Cynthia continued, "your analytical mind is your greatest asset, but also your greatest weakness. You've been working yourself to the bone, missing out on life. This experience pushed you to make a promise to your friends - a promise to cut back on overtime and find a better work-life balance."

Megan nodded slowly, recalling the conversation with her friends. "I did make that promise," she admitted. "And I intend to keep it."

Cynthia smiled enigmatically. "The briefcase, my dear, is a symbol. It represents the choice you now face - to continue down the path of overwork, or to embrace a more balanced life. What you do with it is up to you."

Megan nodded as she contemplated Cynthia's words.

"I need to be kinder to myself," she said.

"And Jess," Cynthia said, her voice softening. "Sweet Jess. Always trying to keep everything and everyone in order. This experience was about teaching you to let go, to trust your friends, to embrace the unexpected. You don't always have to lead. They aren't your students. Let go every once in a while."

Jess opened her mouth to argue, then closed it again, realising there was a kernel of truth in Cynthia's words.

"What you learned about Miles, well... that's all on him." Cynthia said.

"Jess, I would never interfere in your relationship. I introduced the two of you. I thought you were right for each other. I never knew what kind of person he would turn out to be. I'm so..." Rachel said before Jess reached out and copied her earlier gesture, pressing her fingers against Rachel's lips.

"Let's talk that through later," Jess repeated.

Rachel nodded.

"And Rachel," Cynthia said, turning to face her. "Your lesson was perhaps the hardest of all. You were so easily manipulated. I messaged you and you dropped everything to answer. You wanted everything to be perfect, but instead of helping, your constant need to respond to messages and stay in control of the situation left your friends feeling neglected. I can't help but think this isn't the first time this has happened."

Rachel nodded slowly, tears streaming down her face. "I'm so sorry, everyone. I just wanted it to be special."

The room fell silent again, each woman lost in her

308

own thoughts. The Las Vegas sun streamed through the windows, illuminating the tear tracks on Rachel's face, the confusion in Jess's eyes, the dawning realisations on the faces of Lisa, Olivia, and Megan.

Finally, Jess spoke. "I understand what you were trying to do. And maybe... maybe some good has come out of this mess. But it doesn't change the fact that you betrayed our trust." She looked pointedly at Cynthia.

Cynthia nodded, accepting the accusation. "You're right. My methods are... unconventional. But I stand by the results."

"Results?" Megan interjected. "How can you be so sure of the results? You manipulated us, played with our emotions, our memories!"

"Yeah," Olivia added. "How do we know any of what we're feeling is real?"

Cynthia smiled enigmatically. "The emotions are real, ladies. The connections you've made, the revelations you've had – those are all genuine. I merely created the circumstances for them to occur."

Lisa shook her head. "I don't know whether to thank you or report you to the authorities."

"I understand your confusion," Cynthia replied. "But think about it. Lisa, are you not feeling more open to the possibility of love? Olivia, hasn't your confidence grown? Megan, aren't you reconsidering your work-life balance? Jess, haven't you learned to loosen your grip a little?"

The women exchanged glances, unable to deny the truth in Cynthia's words.

"And Rachel," Cynthia continued, "haven't you learned the value of honesty and the dangers of over-planning?"

Rachel nodded slowly. "I have. And I'm so, so sorry, everyone. Especially you, Jess. Can you ever forgive me?"

Jess looked at her oldest friend, seeing the genuine remorse in her eyes. She sighed heavily. "I need time to process all of this. We all do."

FORTY
THIS MORNING

The group sat in stunned silence after Cynthia's explanations. She recounted how Marvolo had hypnotised them, and how she and Jack had taken them back to their room to leave the final clues and set the scene.

"It all seems very complex," Lisa said, almost in awe. "You made sure I used my credit card so we would have that trail to follow?"

Cynthia smiled, as though Lisa had paid her a compliment. "Genius, wasn't it?" she said. "There have to be enough breadcrumbs scattered through the night for you to be able to retrace your steps. That's all part of the plan."

Jess, her mind still reeling from the revelations about Miles, looked at Cynthia with a mixture of anger and curiosity.

"I still don't understand," Jess said. "Why? Why go to all this trouble? Why put us through this ordeal? Just because Rachel paid you to plan the ultimate bachelorette? Didn't you stop to think about the ethical implications and consider just maybe that this isn't what Rachel had in mind?"

"It's not just about the money," Cynthia began, her voice softer than before. "Though I won't deny that's part of it. But there's more to it than that."

She paused, seemingly gathering her thoughts. "I've seen so many people trapped in their own lives, unable to break free from their self-imposed limitations. The elite have everything, and yet they're often the most trapped of all."

Rachel nodded slowly, a flicker of understanding crossing her face. "That's why you agreed to this. You thought we needed... what? A wake-up call?"

Cynthia smiled wryly. "Something like that. Rachel, when you came to me, I saw a group of women on the brink of something. Each of you was struggling in your own way, unable to see past your own barriers. I thought I could help."

"By manipulating our memories?" Megan interjected, her tone sharp.

Cynthia had the grace to look slightly abashed. "My methods are extreme, I admit. But they're effective. Think about it - in the span of one night, you've all confronted fears, rediscovered strengths, and formed connections you might never have made otherwise."

Lisa spoke up, her voice quiet but firm. "But at what cost? Our trust in each other has been shaken. Our memories tampered with. How is that helping?"

Cynthia leaned back, her gaze sweeping across the group. "Sometimes, we need to be shaken out of our comfort zones to truly grow. I know my methods are controversial," Cynthia admitted. "But I've seen the transformations they can bring about. People who come out the other side stronger, more self-aware, more alive."

Cynthia's eyes took on a distant look, as if seeing beyond the luxurious suite. "I wasn't always this person, you know. I used to be trapped in my own life, unable to break free from my fears and insecurities."

The women exchanged glances, surprised by this sudden vulnerability from the normally composed Cynthia.

"What changed?" Olivia asked, her curiosity piqued.

Cynthia's lips curved into a small, nostalgic smile. "I had my own 'ultimate experience'. It wasn't planned like yours, but it shook me to my core. It made me realise how much of life I was missing by playing it safe."

She paused, her gaze sweeping across the group. "After that, I couldn't go back to my old life. I wanted to help others break free from their self-imposed limitations. At first, it was just advice to friends. Then word spread, and suddenly the elite were coming to me, asking for experiences that would change their lives."

"So, you turned it into a business," Megan stated, putting the pieces together.

Cynthia nodded. "Yes, but it's more than that. It's a mission. I truly believe I'm helping people; I've seen the results. Lives transformed, relationships strengthened, dreams realised."

"But at what cost?" Jess interjected, her voice tinged with both understanding and reproach. "You're playing with people's lives, their memories, their trust."

Cynthia's expression sobered. "I know. And I don't take that lightly. Every experience is carefully crafted, every risk calculated. But I believe the potential for personal development is worth it. True growth often comes from unexpected places. From being pushed out of our comfort zones in ways we'd never choose for ourselves."

The room fell silent again as the women absorbed Cynthia's words. There was a palpable shift in the atmosphere - the anger and betrayal were still there, but now tinged with a grudging understanding.

"I can't condone what you've done," Jess said finally. "But I can't deny that this experience *has* changed us. Whether that change is for the better, time will tell."

Cynthia nodded, accepting Jess's words. "I understand. And I want you to know that everything that happened was carefully controlled. You were never in any real danger."

"Except for our relationships with each other," Lisa murmured.

"That's the real test," Cynthia replied. "If your friendships can weather this storm, they'll be stronger for it."

As the conversation wound down, the women found themselves at a crossroads. The revelations of the day had shaken them to their core, forcing them to reevaluate not just the events of the past night, but their entire lives.

Jess looked at her friends - Rachel's tear-stained face, Lisa's conflicted expression, Olivia's newfound confidence, Megan's thoughtful demeanour.

"So what now?" Olivia asked, voicing the question on everyone's minds.

Megan suddenly sat up straight.

"Wait a minute," she said, her eyes narrowing. "What about the flash drive? How does that fit into all of this?"

The others turned to look at her, then back at Cynthia, curiosity piqued.

Cynthia's smile widened. "Ah, I was wondering when one of you would ask about that. Do you have it with you?"

Megan nodded, pulling it from her pocket.

Cynthia held it up, rotating it between her fingers as though she were playing with a poker chip. "This," Cynthia explained, "contains the evidence of your night. Your memories, if you will. It's a collection of photographs that document your lost night."

"How? How did you do that? Get all the photos of us?" Jess asked, her voice a mix of awe and indignation.

"I have eyes everywhere, darling," Cynthia replied smoothly. "It's part of creating the ultimate experience. Every moment is captured, ready to be relived."

The women were silent.

"The experience is designed to push you out of your comfort zones, but also to create moments of joy, of connection. There are plenty of them here on this flash drive."

Megan, ever practical, spoke up. "And what happens to these photos now? To all this... evidence?"

Cynthia turned to face the group, her expression serious. "That, my dears, is up to you. This flash drive is yours to keep. You can relive the night whenever you want, or..."

"Or we could delete it all, like you deleted our memories," Jess finished, her voice quiet but firm.

Cynthia nodded. "Exactly. The choice is yours. Keep the memories or let them go. Either way, the lessons you've learned, the growth you've experienced - that's yours to keep."

The women exchanged glances, a silent conversation passing between them. After a moment, Jess reached out and gently took the flash drive from Cynthia. She held it in her palm, looking at it thoughtfully.

"We'll think about it," she said finally, tucking the drive into her purse.

Cynthia smiled, a hint of approval in her eyes. "A wise decision. Take your time. After all, isn't that what this whole experience has been about? Learning to take a step back, to consider your choices, to trust in yourselves and each other?"

The night they couldn't remember was now laid bare before them, offering a chance to reclaim lost memories or to move forward unburdened by the past.

Cynthia stood up. "Before you go, I have one last surprise for you."

The women looked at her warily.

"It's just a spa day, or at least the full treatment in my own private spa," Cynthia assured them. "No hidden agendas, no secret lessons. Just relaxation and pampering. You've earned it. This is what Rachel thought was going to happen when you arrived. She's already dressed for it, and if you head through to the bedroom, there are robes and outfits for each of you there, too."

"I don't think this is my bachelorette anymore," Jess said quietly.

Lisa put her hand on Jess's. "Then let's make it a girls' weekend. We deserve something good. And to be honest, I'm exhausted."

The girls looked at one another, unsure of what to do. After everything they had been through, the last thing they needed was another surprise. And yet, the prospect of relaxation was tempting. They could use some time to unwind and reflect on the crazy events of the past twenty-four hours. And after all, tomorrow they would have to fly home. They might as well make the most of their final time in Vegas. One by one, they nodded in agreement.

Rachel led the way, walking towards the door. The others followed, their steps quickening with anticipation. As they filed out of the suite, each lost in her own thoughts, Jess lingered behind. She turned to Cynthia, her expression a mix of anger, confusion, and grudging respect.

"I don't know if I'll ever fully understand or approve of what you did," she said. "But I can't deny that you've given us a lot to think about."

Cynthia nodded. "That was always the goal, Jess. Oh, and don't worry about Mr Chen and your Bellagio check out. I've got that all under control."

"I'd forgotten all about that," Jess said, surprised at herself.

"Well, you've forgotten a lot of things," Cynthia said with a dry smile.

FORTY-ONE
THIS MORNING

The warm bubbles of the jacuzzi enveloped the five friends as they lounged, sipping champagne and basking in the glow of their renewed friendship. The Las Vegas skyline shimmered in the distance, beyond the floor-to-ceiling windows.

"Hey," said Olivia, sitting bolt upright in the jacuzzi, sending small waves rippling across the surface. "We were supposed to hang out with Drake Holloway."

Jess smiled and handed her a flute filled with champagne. "I think we had quite enough excitement for one night. Besides, I have a feeling he wouldn't have lived up to the hype."

The women laughed, the sound echoing off the marble walls of the spa, a moment of levity in the wake of their intense day.

"Speaking of excitement," Megan said, her analytical mind never quite at rest, "what are we going to do about that flash drive?"

A hush fell over the group as they contemplated the question. The flash drive, with its promise of revealing their forgotten night, loomed large in their minds.

Lisa was the first to break the silence. "Part of me wants to know everything that happened. But another part thinks that some things are better left in the past."

"I'm torn," Olivia admitted. "On one hand, it feels wrong not to know. On the other, look at what we've gained without those memories. Do we really need them?"

Rachel nodded thoughtfully. "Maybe what we've learned about ourselves, about each other, is more important than the actual events of the night."

"What do you think, Jess?" Megan asked, turning to their friend.

Jess took a long sip of her champagne before answering. "I think... I think we should keep it. Not to watch right away, but to have the option. Who knows? Maybe one day we'll want to see it. Or maybe we'll decide to destroy it together. But for now, it's a piece of our shared history, even if we can't remember it."

The others murmured their agreement, each feeling a sense of closure in the decision.

"Speaking of shared history," Lisa said gently, "Jess, what are you going to do about Miles?"

Jess's face clouded over at the mention of her fiancé's name. "I honestly don't know," she admitted. "Finding out he was behind all this, that he lied about knowing Cynthia, that he tried to manipulate us... it's like I don't even know who he is anymore. And the money laundering. Shit, Rachel."

"You don't have to decide anything right now," Rachel reassured her, placing a comforting hand on Jess's arm. "Take your time, process everything. It

319

looks like I'm going to have some processing of my own to do, too."

Jess nodded in acknowledgement and sighed.

"My heart is telling me to walk away. Is that crazy? To end an engagement over this?"

"*This* was...pretty extreme," Rachel said.

"And no, it's not crazy," Olivia said firmly. "You have to trust your feelings, Jess. If your gut is telling you this isn't right, listen to it. Miles... well, I don't think he is who we thought he was."

Megan nodded in agreement. "And whatever you decide, we're here for you. Always."

"That's right," Lisa added. "If there's one thing this weekend has taught us, it's that we can rely on each other, no matter what."

Jess felt tears welling in her eyes, but for the first time that day, they were tears of gratitude rather than frustration or fear. "Thank you," she whispered. "I don't know what I'd do without you all."

Rachel raised her glass. "To friendships that can weather any storm – even a Vegas-sized one."

"And to new beginnings," Lisa added, a soft smile playing on her lips as she thought of Alex.

"To letting go," Megan chimed in, her work phone noticeably absent for the first time in years.

"To facing our fears," Olivia said, her newfound confidence shining through.

Jess looked at her friends, feeling a warmth that had nothing to do with the hot tub. "To us," she said simply.

Her heart ached with the uncertainty of her future and the loss of what she thought she knew, but in the moment, she was safe with her girls.

As they clinked glasses, the Las Vegas skyline seemed to twinkle in approval beyond the windows.

Later, as they stepped out of the spa and into the cool evening air, a gleaming white stretch limo was waiting for them. The driver, a dapper man in a crisp uniform, opened the door with a flourish.

"Your chariot awaits, ladies," he said with a wink.

As they settled into the plush interior, the limo glided smoothly into the pulsing heart of the Las Vegas Strip. The city was coming alive in the twilight, neon signs flickering to life and casting their multi-coloured glow over the bustling streets.

"Just a quiet one tonight, then?" Rachel asked, with a smile.

"If there's such a thing in Vegas, then yes, please," Jess said. "I know it's not very party hardy of me, but none of us slept well last night..."

She looked over at Megan, whose head was lolling against the window. The stress of the night or the relaxation of the spa had caught up with her.

"We could take a walk to the conservatory in the hotel," Rachel said. "Grab dinner in the Petrossian?"

Olivia perked up at the mention of the bar. "That sounds strangely familiar," she said.

Rachel waved her hand. "It's in the lobby of our hotel. We walked past it last night."

"Something tells me we might have passed it more than once.... or maybe more than passed it..." Jess said, her face a picture of contemplation.

"Well, dinner is on me, if you all fancy it," Rachel smiled. "It's the least I can do."

"This whole thing," Jess said. "It really wasn't your fault. I know you were trying to do your best for me. Cynthia and Miles... They were the ones who..." Jess shook her head.

"Leave it for now," Lisa said. "Let's enjoy the rest of what time we have in Vegas."

"And will you be enjoying that time with Alex?" Olivia asked playfully. "I saw him slip you his number."

Lisa's eyes opened wide, and her three friends laughed, stirring Megan from her sleep.

"Maybe," Lisa said with a coy grin.

"Oh, we're nearly back," Megan said, pulling herself upright in her seat.

They passed the dancing fountains of the Bellagio, their graceful arcs seeming to celebrate the friends' renewed bond. Even though the group had seen the fountain show several times by now, it was still magical. The driver pulled up the slip to the Bellagio, and the replica Eiffel Tower of Paris Las Vegas loomed beside them, a reminder of the dreams and fantasies that Vegas could bring to life.

"You know," Megan mused, gazing out at the glittering cityscape, "for all its craziness, there's something magical about this place."

The others murmured in agreement, each lost in their own thoughts as they gazed at the city lights.

As they pulled up to the Bellagio, the grandeur of the hotel struck them anew. It seemed impossible that just a day ago, they had arrived here full of excitement for a simple bachelorette weekend.

In the lobby, beneath the canopy of glass flowers, they were surprised to see Mr Chen waiting for them, his face softened by what almost looked like a smile.

"Welcome back, ladies," he said, bowing slightly. "I trust your... experience was satisfactory?"

The friends exchanged confused glances before Jess spoke up. "Mr Chen, you knew about all this?"

The hotel manager's eyes twinkled with amusement. "Let's just say that the Bellagio has hosted many of Ms Cynthia's clients over the years. We've become quite adept at playing our part in her scenarios."

"So when you were kicking us out this morning..." Lisa began.

"All part of the experience," Mr Chen confirmed. "I must say, you handled it all remarkably well. Most of Ms Cynthia's clients find the experience quite... transformative."

As they headed towards the elevators, still processing this final revelation, Mr Chen called after them. "Oh, and ladies? Your suites have been upgraded for your last night. Compliments of Ms Cynthia."

The friends paused, taking in the grandeur of the Bellagio lobby. The air was cool and crisp, a stark contrast to the desert heat outside the revolving doors. The soft tinkling of the Dale Chihuly glass sculpture overhead mixed with the distant chimes of slot machines, creating a unique symphony of luxury and chance.

The subtle aroma of the Bellagio's signature fragrance enveloped them as they approached the elevator bank. The mirrored doors reflected their images – five women, dishevelled but smiling, forever changed by their Vegas experience.

In the elevator, the friends looked at each other, a mix of exhaustion and exhilaration on their faces.

"I didn't know they had any suites better than the ones I booked," Rachel said, with curious surprise. "I'll have to ask about them for next time."

"Next time?" Jess said. "I'm not sure I'll be ready to come back here in too much of a hurry."

As they burst into laughter, the elevator doors closed on their wild weekend, leaving them with memories — both remembered and forgotten — that would last a lifetime.

Thank you for reading **WAKING UP IN VEGAS.**

If you have enjoyed this book, please visit Amazon, Goodreads or wherever you leave reviews. Reviews help readers to find my books and help me reach new readers.

If you're posting about this book on social media, I'm @jerowneywriter
On TikTok I'm @jerowney
Tag me!

For further information about me and my work, please visit my website: http://jerowney.com/about-je-rowney

Best wishes,

JE Rowney

.

Made in the USA
Las Vegas, NV
13 November 2024

11777664R10194